Patrick Loper

or the altered whale

Chicago

USA

Illinois

Autograph Page

pen
gym

to Tara

Novo-Cetus

or the altered whale

By
Patrick Loper
In association with Jo Anne Loper

Loper Publishing 2014

Chicago Illinois

978-0996854207

For the whales I admire . . .

May they always thrive.

Acknowledgments

I am so grateful for the support of my friends and family members who read my book from early manuscript to finished product, and always provided useful feedback along with tons of encouragement. Without them, I would have no book.

I do have to single out a few people for their specific contributions. My mother, whose hard work and dedication helped make this book possible. I would also like to acknowledge the hardworking individuals who spend months at sea studying Cetacean.

My critique group the North Side Evanston Writers Group; their valuable feedback help flush out the story's plot moving it from a novella to a full-fledged novel.

I especially want to thank the many people and organizations that have supported my education and mental health along the way. I fondly remember Cove school and their dedication to my education. They helped me defy an early verdict that I may never learn to read. Counselors, teachers and therapists who taught me and kept me safe as I learned to manage my mental illness; and Dr. Shara Kronmal, her constant support and encouragement helped me finish this book

Lastly, I need to mention the British broadcasting documentary *Ocean Odyssey,* the inspiration for this thrilling tale. Its brilliant detailed exploration of sperm whale life inspired my love of Cetaceans.

Preface

Novo Cetus, or the Altered Whale was inspired by the BBC Documentary Ocean Odyssey. The documentary highlights the life and eventual death of a male sperm whale though his viewpoint over eighty years. The documentary uses computer graphics to produce a picture of an intelligent yet threatened species of cetacean living in a world humanity knows little about. The portrayal of the sperm whale pod also known as a Cian inspired me to write from the viewpoint of a sperm whale calf living within such a social unit.

Whales lob-tailed nervously at the surface. Elders sensed a storm brewing above the waterline. A score of sperm whale headed leeward.

Chapter 1

For days, the pod skirted a weather front that churned up small fish, crab and shrimp from the deep waters, which in turn, produced hundreds of squid to eat. During this feasting time, a mother sperm whale taught her calf to dive deep. The sensation created as his ribcage condensed and his lungs flattened startled him. He entered the midnight zone, the depth where light no longer shone, and the total darkness felt empty and cold. In contrast, he was thrilled as he powered through the surface and felt the dry, warm air on his cold, wet skin.

The hurricane edged closer and the matriarch Gray, named for her smooth gray dorsal, drove her family out to sea. She watched the mother, named Hope, prod her new calf to keep up. Hope delivered the only calf to survive this birthing season. Marauding tribes of killer whales were relentless and picked off all the family's new ones. Years ago, Hope had been an "only" as well. She survived through a season of violent storms — one after another, each storm snatching a baby. The clan saw balance in Hope's delivery of this lone, surviving calf. They looked forward to the meaning this would have for their clan.

With no other calves to nurture and teach, every mama fostered him. They amused him with their name-stories. Each tale carried a warning or a celebration born from the experience of the individual. His favorite stories boasted epic battles with giant squid of the deep that flared many colors, from the angry warning-red of the morning sky to the putrid-purple of dying flesh. These clashes left many clan members scarred deep with pockmarks from the beast's serrated suckers and yawning gashes from clawed tentacles that tore away flesh.

The front edge of the storm produced huge waves that rolled over Hope and her calf. Scared, the calf swam erratically – randomly clicking. Hope pushed and prompted her baby away from the approaching storm. He became confused as the murky top-water boiled and the storm swept over them. Hope dove to avoid a swell poised to slam into her. She clicked a dive command – and dove.

Disoriented, the calf lost track of his mother. The colder saltier water, upwelled by the hurricane, tricked him – his senses telling him he was deep when in fact he was not. The water roiled around him, and he somersaulted through the storm surge.

Fighting exhaustion; punishing waves in the eye-wall of the storm shoved him underwater. He remembered the game he played with his mother and powered to the surface. Instead of breaking through the top-water into the warm and dry, the hurricane's strong winds and driving rain slammed him back underwater. Determined, he raced to the surface, never feeling the warm, but always getting air. The storm moved on and towed the little one along with it.

The calf tried to stay alive in the violent storm. He was well fed and well taken care of before he went lost. Everything he learned with his clan had seemed like a game, but now he used his games to stay alive. He remembered the story one mama told of her brother who went missing for a while. The brother was young and only suckled. The brother returned weak, eyes sucked back into his head and his smooth youthful flesh furrowed and sagging. The brother had not thought to eat the fish while he was lost. The mama cried when she told that he had not learned from the games he'd played, like the fish game – taking the fish into his mouth and swallowing great gulps, holding still to feel the fish wiggle and flop all the way down. She grieved still, because brother had not lived many seasons after his return home. This lost calf had learned the lesson of the fish game – he would die of thirst if he did not eat the fish.

Meanwhile Hope's survival instinct took over as the storm raged around her. The hurricane churned the water to a tenebrous soup. She questioned whether she'd practiced a blind swim with her calf. She made as much noise as she could, hoping he would hear her over the clamor of the thunder and crashing waves. She moved away from the storm at a pace her baby could keep up with. It was a long underwater swim through muddy water. As soon as the sea cleared, she headed toward the surface. *He loves this game*, she thought. She broke the surface and felt the dry on her wet skin. She turned to see him fly up out of the water. It never happened, and her heart sank.

Hope found her clan far from the storm's path. Her sisters happily nudged her; thankful tributes of her survival joyously clicked throughout her family. The happy clicks and boings trailed off as they realized she was alone. Like a thick fog, sadness rolled over the pod. Heartbroken leviathans launched their bodies toward the surface, breached the top-water and then crashed back into the sea. Gray knew the rhythm of the water. She called on the clan to search for the lost calf. Several whales followed Gray and the current, while others followed Hope as she headed back into the storm. Adults and adolescents fanned out in search of the lost calf. The sea was thick and gloomy from the tropical storm. Gray knew her clan's sonic clicks would fall a short distance, pushed deep by the heavy water. For several days, they sifted through the dense sea. Their haunting coda echoed for miles as the clan called out for their lost little one. Days of searching produced nothing. Gray and her tribe circled around and joined Hope and her group; their quest was over. This season's only calf was gone.

Hope continued her search alone. She knew the routine of her pod – where they would head when the water turned colder. Previously, she and the others hunted for the calf where he should have been, so she headed in a direction he should not have gone. Against the current, she swam clicking a mother's coda.

The tribe prepared to celebrate the life of the little one they'd lost. Generations of loss – the strong to whalers, the weak to predators and the environment – resulted in a culture that celebrated the lives of those who passed on. A joyous celebration of the bold and confident calf replaced the sadness displayed when they discovered he was missing.

The clan focused their sonar. At the intersection of this sonic convergence appeared the playful image of the calf as he corkscrewed up to the surface and exploded into the warm dry topside. The broadcasted image of the small whale playfully lob tailing and breaching brought high praise and loving comments from the clan. Many shared stories of his life and his disappearance. His time would be archived and re-counted for generations as a cautionary tale.

Chapter 2

The calf drifted with the flotsam and jetsam regurgitated at the backside of the hurricane. Drifting side-by-side, were natural items, like the orbs created by turbulent water that whipped palmetto grass and seaweed tightly around a shell and man-made junk, like blown-glass Japanese floats and plastic mermaid tears. He welcomed the return of the remora fish as they battled their way through the marine debris to latch onto his skin.

Orcas followed the gyre – the circular water current where the calf floated. He was not alone adrift in the debris; seals, turtles and dolphins also took shelter there. Safely nestled within the nurdles and rubbish, the small calf heard the terrified barks and high-pitched whistles as the sea's black and white assassins picked off those at the edge of the ocean garbage patch. Tightly cocooned in the litter, the calf also heard a hum rising from the deep; in the distance, he saw something large and gray breach the surface.

At the edge of the garbage patch, the U.S. Navy's largest Marine Remotely Operated Vehicle (MROV) bobbed to the surface, scattering the Orcas. The hurricane had freed the post-World War II submarine from its deep-water tether. Redesigned as a stationary science laboratory, this freed underwater test site pushed through the ocean.

The calf stirred; the melodic whir and forward motion of the MROV pulled at him. He remembered when a blue whale and her calf swam with his pod for an afternoon. He and the young blue had breached and flopped onto the surface for hours. He'd watched in awe as the blues unhinged their giant mouths and skimmed the water for krill. The blue whale's mother had hoo'd and hummed directives to her calf. *Maybe this is a blue whale;* he thought and let himself float away with the submarine.

Hope heard the mechanical song she'd learned to stay away from years ago. Did this calf know the danger of the deceptive song? This creature had been far from the pod's thoughts this season – Orcas were the danger they avoided. She headed toward the artificial sound and saw her baby floating next to the sub. She clicked out to him with joy. He saw her and snapped his jaws together frantically, clicking his delight to her. Instinctively, she moved her massive body between her little one and the deceitful ocean swimmer.

The false song stopped. The ocean was eerily quiet; and then the submarine exploded. There was time enough for the calf to notice the quiet. He turned to his mother for an explanation and saw sadness in her eyes; she knew death was upon them. She offered up a prayer to the ocean's wisdom to spare her calf from suffering. Ahead of the flames, a powerful surge of water pushed the calf. He heard a horrible hiss as the water around his mother turned to steam. The sound his mother made as she cooked to death imprinted into his brain. The surge dissipated; fire and debris swept over him. It engulfed his body and burned his flesh. He screamed out as flames burned into his eyes. As the calf drifted to the bottom of the ocean, parts of the sub fell down around him. He was in agony, alive and alone.

Minute metallic fibers inched out of the debris; several slowly twisted their way to the calf. When they reached him, the strands jacketed the injured body like spiderwebbing. More filaments stretched out from the ruins; they burrowed, and raked through the debris field…searching. As they gathered fragments into their fibrous web, a camera poked up out of the rubble. Designed to withstand explosive impact, the camera turned in each direction and assessed the damage.

Concussion from the blast left the calf disoriented. He thought he felt Red Algae Seaweed surrounding him; indifferent to the ocean current, it moved with malevolent purpose, tugging and burrowing into his flesh. The calf remembered playing in the algae, letting the fronds caress him as he glided through a meadow of the deep-water sea grass. This grass did not caress him; it tormented him.

He was on the bottom; he sensed this for sure.

Noise overwhelmed him. There was more noise in his head than what the gulls made when they feasted at an anchovy ball. Strange noise mingled with memories. He struggled to escape the clamor and clawing, but the algae anchored him. He fell into an unnatural sleep.

Nano-machines were hard at work inside his body

These were underwater repair nano-machines, specifically designed to work independently – without human or computer direction – to be mechanically resourceful. Submarine repair was time consuming. Replacement parts occupied valuable cargo space and added unwanted weight to the new specialized submarines. Theoretically, in an emergency, these nanos deployed spontaneously to assess damage and use materials at hand to do repairs. When the hurricane ripped the MROV free from its tether, the functionality testing taking place in the deep-water research site was interrupted. The nanos detected the need for navigation and engineered simple propulsion to move the submarine forward.

A camera evaluated the damage: *extensive*. Assessment nanos noted strong energy readings coming from a biological source in the wreckage. Linking to fiber optic cables imbedded in the seabed, communication nanos connected to the internet. Search nanos followed electric signals from nerve cells into the calve's brain. Collectively, the nanos judged the biological energy controllable. They would combine the biological matter with salvaged material from the explosion to achieve their goal: repair and rebuild the vessel.

Research nanos identified the energy source: *infant sperm whale, age: between second and third year, weight: estimated two thousand kilograms of biologic material.*

Vital internal organs sustained minimal damage; however, there was extensive injury to the skin and skeletal systems. Repair nanos reprogrammed, tasked to gather medical and veterinary data. The medical nanos stabilized life signs while engineering nanos focused on tissue manufacturing. These nanos developed high-performance bio-nano mesh skin by combining organic material with carbon nanofiber lattices. They renamed the material nanoflesh.

They would create more nanoflesh by increasing the chemical and electrical signals in a cell's nucleus during mitosis. This would allow for anticipated changes in size and shape.

The nano machines determined whale structure enhanced the function of the submarine and expanded on that biological model. Thus, the fore of the vessel was large and blunt tapering to a smaller aft section. The nanos papered the inside of the newly constructed framework in nanoflesh thereby creating an airtight cavity to house the fragile, biological mainframe. The nanos swaddled the calf in the newly formed nanoflesh to protect their central processing unit from infection.

Impressed by the agility of a sperm whale, specifically the broad tail pattern; a replicated fluke finished the vessel's design. Bone and craniofacial tissue engineering depended heavily on bone cell-infused tissue scaffolding, which functioned as an expandable framework.

Through the development of biosynthetic neuromuscular synapses, simple Romex wiring salvaged from the wreckage and placed in the biological backbone would link systems into the mainframe. Based on its ability to organize, store, access and process information, the nanos used the organic brain as the mainframe.

Search nanos collected biological materials, such as phosphate, proteoglycan and calcium, along with synthetic materials recovered from the rubble to develop a neuromuscular junction to receive and send the signals required for movement.

The nano's developed a simple respiratory system by combining lung tissue with carbon nano fiber tubes creating a set of super lungs. These lungs worked using the same principle as normal lung function; muscles contracting to take in oxygen and relaxing to release carbon dioxide.

Rods salvaged from the wreckage connected the propulsion system to the fluke. The engine relied on the fluke muscle's ability to contract and relax to manipulate the rods.

The nanos chose Long Range Acoustical Devices (LRAD) as the primary weaponry. They made use of the organic spermaceti, the oily substance inside the whale's head, to enhance sound waves, similar to its original function. Sound-emitting nanos inside the junk partitions of the whales' skull, along with a well-charted course of fluid-filled knobs, were placed inside the whale's melon - the rounded fatty domed part of the head - just below their modified spermaceti organ. These knobby surfaces reflected sound waves coming through the spermaceti. This new system functioned as a sonic cannon. Increasing any sound that passed through the nano-altered spermaceti case to a destructive level. The main computer, or mainframe, controlled sound intensity by changing the consistency of the spermaceti. The more oily the spermaceti, the more powerful the sonic wave. Conversely, less oily spermaceti produced a less powerful sound wave.

Construction of a vision organ was difficult since the explosion badly damaged the biological tissue necessary to construct modified eyes. The nanos adapted the working camera to create a graphing system. This system lacked the visual acuity of a normal eye and depended heavily on infrared light waves due to its inconsistent reliability with normal light waves. The nano-machines compensated for this unreliable vision system with additional sensors devoted to hearing.

When the nano-machines opted to utilize the calve's brain as the mainframe, they could not have anticipated how, with its memories and instincts, the organic brain would react.

Repair finished; systems waited for activation.

The calf woke up. Instinct propelled him to the surface. All systems worked in synchronicity; the intricately structured relationships between the rewired brain and the reconstructed systems moved the vessel flawlessly.

As he maneuvered to the surface, his new body creaked and groaned. Anticipating his every move the nanos retracted the protective cover over the S-shaped blowhole; the calf took in a great gulp of air, then the nanos closed it again as he dove underwater. He listened for the sound of his pod.

The nanos choreographed movement of the newly engineered pectoral fins with the remade fluke to steer and propelled him through the ocean. The calf heard his pod in the distance and headed in that direction. At a glance, this biological sub looked like an overfed whale calf swimming effortlessly through the water as sun glittered off his nano-infused skin.

The nanos analyzed all systems as the calf moved easily through the ocean. The only glitch in the system lay deep within the amygdala of the computer. Memories of the explosion generated enormous energy. The nano-machines labored to keep that energy in check.

The calf approached his clan and clicked their unique coda greeting; he wove his way through the pod searching for his mother. Moving from female to female he scrutinized each nuanced expression, hoping to see her eyes, crinkled too much at the edges but filled with love for him.

Chaos erupted as this stranger invaded their territory; his appearance disturbed them. His skin was too shiny, his fluke too long and an unfamiliar hum surrounded him, yet his argot was familiar – a dialect used only by this pod.

The clan moved away from him. Mothers corralled their young and circled them, anxiously slapping their tails on the surface. The matriarch positioned herself between her band and the outsider and listened. His story differed little from that of many orphaned whales. Lost for a while before returning scarred and deformed. This oddly shaped baby with glistening skin knew his family and they knew him. There was no denying this was the baby lost in the storm.

The massive fluke of the oldest member of the clan slowly waved up and down as she propelled herself toward the familiar stranger. Deep gashes and circular divots from razor-sharp beaks and the tooth-lined suckers of giant squid decorated her from stem to stern. She stopped inches from the peculiar calf; nose to nose.

The nanos received information from deep within the parietal lobe of their rebuilt computer. *Recognition and categorization – family member.*

The calf listened as the old female told the story of how he went missing.

". . . you were stolen away by a giant wave in a violent storm. We hunted for you, calling you. . . Our Hope left us to search for you . . . gone.

Chapter 3

The pod allowed him to swim with the clan, but most kept him at a distance. The integumentary system created by the nanos worked perfectly, creating nano-laced skin cells complete with thermo-regulation and sensation. The nanos moved closer to their goal: a biological submarine.

The strange calf swam deep, taking advantage of the extra pressure hundreds of feet of top water provided to compress his ever-changing body. He grew quickly and at times parts of him shifted, wagged or rolled as the nanos synchronized their efforts to build systems within the vessel.

The clan's curious kept company with him throughout the day. Young and old took their turn swimming with the unique calf.

The organic matter of the submarine required protein. Nanos dedicated to biological fueling used enhanced echolocation to find deep-sea squid. The pod grew fat from the abundant supply of giant squid he located. Security nanos lodged themselves in the hypothalamus, primed to alert the sympathetic nervous system. This provided a perfect framework for a defense system.

Nano security detected GPS sonar focused on the pod.

Locate origin of tracking device and identify: Seventeen meters off the starboard bow. Asian Whaling boat; a converted trawler designed to process ambergris; outfitted with a one-ton harpoon shooter and high caliber automatic weapons. International Whaling Commission (IWC) identifies this particular vessel as pirate.

The huge whaler coasted through the water, drifting without destination. Sunlight glinted off the metal harpoon turret that dominated the starboard side. Recent sanctions leeved by the IWC rendered this ship useless to the "research" fleet that harvested blue whale. The IWC discovered several dead whale calves aboard this ship during a surprise inspection. Encountering these sperm whales while off the grid was a boon for the crew. They prepared to hunt within the pod.

Assessment of the approaching whaling ship's arsenal: Rudimentary weapons system. Likelihood of damage/injury: low.

The nanos devised a counter defense and planted their biological sub between the whaler and the pod. The whaler fired an armed 30-gram penthrite grenade harpoon at the young male sperm whale in the direct sight of the cannon. It struck the altered whale's enhanced skin and exploded. A fireball flashed and the water agitated to a foamy white, snuffing out the fire as thousands of bubbles formed and roared to the surface.

The whales scattered as the reverberation from the shockwave roiled through the pod. Capillaries in the whales' lungs ruptured from the grenades concussion and mothers nudged disoriented calves to the surface to take a breath. Frothy water dissolved and the crimson bloom the pirates expected to see develop never did. A shimmering sperm whale hung in the water undamaged by the harpoon. His eye, emptiness highlighted by impenetrable blackness, stared back at them in defiance.

Chatter scuttled through the superstitious crew; what ill omen did this herald? The trawler fled the area with its terrified crew members, each with magical tale to tell.

The small explosion stimulated activity in the orbitofrontal cortex of the bio-ships organic computer. The nanos directed the surplus energy to different systems in their vessel.

The calf followed its pod's wake. When he reached them, they greeted him with unusual silence. The explosion impaired their ability to vocalize, however they bumped and nudged him in joyous reception.

It had not escaped the matriarch and the elders that their peculiar calf had placed himself between the pod and danger. Having been busy guiding her family to safety, she had not seen the explosion; but its effect still resonated through her melon. The calf seemed unharmed by the blast. She listened and watched as he greeted each family member by name. His eyes moved quickly, one eye greeting an old friend while the other moved on to acknowledge the next. He shimmered slightly as the sun reflected off his unblemished skin. Her pod had grown fat from the calf's ability to locate easy prey like large schools of Cownose rays that moved like surface birds with slowly beating wings.

In her life, this matriarch had experienced many seasons of too little to eat and too much danger. So she gestured welcome to the returning calf, and one by one, the elders acknowledged their glittering kinsman.

Nanos systematically modified the mixture of chemicals dumped by axons. Monitoring and modifying this cocktail that flooded dendrites and neurons should keep the computer on line. Power surges that sprung from emotional pathways needed constant observation. The nanos discovered some emotions so powerful they sent the system off line.

Chapter 4

The family of whales enjoyed the cooler sea-surface temperatures, deep canyons and pitched drops of the continental slope in the Pacific. They alternated between resting and foraging. The more restless whales dove deep for giant squid, seeking out depths where the eerie glow of iridescent fish and the florescent bodies of squid replaced the brightness of sunlight. Wrinkled skin puckered further as the crushing pressure of the deep compressed their bodies. Blubber contracted against the weight of the water as the sperm whales' flexible ribcages folded in against deflated lungs.

Each whales' sonar pinged and sent back ghostly images of towering peaks and steep drop-offs along the ridge. Excitement reverberated throughout the hunting party; giant squid had been located. One by one the whales positioned themselves and surrounded the squid, their behavior evolved by centuries of cooperative hunting.

The Giant squid felt the echolocation ping off his boneless body and flattened himself against a ridge, brightly flashing red and white. Its hard gladius, the internal structure of the mantle, stopped it from completely disappearing into the structure, however the tentacles and tail fin settled into the crannies of the erection.

Water whooshed out of its funnel at an exaggerated rate as its respiration increased. Instinctively, this squid knew he was in mortal danger.

Gray pumped her tail up and down as she hurtled through the complete blackness of the deep abyss, her sonar focused on the beast. She bared down on her target, prepared to suck the creature down her gullet at the very moment she reached it. A hammer in the deep; she smashed into the protruding gladius and knocked the giant out of its cranny. Gray grabbed the monster by its head as it attempted to flee; wiry tentacles slashed backwards tearing chunks of flesh from her face. She sucked in the architeuthis, her stomach muscles crushing its internal shell as it traveled down the digestive tack. Acid in her guts dissolved the cephalopod skin and muscles leaving only the horny beak as evidence of its existence. The clan watched; pleased to give their mentor the first kill of the day. Confident all would eat their fill today.

The clan continued its journey south, pausing along the Tropic of Cancer. They enjoyed all the ocean provided, relishing cooler air and the warmer top water of the coastal region. They stopped for rest and refueling before making the long trip south past the equator to the Galapagos Islands.

Several healthy bachelors grew restless. Biology urged them to break away from the confines of the pod. Adolescent males reached record size, nearly that of adult females – thirty feet in length and fifteen tons heavy. Successful hunting had led to exponential growth for all pod members.

Young males, ready to leave the pod, squared off and rammed each other in mock battle -- repeatedly ricocheting off each other's bulbous brows. Young females on the edge of sexual maturity watched the affable rivalry. They slapped at the surface delightedly with their tails and pectoral fins, and clapped their jaws together in appreciation of the display. Slow clicks from the usually silent males and elongated creaks from vocal females were a constant background noise.

The whales in the nursery practiced synchronized coda. Mamas and babies faced each other and reflected each other's clicks and creaks. A symphony of duet chains, reciprocal coda and matching vocalizations pealed out from the nursery. All of this activity reinforced the social bonds of the pod.

The glittering calf hung in the deep. No longer unblemished, his skin bore hard-won battle badges from the clawed tentacles and razor sharp beaks of the giant architeuthis. He stretched over forty feet in length and weighed twenty-five tons. None of the males challenged him in competition, however every so often the calf rose to the surface and lob-tailed around the mock battlefield in spectacular pageantry.

The calf enjoyed the days of play. He particularly liked the constant sounds and voices echoing through the clan. These friendly noises almost drowned out the relentless whir and rattle in his head. Nanos intercepted his thoughts when consciousness edged him toward examining what had happened to him or why he was different. Nonetheless, he knew he was changed. Whales visited daily and told him stories of the surface. They described the stampede of dolphins when tens of thousands of white-sided dolphins crisscrossed through the pod. He particularly loved their story of the group of high-spirited blue whales that passed through their clan. Pod-mates revealed how the blues had rollicked and rolled through the pod, unhinging their lower jaw and scooping up tons of krill that swarmed the surface.

Coached by a twisted combination of nature and nano nurture, he co-existed with his pod.

Steve Martinelli captained the cruise ship *Ali-Goren*. Several hours ahead of schedule, he allowed the unusually swift current to move his ship silently along the continental shelf. Coasting with engines cut, provided an eerie experience. Accustomed to the constant hum and forward motion of the powerful engines, drifting provided all aboard the opportunity to enjoy the quiet and stillness of sea life. This practice evoked Captain Martinelli's childhood memory of sailing his beloved blue and yellow skiff when the wind happened to die. Stalled for hours, he learned that when completely quiet; the fish in the water didn't seem to notice him.

The whales logged in the water, resting as the cruise ship with the diamond logo displayed on its side approached. Unaware of the silent danger gliding toward them, the pod drifted motionless on the top-water, their heads, blowholes and dorsal knuckles exposed to the surface.

The ship knifed into the clan. Its bow sliced the matriarch, slashing open her melon and cracking her skull. Wax oozed out of the spermatici organ and air hissed as it escaped from her torn distal sacs. The impact lacerated her blowhole and exposed the folds of skin, called monkey lips, which lay deep within the blubbery exterior of her blowhole. The ship severed the tendons holding her lower jaw in place, and her mouth hung open in a never-ending scream. Where her blowhole used to be, let loose a mournful wail. The intensity of the cry, so similar to the sound of his dying mother, jarred the calf's memory. His hippocampus flooded as his mind flashed back to the explosion. Nano linemen systematically rerouted energy, to maintained order as chaos flared up in the mainframe. They disconnected and interrupted the pathways recalling the shocking trauma.

Anguish quickly turned to anger and nanos knew what to do with anger. The energy it created went directly to the defense system. Incorporated into the pectoral fin's design, were missile launchers. The nanos sent a message to a muscle in the fin. It contracted, firing a missile into the cruise ship.

Captain Martinelli needed no military training to recognize they had been fired upon. He issued a ship-wide emergency action command and sent out a distress signal. He ordered the crew to engage the engines in an effort to get closer to shore. He hoped the passengers paid attention to the mandatory emergency information meeting at the start of the cruise and would find their way to life vests and vessels if needed. He scanned the waters to get a glimpse of what and who had fired. The only activity he identified was a pod of sperm whales as they swam frantically away.

The pod went in one direction, and the cruise ship in another. The rebuilt whale waited until the cruise ship wobbled away, then followed his pod. As he approached, he could see several matrons under the matriarch holding her at the surface. Clan members crowded around her, touching and caressing her, each nudge and stroke a loving tribute to their leader. Several males formed a rosette around their family, warding off predators attracted by the scent of blood.

The rebuilt whale approached the cluster of clan members and reluctantly the whales moved out of his way.

Nanos examined life signs from the dominant whale: *marginal signal emitted from cerebral cortex, body temperature cooling, breathing labored, circulatory and respiratory systems failing. Conclusion: Death.*

The altered whale skimmed softly along the length of his mentor's body and gently nuzzled her injured frame. Perfect vision was unnecessary to see what was happening; the life spark that shone in her eye was dark, and she quaked with each intake of air. No click or coda could convey his grief as he sensed her life slip away.

Chapter 5

The pod continued their journey to the Galapagos Islands without their
matriarch. Urged by several males ready to leave the clan, the calf joined a
bachelor unit. Driven by instinct, this band of youthful males, some sexually
mature – most socially immature – charted their own course south.

The calves' developing form designed by nanos, produced an impressive
silhouette. Twenty feet high from blowhole to belly and forty feet long from snout
to vent with a magnificent fluke completing his framework. There was no doubt he
would be their Leader.

Nanos assessed the situation: *Smaller, specialized fleet noted (males between six
and sixteen years); migration patterns indicate a higher latitude course, probable
cause: increase in species diversity producing ample fuel for the convoy.
Biomechanical vessel in command.*

The Leader directed his new clan along the East Pacific Rise. This mineral rich
water supported a wide collection of life. Peppered within the hydrothermal vents,
communities of tubeworms, crabs and shrimp thrived. The dense clusters of
tubeworms, resembling a wad of lipsticks wafting in a breeze, fed the swarms of

shrimp and crab that thrived within the ecosystem. These bottom-dwellers nourished the deep-water tuna and sluggish Zorarcid fish, which the top predator – the giant squid – preyed upon.

The Leader's reconstructed body needed extra blubber to keep it buoyant. Recognizing the need for regular fueling, the nanos researched effective tracking plans. Clearly articulated, coordinated attacks were successful in keeping the newly formed fleet fueled. This ability to maintain a plentiful food supply benefited all members of his clan. His newly formed bachelor pod continued to grow fat from the bounty.

The Leader had a secret to consider as he swam with his new clan. He knew he'd injured the surface creature that killed his matriarch. He didn't know how he managed it, he had thought of murder and then there was an explosion.

He lead his pod through the ocean's sun-streaked Mesopelagic zone into the total darkness of the Bathypelagic zone. Sonar pinged against towering mountains of boulders and entered the deep chasms of the ridge, providing him with a topographic map. A seventy-five-foot black smoker belched blistering hot water and minerals out its vent. He focused on a growing fissure in the tall thermal chimney.

Probability of collapse: high.

The nanos examined their options. Data showed more than enough giant squid in the area to fuel the fleet. *Options for continuation: missile deployment to destroy the pillar or deployment of sonic weapon to achieve the same.* Option two was brought on-line: sonic cannon deployment. The nanos calculated timing for detonation, aimed and fired. The result would have pleased any demolition expert; the towering hydrothermal vent collapsed in on itself with minimal damage to the immediate surroundings.

Without a doubt, the Leader knew he'd caused the column to collapse. As clearly as he knew that when he torpedoed up to the surface he breached the top-water, he knew when he saw the crack in the rock formation he would destroy the structure.

Clouds of sediment swirled around the crumbled chimney. Throngs of eyeless thermal-vent shrimp and ghost crabs scuttled away from the wreckage. Panic crept into the whale's consciousness. Quickly, he assessed the effect of the explosion on his clan. Finding no injuries, just confusion, he fled the area.

Nano linemen rerouted energy away from the small almond-shaped region of the medial and temporal lobes that process memory and emotions. Energy persisted in creating a neural shortcut to fear and anxiety. Research and Development nanos rewired neural pathways to direct energy to the frontal cortex, which govern reason and caution.

Surplus emotional energy was converted to movement to transport the vessel away from the fleet. The sonic cannon had worked remarkably well but the organic material in the mainframe was misfiring; energy needed to be dispersed. Movement would release the energy in a productive way.

Several miles from the explosion site, the Leader stopped and logged at the surface. He spouted noisily, trying to drown out the unnatural hum that shrouded him. Swinging and slapping his tail on the water, he lob-tailed anxiously; warning others to stay away. The danger he warned others of was himself.

The Leader considered his past. Memories of his life before the storm were strong. His relationship to his mother and the others, and the stories and lessons he'd learned were cogent memories. He remembered his return to the pod – greeted at first with suspicion – and the moment of his acceptance. The matriarch. She'd remained silent when the pod spun his tale of victory over the whaling ship. Additionally, she had never celebrated his resiliency or his hunting skills. He had so many questions: had *she* agreed when the others announced he was resourceful just like his mother, Hope? Had she boasted to other swimmers, like the white-sided dolphin, that *he* was the pod's deepest diver? Never.

She knew he was different, and now he knew he was different. The bachelor pod looked to him for leadership, protection and provisions. Despite his size, he still needed a clan. He contemplated what to do next.

The nanos' primary program: to assess problems and adapt.

Perception and experience proved to be a convincing influence in biological data processing. In contrast, the nano process of systematic enquiry to come to a conclusion, proved ineffective in problem solving.

In an effort to modify the negative effect of emotion on managing the flow of information through the CPU, the nanos created a link between perception and the computer. This adaptation viewed information as intelligence and introduced intuition into the processor. This kickstarted the assimilation of nanos into the whale's culture and traditions' and began the mental process of using perception, reasoning and judgment.

Nanos pinpointed the obstructions: cognitive incongruity; or trouble integrating an event, for example, the loss of a loved one. Attempts at thought suppression were difficult because ironic processes (the practice of monitoring whether information has been successfully suppressed) defeats suppression of an idea, by keeping the matter in mind.

Nanos worked to regulate anxiety. However, research showed anxiety to be ambiguous and anxiety was central to the misfiring of organic material.

The Leader heard his bachelor pod approach. Excited chatter, filled with wavy boings and staccato clicks, reverberated through the ocean as stories of the collapse echoed through the group. The boisterous band of males arrived en masse, nudging and bumping their greeting while boasting the tale; hadn't it been lucky that no one was injured? None of them had ever seen a collapse. Excitement, triggered by the near-deadly encounter with the crumbling chimney, prompted a large male to breach the top-water several times and belly flop back to the surface. A smaller male, his head encrusted in barnacles like a crop of curly white hair, circled the group and slapped his fluke against the surface with bravado. This magical tale would enhance the growing story of the clan.

They arrived in warmer waters of the Galapagos Islands and mixed with young females and bull males. Hunting parties comprised of whales from different pods formed and shared expertise as they stalked the giant squid. Large bulls near the Islands were aggressive, more than willing to prove their supremacy to any contender. Unwilling to provoke a challenge, the Leader stayed in deep water, far from the social circle surrounding the Islands.

The nanos swept their system for errors. Structure scans reported mechanical systems within a satisfactory working range, while repair nanos searched for and deleted erratic emotional responses embedded in fear structures.

The nanos sifted through the biological mainframe, sorting and filing information to integrate into their new collaborative system; migration patterns, hunting grounds and safety protocol were merged into the system. Nanos analyzed and rejected experiential knowledge – data gained through the whale's firsthand experiences. They found this information fluctuated and deemed it unreliable. This exclusion ultimately limited the Leader's capacity for insight.

The clan left the Galapagos Islands and headed towards the coast of the United States. The Leader anticipated several days of peace as he and his clan mates cruised through the crystal blue water along the Pacific Rim. He felt content after his time in the waters of the Galapagos.

Tales of the charmed pod resonated throughout the Cetacean communities from the Tropic of Cancer to the Aleutian Islands. The Leader's troop of ten strong males doubled as bold and brash adolescent sperm whales left their family pods and joined the bachelor pod.

Most clans urged their young to stay far away from the mythical clan. The wise were wary of anything different. The dangerous, false creatures of the surface are drawn to large whales. Some stories are shared as a warning, they cautioned. Fishermen were superstitious. Stories circulated of a pod of fat male sperm whales. Like the pod leaders, whalers steered clear of this pod. Most cultures possess a tale of a giant whale, and too many of these yarns end tragically – especially when they start with a giant whale.

Chapter 6

John Brasco entered the lobby at the Department of Homeland Security (DHS). With a wink, he flashed his ID at the security guard. She nodded him past her checkpoint, apparently unimpressed with his flirting. The briefcase he carried contained files, charts, and video footage revealing an unidentified craft. He would present this data to an assembled Homeland Security Panel. Their role: to determine any threat to the United States. If they determined significant threat, the case would go to a DHS Inspector General for further investigation.

A veteran at presenting information to DHS Committees, Special Agent Brasco was familiar with the conference room setup and unimpressed by the political and military clout sitting at an imposing rectangular conference table. There was no room for him at the table; however in a corner of the room was the necessary equipment for a PowerPoint presentation. He linked his computer to the network as the members finished reviewing preliminary reports on the secure tablets he provided earlier. He waited patiently until they finished, then directed their attention to him.

"Good Morning. I am Federal Homeland Security Agent John Brasco. I will highlight some of the information contained in the folder in front of you.

"Our southern satellites are tracking this UIC moving along the southern oceanic ridge, specifically the Pacific Rim. A naval satellite monitoring its movement detected an explosion. Pinpointed in close proximity to the explosion was the UIC. An unmanned submarine, The Wolf trailing the craft was close enough to gather underwater photos. Moments later we lost contact with The Wolf through what we believe was a large sonar blast."

Brasco, a veteran at highlighting visual information for these committees, slowly clicked through photos of the UIC. There was no noticeable response from the panel. Each had arranged their face in detached boredom. He continued.

"We've attempted to send other underwater vessels to gather more information and are unable to covertly penetrate the large concentration of whales that surround the UIC. We are currently investigating several methods of scattering the whales, including stunning them with sonar, killing one or more to frighten them away, or anesthetizing them with chemical agents. We recently located the UIC near the Galapagos Islands. It seems to be following sperm whale migration patterns using the whales as cover.

"Our hands are tied since it is not in U.S. waters. We have no jurisdiction in the Galapagos, but its trajectory is on course to arrive in the North Pacific. It is my understanding that this committee will be able to fast track the use of extreme force outside of U.S. jurisdiction if needed."

Brasco took his time closing down the presentation. When the overhead screen went blank, he continued, "You have all the relevant information on this subject. Do not assume that the U.S. is the only government assessing this situation. Any questions?"

Senator Sessmen, a senior diplomat from Illinois, gave a slight jerk of his head, indicating he did have a question. "This does not look like a 'craft' to me, and even in these pixilated, fuzzy satellite photos I think I can identify it, so why are you calling it an 'unidentified craft'?"

Anticipating this question, Brasco had prepared an answer. "The Office of Homeland Security has no comment on what the craft 'looks like' in pictures and video. *I can* report that these are the clearest images available and there is credible intelligence that there has been hostile action generated from the UIC."

Assuming Brasco did not have the clearance to be present for the discussion, the panel was cautious. Allowing the information guy to be privy to discussion, inhibited dialogue, therefore Brasco was asked to leave the room for their classified conversation. This was going to be a heated debate.

Sperm whales were still on an endangered list. Killing the whales would be out of the question. "Save the Whales" was still a euphemism for fanatical animal rights groups. Stunning them was also out of the question for the same reason.

"Based on relevancy" was code for "there was a whole lot of information they had not been told." More than likely, there was another panel assembled somewhere else, being briefed with similar, but slightly different information.

Colonel Jacobs wasted no time getting to his point. "This looks like a God damn trailer to some God damn horror movie to me." His red face ballooned above his starched collar and tie. "This dang relevancy thing is pissin' me off." Jacobs had been on this panel through several administrations and relevancy was a new instruction.

Governor Childs looked older than her sixty-four years. Deep furrows between her gray eyes and parentheses carved around her mouth exposed years of making tough choices. She had always liked Walter, but also dreaded their rotation together through this Homeland Security Panel. Since 9/11 what DHS considered "relevant" sometimes bordered on the absurd. She knew Walter was as impatient as he was intelligent and did not suffer fools gladly; revelency was a spark to tinder for Walter.

Sean Anderson, first-term congressional representative from Oklahoma, interrupted her thoughts. "I'm pretty sure it isn't a Michael Moore film this time, Wally. I watch Ocean shows with my kid all the time – he loves sharks – anyway, I've seen those stalactite-things crash because of underwater earthquakes. They happen all the time, you know – underwater earthquakes." His Adam's Apple bobbed as he swallowed hard with the little spit he had in his mouth. Sean had lobbied hard to land a rotation on one of these panels. His media team thought he needed experience and confidence dealing with political "big boys."

Childs said, "Regardless if it was an earthquake or an explosion, I don't see how it affects our security."

"The information presented to us does not warrant any action from the United States" said Monroe Feldman, a securities broker in his fifties. He carried an expensive Beau Reed hand-tooled leather briefcase that contained nothing more than his golf shoes and the most recent issue of Golf Digest. He looked at his watch; he could still get in nine holes if the committee made a decision within the next hour. "Any more discussion?"

Without pause, Feldman snapped shut his briefcase and stood up.

If the two remaining members were suspicious of this assignment, they made no comment. The objective of this committee was to consider the danger to the country and give a green light to "use whatever means necessary to secure the waters of the United States of America."

They concluded that, given the information provided, there was no immediate threat to the United States.

Chapter 7

As soon as the group of whales containing the UIC entered United States territory, the US Navy deployed three attack-grade submarines to confront an unidentified craft, imbedded into a sperm whale pod, on the move along the Pacific Rim. These submarines, their bulbous hulls cloaked in black paint, knifed through the water like bullets aimed at the whale pod.

The captain of the *Edison*, Gil Rogers, coordinated the confrontation. His resume included decades of military experience, active warfare duty during Operation Desert Storm and the conflict in Kosovo. The *George Washington*, with its relatively new crew, would follow closely behind Gil. However, Gil knew the young Captain and was confident with her at his flank. A third attack-grade submarine *The Custer*, would make a surprise approach from the rear. If the UIC failed to surrender, they had the authorization to fire.

During strategic planning for this assignment, Gil favored a "mine laying" expedition. He recommended his crew bury a strip of explosives, retreat to a safe distance and detonated when the craft moved over it. Decisions were made based on collateral damage to the environment, and therefore the more targeted attack was settled on.

The subs moved into position and sent out "surrender or prepare to be fired upon" in several languages.

The nanos intercepted the message – the attack submarines were going to fire. The nano craft was a perfectly tuned, biomechanical, weaponized vessel with each system working in harmony.

Nanos detected three submarines approaching: *attack grade; capable of high speed, unlimited endurance and maneuverability; currently using the protective cloak of stealth. Conclusion: A lethal opponent.*

The emotional response to the threat from the submarines activated the defense system.

The unidentified craft failed to respond to their signal and the submarines cued up in a classic military-strike stance. Gil commanded the *Edison* to fire a torpedo. Immediately after launching their missle, the *Edison* swung to the left and allowed *The George Washington* to take center stage; Donny took aim and fired a torpedo as well. Dislodged fragments from the unidentified craft floated to the surface.

The nanos' newly acquired mindfulness reached a conclusion: the fragile makeup of the biological fleet – the clan – was in danger. *Employ sonic cannon.*

The first sonic wave hit *The George Washington* from below. As the wall of energy penetrated the sub's hard metal exterior, every screw, bulkhead and brace came apart. Gil looked on in horror as the *Washington* exploded. *The Custer* swung into place in the battle zone as the menacing craft emerged from the falling debris of the shattered ship. Before *The Custer* could respond, a soundwave rippled through the submarine. This time the pressure killed the crew as the wave crushed their organs. The crew was dead, and all systems shorted out within seconds of the wave sweeping through the ship. Without power or people directing it, *The Custer* drifted to the bottom of the sea.

The *Edison* held its position at the left wing of the battle zone, exposed and vulnerable. A young midshipman fired two torpedoes; Gil watched as they ricocheted off the craft.

The UIC fired a third sonic blast. All electrical systems flashed and crashed as the soundwave rumbled through the *Edison*. Waves of nausea rolled through the crew; noses bled and small blood vessels popped as the weakened blast coursed through the submarine.

Bile rose from Gil's gut. He wrestled the waves of nausea that threatened to make him wretch. Visual assessment of his crew showed some were puking, others were weaving from the effects of the invisible blast that had slammed through their sub. Auxiliary systems powered up and the submarine retreated.

Nanos assessed the situation: *All danger crippled or destroyed.*

State of mind no longer hobble the vessel. As emotions emerged, the system sorted, processed and interpreted them. The nanos acknowledged the regret generated by the hypothalamus in response to the destruction it had caused.

The Leader relied on his echo-location system to track his pod. He monitored their safety from a distance.

A cleanup crew salvaged a piece of the unidentified craft floating at the surface and sent it to Brasco.

Chapter 8

Twenty-five miles southwest of Virginia Beach sat the newly opened Nash Research facility. Its Director, Dr. Clair Lofton, had spent endless hours working on the business end of running this research facility.

She was in her office reviewing the new website when her secretary Sharon interrupted her.

"Clair! There is a Lieutenant John Brasco of Naval Intelligence on line one, what should I tell him?" Sharon's voice was breathy with excitement; having worked as hard as Clair at organizing the office she was eager for a profitable contract. Working together, busting through the good old boy network of military contracting, helped the two become best friends.

"Hopefully this is the big one we've worked so hard for" Clair said. "Forward the call to me."

Big government assignments included built in outrageous overheads and wildly lucrative.

"Dr. Lofton here," she said.

"Brasco here." He launched into his task. "Have you worked with Naval Intel before? It says in my catalog of providers that you have Level A clearance. Are your people current? Who have you worked with?" He waited a nanosecond before saying, "Dr. Lofton -- are you there?"

Clair answered, "Yes – yes I'm here, and we do have Level A clearance, and staff credentialing is current." She stopped. Her list of former clients was nothing special, and she wanted to sidestep the question.

Brasco interrupted her thoughts. "My go-to Virginia Beach research lab is backed up and I need this job done ASAP. I can get the job to you this evening." Brasco was rushing this. He did not want this Dr. Lofton to ask too many questions. "You do take overnight deliveries?" he pressed.

Her parent company Global Nash Research held several standing contracts with the government. Getting her facility a government contract would put her laboratory on the fast track to more significant research projects – and her on the fast track to owning her own lab and doing her own research. Clair was determined to make this connection.

Sharon tip-toed into the office and boldly pressed her ear up against the other side of the phone. As if she read Clair's mind, Sharon elbowed her and gave her the thumbs-up sign.

"Yes, we have a twenty-four hour dock," Clair said. "Lieutenant, you know there is paperwork to complete before we can accept delivery, do–"

"My people will fill out all the necessary paperwork and get it to you immediately. This is a simple analysis project, Ms. Lofton. We have a piece of – for lack of a better word – mechanical junk we need analyzed. It'll need to be – never mind, I'll brief you by e-mail. I've got to go–" Brasco disconnected the call. He did not intend to forward any information on the "junk" he was shipping to the lab.

Familiar with the meaning behind the term "junk," Clair was surprised Brasco had asked her lab to analyze it. Not that this lab wasn't equipped to do the job, but it sounded like a standard "identify the country of origin" job, typically done by military lab grunts.

"Woot Woot! Our first big job." Sharon gave a pull on Clair's office chair and spun her around. Clair allowed herself to twirl happily in her chair, thrilled her lab had finally landed a real research job. For the past few weeks, analyzing urine and blood for a city contract was the only work they had seen.

"Okay, Okay, we've got to prepare," Clair said. "The sample will be here tomorrow. You follow up with Brasco on the paperwork and I'll get to work on putting together a research team." She hugged Sharon. "Our hard work really paid off. Thanks for everything you've done."

Clair reviewed several resumes, each from experts within different specialties. She focused on mechanical and computer engineers as well as chemists. Brasco gave no indication they would be analyzing something biological in nature, however she chose one biologist who held dual doctorates in mechanical science and biology.

On a SmartBoard in her office, she grouped the researchers into three teams. Ted Banks, a mechanical engineer, headed up the group tasked to analyze construction. Lily Benton and the chemist group would analyze the chemical makeup of the sample. The biologist group, headed by Buck Sparkinsi, would review all data and project any environmental threat.

Clair considered asking Sharon to review the list she had finalized, but decided against it. She felt confident with her decision and didn't feel like rehashing each name with Sharon, who had an opinion on everything. She drafted a memo and e-mailed it to each of the researchers. Clair called the loading bay and told the supervisor to notify her once the sample arrived; she left the office with plans to return early the next day.

The following day, Clair carefully picked through her closet for the right outfit. She was very tall and boyishly slim. These were science guys so her power suit would be lost on them. She found sexy worked to get their attention, but tended to piss off any female researchers she may have hired. She chose low-slung black trousers with a chunky belt, a white, fitted button-down shirt and flats – always flats for shoes.

When Clair arrived at Nash, Sharon was standing in the lobby and waving an invoice about spasmodically.

"I opened it," she said referring to the invoice, "it's from the night manager. I guess he didn't know to call you as soon as it arrived. I didn't call down and give 'em hell. I left that to you."

Crap! thought Clair as she read the note. Someone had put the package in holding on the dock. She hurried to the loading dock to get a look at the sample. Once there, she learned they moved it to cold storage and that it was huge and weighed a ton.

She rushed to cold storage, located the sample, and stopped in front of the box for a moment. She needed to be thoughtful about her course of action. Her career depended upon it. Security was of utmost importance. Clair wondered whom to call from the loading dock to move the sample.

She turned to Sharon and asked, "Does Pete have security to move this thing?" Sharon assured her that he did. They decided to have Pete on standby to move the sample when necessary.

Why frozen? she wondered, but there was no time to investigate. She headed to the conference room to meet with members of the teams. She felt confident. Each member had government clearance and was an "out of the box" thinker. She looked forward to working with them.

Team members arrived at exactly nine-thirty. Clair didn't waste any time in giving each their assignments. She gave them a few minutes to review the data and then they headed down to the loading dock, where the sample awaited analysis.

"Sharon axed me to crack da lid so you guys could see it right away," explained Pete, who stood over the open crate. Sharon stood next to him with a crowbar and a sheepish look on her face, knowing she should have waited. Clair peered into the container.

What the fuck? – It looks like skin!

Too stunned to say anything to her assistant she redirected her focus.

"Buck, this looks like a biological project at first glance. Are you up for it?"

"Christ, where'd this thing come from?" Buck asked. He directed his group to take a sample up to his lab for a DNA test. "The others should take samples and see how they correlate in their disciplines."

"I'm still waiting for briefing material," Clair admitted. Earlier, she reviewed the recording of her initial conversation with Brasco to extract any additional information and discovered nothing.

"Should we wait?" Buck asked. He hoped not, this promised to be a very interesting project. "I'd like to start now with DNA testing to determine whether the material is biological or synthetically engineered to resemble living skin."

Ted said, "My team can start on how it's constructed."

"I can get you a preliminary chemical analysis within a few hours," Lilly interjected.

It seemed there was going to be a healthy dose of competition among the groups. *Good*, thought Clair; in her experience, a little competition always helped a project. "Don't wait. I know I don't have to tell you that we're under an unrealistic time constraint."

There were harrumphs and snorts from the team members. Buck said, "We've all worked for the feds before, Clair. Thank god it's your job to deal with them."

He headed up to the biology department as Ted and his team picked up two of the larger pieces and took them to mechanical engineering. Lilly had chosen a few smaller pieces for chemical analysis and called up to the chem lab to kick out anyone without clearance. Clair decided to follow Buck and his team and get their preliminary observations first.

Inside the mechanical engineering lab Ted prepared to dissect the first sample.

"Carla, you're in charge of documentation. This job will require audio as well as video recording," Ted said and turned to the rest of the team. "You, guy in the green shirt, get me several different dissection kits. We don't know what we've got yet. All of us will suit up in biohazard gear. Better safe than sorry is my motto!"

The team started to grumble about the hazmat suits, and Carla whined she did not want to be stuck recording while everyone else got to cut into this thing. Ted let them grumble. He didn't want to wear the suit either and probably wouldn't have if he'd been working solo.

"Carla, I'll be sure you get your tweezers dirty today." he said to pacify her.

Lilly's team was stuck in a small educational lab. The lab she needed for this analysis was in use for the next few hours. She would perform preliminary testing on her sample in the educational lab, but more comprehensive testing would be needed. She called Clair to oust the other scientists by noon.

Clair was in a lab in the biology department. It was one of the largest, fully equipped laboratories in the facility. She marveled at the high-tech equipment networked to scientific laboratories on site with the advising and administrative offices.

Three stainless-steel counters occupied two-thirds of the room. Each one housed state-of-the-art microscopes and two "slop sinks." Audio/visual equipment had been artfully included in the designer lighting and cooling systems, and the dun-colored floor tile had been padded to relieve any back or leg fatigue. Specifically chosen for the walls was a soft celadon color, selected for its calming quality.

She watched closely as each member of Buck's team tested the substance. Buck had a great system going; he had not taken his own sample to analyze, but moved from one member to the next, questioning, encouraging and taking notes. *He'd have been a great teacher*, she thought as she watched his peers look to him for direction and support. Clair smiled slightly as she noticed his combover became stringy bangs as he bent over, quietly assessing each researcher's findings. Forty minutes passed as the team dissected and examined the matter. Buck finally straightened up and focused his attention on Clair.

"It appears that there are several types of material in the skin, bone on the underside and nerve cells in the center. There is a thickening of the tissue at the edges – like it is healing and scarring. There is just as much non-organic material, but we were able to easily pick through it and examine the tissue. Clair, it looks like the non-organic material is partially integrated into the organic material though biosynthetic conduits scattered throughout the tissue."

Before Clair could respond, her cell phone rang; it was Ted.

"You got to see what we got down here. Where'd you say this thing came from?"

"I'll be right there," Clair answered. She turned to Buck. "I'm going to see what Ted has on the synthetic material. You guys sit tight. I'll be right back."

She arrived in the mechanical engineering lab, momentarily startled to see Ted in his hazmat suit.

"The bio guys aren't wearing hazmat suits," stated Clair.

"And all their babies will probably have three eyes," shot back Ted. "Anyway, forget the suit and take a look at this," he said and directed Clair to a microscope.

"I read about these several years ago. These are high grade, maybe even military. We've stumbled upon something pretty complex, Clair," Ted said.

Clair looked closely into the microscope --there she viewed a swarm of microscopic machines. She immediately recognized the nano design. A few years back, a member of her doctoral committee presented some research on them to her for professional review. She'd provided a short generic supposition. She'd spent little time on it; nano design was too expensive for most private research companies.

"I told you this was a government project, Ted. And we didn't 'stumble upon' anything – they gave it to us. I've got to figure out why we were sent the sample." Clair was furious. She was putting two and two together and the four she came up with made her look the fool.

"You guys sit tight while I make a few phone calls. Keep your sample frozen and take off the suits." Before she left, Ted asked for information from the other teams. Clair opted to keep the discovery of information independent and declined his request. She needed time.

One of the guys in a hazmat suit spoke to her as she left, "Is it true the bio guys aren't wearing these suits?"

"Hey, green T-shirt guy, it don't matter what the bio guys are wearing. I'm requiring all my team to keep them on. I don't want to get a call from your wife six years from now, cussing me out because your kid has three eyes – because you didn't wear standard cautionary gear today," Ted said as he walked Clair to the door. She hurried back to her office.

Bone tissue and nano-machines, Clair thought. She needed to call someone to find out how these tiny machines ended up in her junk.

Sharon was away from her desk when Clair entered her office. *That's a good thing,* she thought, *I don't want to explain what the hell's going on to her right now.* She scanned her desk for any additional information from Brasco – nothing. She grabbed an expensive fountain pen from her collection that sat in a display case on her desk. This sleek, bright-blue pen was her favorite. It was the size of a cigarette and fit perfectly between her pointer and middle finger. Having quit smoking five years ago, she often craved the calming effect of nicotine. She held the pen like a Parliament 100 and took a deep breath. She had been certain Ted's team would uncover some new kind of synthetic fiber. What he showed her was organic cells working together with the nano-machines.

She had two choices, and she was on the edge of making the risky one. *Go for it,* said a voice inside her head. She dialed up the only person she knew who could shed some light on this.

"Dr. Harden," said the man at the other end of the phone.

Clair jumped right to her point. "Yeah, Dr. Harden, this is Clair Lofton; you sat on my doctoral committee. Anyway you're the only member of Project Nano I know of."

There was silence, then Hank reacted,"What does the Nano project have to with you?"

Clair was annoyed; she didn't have the time to play the game of Who Knows What before I Speak?

"Look, my lab was hired by a government agency to identify a sample of something," she said, "and there are pieces of Project Nano all over my sample."

Hank seemed unfazed. "Fax me over what you have and give me the name of the person you're working for."

Clair hesitated only a minute. She had decided before she made the call that she would be transparent. "His name is John Brasco, and you'll get any information when I have time to send it."

Hank ignored Clair's last sentence. "I know John." He gave the impression he was talking to himself. "I'll give him a call. The Nano Project is classified Dr. Lofton. I'll need clearance to talk to you."

"Whatever," replied Clair and hung up the phone.

She needed to get back to the laboratories. It was hard to decide which lab to visit first. She fiddled with her pen a few more minutes, deciding which to choose; *Buck in biology,* she concluded. She really liked the cooperative work done there. In addition, she was pretty sure Ted still required his team to wear the bio-suits. Clair carefully returned her fountain pen to its case.

"Clair!" Sharon called into her office. "Brasco's on the phone. He needs to talk to you—NOW." Sharon continued, "I've been trying to get a hold of him – like – forever, and he was never available, and now he's in a hurry and I'd like to put him on hold for – like – forever, but it's your call." By now, Clair was standing next to Sharon's desk. Today, the nut-brown color of the reception area did not provide the comfort the decorator had promised. Frustrated, she grabbed a handful of her auburn hair and tugged at it. *Be professional*, she reminded herself and took the phone from Sharon.

"Brasco, where's my briefing? Do you have any idea what we've got here," she said, certain Brasco knew what he had sent her. *If he thought she would ignore the elephant (or Nano) in the middle of the room, he was about to be disappointed.* Before she could continue, Brasco cut in.

"Dr. Lofton, I don't really care that you're annoyed by my lack of full disclosure when I sent you the sample. In addition, I don't have time or the inclination to explain anything more to you over the phone. Dr. Harden is on his way to your lab and he will take charge of this project. You have two very viable options Clair; you can take off your lab coat right now and go home. I'm sure Dr. Harden can be updated by your more than competent staff." He let the option sink in.

Clair was stunned; she had not expected to get kicked to the curb so blatantly. Walking out the door would ruin her career. Sharon, ear pressed up to the back of the phone again, gasped and flipped up her middle finger, enraged.

"Or you can stay on and assist Dr. Harden as needed," Brasco continued. He stopped talking and waited for Clair's response. He knew he had profiled her correctly. She was a risk taker, yes, but career advancement was extremely important to her. Having this project on her resume would boost her reputation within the research community. "You need to make your decision Clair. Dr. Harden is about one hour out. Prepare your staff. He'll either see you or he won't." He waited.

"My assistant Sharon will meet Dr. Hardin in the lobby," Clair said. "I'll be in the biology lab with Buck – I mean Dr. Bruce Sparkinski." She hung up. Her mind reeled. Brasco had played her from the beginning. When she thought about it, Brasco must have known she knew of Dr. Hardins' work and he probably assumed she would call Hardin if the samples contained nanos. Now, phone records would indicate *that she* was the one to called Hardin in. She had taken several professional development courses providing guidance on working with security agencies and classified material – none of this followed procedure. She was certain her lab had acquired top-secret data and Brasco was not playing by the rules.

"Who the hell does he think he is?" Sharon growled. "And what are we going to say to the team?"

Clair didn't wait to rehash the phone call with Sharon. Figuring out what to tell her team about her demotion was the least important complication on her to-do list.

She rushed up to the mechanical engineering lab to speak to Ted.

"Did you record all your findings?" she asked. Ted ignored her; he was deep in research mode.

"See this nerve tissue here? It's configured to resemble basic mechanical wiring, and this group here is in a configuration resembling a computer port. The skin itself has been reinforced with a network of carbon nanotubes, as have the other tissues." Ted's team was studying their sample on a screen at the back of the lab.

Clair surveyed the screen. "This is incredible."

`Ted turned toward her and scrubbed his head where his hair should have been -- he had any. The action caused waves of skin on his skull that kind of hung there fleetingly, and then receded back into his scalp.

Yeesh, thought Clair, *he should drink more water.*

He continued, "This kind of biological engineering is extraordinarily advanced. A machine using this kind of engineering would not only be able to repair itself, we can assume it would manufacture anything it needed to be operational. I have Uber scientific clearance and I have to say I've never seen anything close to this."

"I know, I know, Ted. I have an expert coming ASAP," Clair said. "He should shed some light on what the hell is going on." That was not exactly a lie. Dr. Hardin was probably coming here to assume control, not shed light, but he was an expert on these nanos.

Looking around the room, she saw who she hoped was Carla in a hazmat suit, checking the audio-visual control panel.

"Carla? When did you start recording, and can I get an electronic copy of what you've got?" she said. Reviewing every moment of discovery was top priority now. *Fool me once shame on you, fool me twice shame on me* was an adage she'd lived by since graduate school. Hours of research could be stolen by trusting the wrong colleague, fellow student or lab partner. She would comb through data in the discovery stages; hopefully that would shed light on why Brasco misled her from the beginning.

"I have tape from the beginning," Carla answered. "But I'm not exactly sure where the final product ends up." She turned her palms up and visually scanned the lab. Clair looked around. This high-tech lab had artfully disguised the equipment, such as computer keyboards, monitors and audio-visual devices. It was a little like "find the hidden object" to ferret out such equipment.

Clair moved to the control panel. She pressed "Format Options,", typed into the search bar "Item from Content Library" and opened that tab. "Did you name this file?" she asked.

"No. I just started recording. " Carla was sweating inside her haz-mat suit. The suits adjusted to body temperature, so the sweat was from anxiety. It didn't take a brain surgeon to know they were on to something big.

Clair found the file created this morning in the lab. She created a duplicate copy, and sent the copy to her e-mail. "This program is similar to Microsoft Publisher. Several of the office staff and I received a tutorial on the system a few months back," Clair said. She looked around; no one was listening to her nervous chatter. They were all genuinely engaged in the research. Her cell phone "pinged" as an e-mail hit her inbox. She left the lab.

Sharon met her in the stairway. "I knew you'd be here. Buck's looking for you. He's got the results of the DNA testing; you know, 'who da baby daddy?'" Sharon joked. Clair kept walking.

"Well, Buck didn't think I was funny either," Sharon said and held the door for Clair as she walked through and headed silently toward the offices.

"I'm sorry Clair," Sharon said. "I'm just nervous, and you know when I'm nervous I joke around." Clair stopped, turned and looked at Sharon – she looked pathetic standing there wringing her hands. As much as Clair would've liked to put Sharon's hurt feelings at the bottom of her to-do list, she decided to address them.

"Honey, we're all under a lot of stress here, including you," Clair said. "But let me give you a clue as to what you will encounter today. Most of us are scientists with a huge discovery unfolding. On an average day, we can be buffoons in the social realm. Today, there will be no polite social banter, no back-and-forth communication, and mostly no joking." Sharon stood by the stairway door, still wringing her hands. Clair leaned in and gave her a hug.

"I just don't know what to do, Clair," Sharon whispered.

"Just remember that you like us! And regardless of how you may perceive the way you're being treated today, remember that we like you too. Put your feelings away." Clair continued, "They will only be hurt on a day like today."

Clair walked on. "I'm going to Buck's lab," she said. "Dr. Hardin will be arriving any time now. Go wait for him and greet him with all the brazen moxie you have, then let me know he's arrived." Clair took time to turn and smile. Sharon's shoulders relaxed in appreciation of that simple act.

"Thanks, Clair. I may even be nice to him. . ." Sharon was still talking as Clair walked away. She heard something about "ex-lax and coffee" as she entered the hallway that led to the biology lab.

Buck's team was huddled around a cardboard "Karaf of Koffee" from the Kluck-Kluck Koffee Kafe, a chain of premium coffee houses. Many scientists favored these shops because they marketed their careful attention to the scientific method of coffee brewing, which focused on extraction, acids, sugars and bitters, and ultimately promised that their extraction rate was between nineteen and twenty-two percent – coffee's ultimate brewing "sweet spot." Clair didn't drink coffee.

"Sharon says you have some info for me," Clair said as she approached the group of researchers. No one looked at her; they all kept their eyes fixed on Buck.

"The DNA was an exact match to a sperm whale," Buck said, filling up his coffee cup. "Extensive testing shows no signs of mutation or genetic modification. When do we find out what they have in engineering?" he said as he ripped open several pink packages of Sweet'N Low to pour into his coffee.

Now all turned toward her. Hopefully her poker face hid the fact this was not what she expected. She'd expected scientifically modified or synthetic DNA. Now they had whale DNA with nano-machines. Who would modify a whale in such a way, she wondered. She had too many questions and not enough knowledge of nano-machines to guess.

"I've got an expert coming in," Clair told the team. "He should be here within the hour. We'll meet with him and Ted's team to settle on the next steps."

"An expert on what?" Buck said, then took a sip of coffee. "We're feeling a little like mushrooms down here, Clair. You know, kept in the dark and fed–"

"I know! I know!" Clair cut him off before he could finish. "It won't be much longer I promise. Please send all the tape you have on your discovery to my e-mail." She scribbled her e-mail address on a piece of paper and handed it to Buck. She looked around. "Anyone know the video system?"

A young researcher with sandy hair and very green eyes spoke up. "Yes, I do. I learned this system in grad school. I'll send a copy ASAP." Clair left the biology lab and headed for her office.

She was exhausted. It was barely 2:00 pm and she had been juggling this discovery for the last eight hours. Now that she thought about it, she was also hungry. The vibrating phone in her pocket interrupted her thoughts of lunch. It was Sharon.

Sharon spoke in a sugarcoated voice, "Dr. Lofton there is a Mr. Hard-On here to see you. I know you're *extremely* busy, should I ask him to wait?" The emphasis on "extremely" was outrageous, and the "Mr." wasn't lost on her either.

"Sharon, tone it down," Clair said. "I'm in the hallway – right outside." This was one of those times she was thankful for her six-foot frame. *Deep breath,* she told herself, then squared her shoulders and entered the reception area. Hank Hardin hadn't changed much in the past several years. He had the stereotypical "research look" about him; tall, thin and pale. His jet-black hair, slicked back from his face, and ice-blue eyes left him far from nondescript. However, his saggy hound-dog cheeks and thin lips kept him from being handsome.

"Good afternoon, Dr. Hardin," Clair greeted her former advisor. "We met several years ago."

Hank grabbed at her hand and managed a halfhearted handshake. He moved around her and exited the office area to the hall where Clair had just come from.

"Yes we did," he said. "Now, I'd like to see what you've found so far."

Great, he's rude, Clair thought. *Whatever. S*he wanted to be included in this research. "Yes, of course, you'll need to follow me." She waited for him to stand aside and passed him to lead the way to Ted's lab. Hank read a file he'd brought with him as he walked down the stairs. She wondered if she had any of the information it contained.

Mechanical engineering was closer, so they went there first. Ted paced throughout the lab; the top half of his hazmat suit now hanging off his hips. He had cleverly tied the arms around his waist to keep the suit from falling off. The headpiece bounced against his butt.

Ted did not wait for introductions, or for them to sit, but guided their attention to a large video screen. "We've been watching these for a couple of hours," Ted said. "Every movement is orchestrated." He zoomed out the image and the screen showed what appeared to be microbial matter. He then zoomed in closer and micro-machines materialized. He waited for Hank to join in his enthusiasm. It didn't happen.

Hank stared at the tissue sample. "What else do you have?"

Ok, he's officially creeping me out, thought Clair. If her assumptions were right and this piece of tissue housed real application of his research, he should have been over the moon happy, or over the moon angry. *Oh well*, Clair thought, *I too can pretend this is no big deal.*

"More research is being done in biology," Clair replied.

Hank followed Clair, timing his breathing to his steps. If he didn't, he thought, he might hyperventilate. *I can't believe I'm seeing this*, thought Hank,. This project was literally dead in the water years ago. He kept a dedicated ear to the research chatter and was sure no money had been filtered into any new projects. He spent a few minutes staring at the sample, then spoke.

"Clair, secure us a conference room where we can speak." He looked at Ted. "You're Ted, right? I will meet with you, the biologist and Clair." He returned his attention to the microscope. "I'm keeping just the two researchers on the project. Let go all other team members involved." There was a collective gasp from the room. Hank looked around, blankly, startled by the noise. He noticed three other researchers with very angry faces gaping at him.

"Thank you all for your time," he said. He needed to dismiss them quickly. The team members were quite young; he knew they would be concerned about their reputations. If they made any fuss about leaving, he would threaten to discredit them.

"Please see the receptionist in the office before you leave. There is a military confidentiality contract you all need to sign before you leave here today. Your compliance is essential. There are significant legal and personal ramifications if you do not sign this contract. Do you all understand?"

He turned to Clair. "Where can we go?" He needed to exit the room before there were any questions. Clair grabbed him by the elbow and swept him out of the room. She turned into a small lab and deposited him there.

"This is not where we will end up Dr. Hardin, but we can hide out here until I can secure us another spot. You're not very popular with my staff right now." *Or me either*, she thought.

Clair called Sharon with a heads-up that supporting members on the engineering and biology teams were on their way to check out of the project in reception. "Have routine confidentiality available, and be prepared for plenty of bitching and moaning. I'll be in conference room four with Buck, Ted and Dr. Hardin," Clair finished.

Sharon was uncharacteristically, and thankfully, cooperative.

The two-team leaders met Clair and Hank in the conference room. Hank asked for a PowerPoint setup and all eyes turned to Clair. *Maybe I'm going to be the AV guy for the project*, thought Clair grumpily, revealing the computer monitor concealed behind a retractable panel.

"It's here," she said. "Just insert your presentation." Hank handed her the disk. A woman in a typically male-dominated field was often relegated to office tasks. Often she politely, nonetheless firmly, declined such duties, but not today. *He's not a sexist*, thought Clair, *just an oaf*. She started the presentation. The disk contained official information on Project Nano. Hank felt little need to speak during the presentation since the viewers were scientists.

He signaled Clair to stop the presentation, and without waiting for questions, provided details on his background. He told them one of his doctorates was in microcellular engineering; as a graduate student, he focused extensively on theoretical research on nano-technology and had been part of the government Nano Project since its conception. The military-funded project worked solely on military implications for nano technology. The primary focus of Nano Project had been to assess and repair damage. Small-scale experiments conducted in the lab proved hugely successful. However, the first field experiment turned disastrous. A catastrophic explosion caused a sperm whale's death and destroyed a nearby rare coral formation. A huge public backlash developed. Green organizations got wind of the explosion and it resulted in negative media attention.

Clair watched as he droned on. Not a muscle twitched as he explained himself. He carefully made eye contact with each of them as he stood as still as a statue and described how he had lost control of a sensitive project. Clair chuckled as she found herself in a similar situation.

The military was able to cover up their involvement. Hank reported that the monetary loss exceeded one billion dollars – this included the loss of the military sub, the research, and the cover-up money. With that kind of monetary hit, there needed to be some "head rolling." Losing his job was inevitable, but he was astonished they scrapped the entire project. They dismissed him and the team within days of the explosion. He assumed the military secured all nano material recovered. Hank stopped and let the information soak in.

"You *assumed*?" Ted's face flushed and his voice rose. "You were a lead scientist. It was your responsibility! How could you leave not knowing?" They all stared at Hank in disbelief.

Deadpan, Hank continued his explanation. "After the explosion, it was no longer a scientific project; it was military recovery, and I was bounced to a nearby private lab and stripped of any military clearance. No one would talk to anyone on the team. It was days before we were debriefed. There wasn't much of an opportunity for us to ask questions but we were assured any information on the project would be forwarded. My team and were let go the same day we were debriefed."

Eerily similar to the treatment of her researchers today, Clair thought.

"What did they do with what was recovered?" Ted asked.

Hank replied, "Oh, I asked several times. However, I never regained military clearance to receive that information."

As stunning as this announcement seemed, Clair ignored it. "How did you get involved with Brasco?" she questioned.

"Brasco floated at the edge of the original Nano Project," explained Hank. "He contacted me shortly before you did." He ignored the researchers and fixed his eyes on a Renoir print at the back of the room.

"Who's Brasco?" Buck asked.

"He's the guy who sent me the sample," Clair replied.

Hank moved to the back of the conference room toward the door. "Look, we've taken a lot of time to review who I am and what happened several years ago. We need an explanation for what is happening right now. If you three are interested in continuing on this project – fine; I need a biologist and an engineer and you people are here. I can find in new scientists but I'd hate to waste more time bringing them up to speed." He turned to Buck. "I'm going to start with the biology of the sample. I already have a good idea of what the mechanic's look like. Are you coming?"

Without hesitation, Buck followed Hank out of the room, and Ted quickly followed.

Clair was keenly aware there had been no mention of a need for her expertise on this project. She had sold herself as an administrator long ago, however her doctorate in bio-molecular/chemical engineering would prove useful on this project. For what seemed like the one hundredth time today, she stuffed her anger down into her pancreas and followed the three men out of the conference room.

They decided to approach the sample with the same question in mind – how did the biology fit into the nano's equation? The three men worked independently at their state-of-the-art microscopes while Clair searched her tablet for scientific sites and related articles.

Buck hypothesized aloud, "We can assume that whoever was supposed to sweep the area after the explosion did a half-assed job. I mean, something was missed and this was created, right?" He poked gently at a chunk of the specimen with a scalpel. As a biologist, he was used to working from concept to creation. This project forced him to work backwards, and he enjoyed the exercise.

Hank pulled his attention away from his microscope and thought back to the time of the explosion.

"Some green organizations rallied several anti-whaling vessels to the site and interfered with the recovery, bumping into military vessels and generally causing chaos." Hank remembered television news shows, like Dateline and 60 Minutes, had aired interviews with animal activists relating what they suspected the agonizing final minutes of this very intelligent mammal were like.

Buck stopped poking at his specimen. "What if there were two whales instead of one?" he said.

Hank scowled and shook his head. Ted picked up on Buck's line of thinking and pressed further.

"Like, maybe a mother and a calf?"

Now Clair looked up from her computer screen. She appreciated the out-of-the-box thinking. The team needed more information on the sample.

"Where did Brasco get this?" she asked Hank.

"My information reported a skirmish between an unidentified craft and three military submarines, ending with two destroyed subs. This was recovered," Hank said. *Unrestricted information*, he thought, *released to security agencies. Easy to find if anyone searched for it.*

"But your theory is impossible," Hank said, turning his attention away from his sample and on to Buck. "We tested my nanos for negative effects on the environment or animals and they proved harmless. For Christ sake, they were constructed in a green lab!"

Buck, now up and away from his microscope, paced the laboratory. "These nano-machines are out there Hank; part of something," he reminded.

"Without a power source, my nanos are programmed to sleep, turnoff, go dormant," Hank continued in defensively.

Buck kept pushing. "Would they search for a power source?"

Hank shook his head, denying the concept. "Not outside of the program design – to analyze and repair damage."

"What if, during analysis, the nanos encountered two damaged objects?" Ted said, swinging his chair back and forth in an arc.

Clair pushed it further. "And what if they found a power source? Like the electricity in an animal brain." Her leg bounced up and down, a nervous habit she'd developed in graduate school.

"In biology, analysis is often used to identify key factors and then employ those key factors to make critical decisions," Buck said.

Hank thought for a minute. "Critical thinking for my nanos isn't a stretch, but this application," he nodded to the sample, "this is the stretch."

Clair's leg stopped jumping. "Could the energy of a whale's brain power your nano-machines?" she asked.

"We never tested for that specifically," Hank said. "I suppose it would depend on how much power the brain was producing." He scrubbed hard at his forehead with the heels of both hands. *How did this happen?* He wondered.

Clair pulled up a page on the sperm whale brain on her tablet.

"The sperm whale brain is the largest brain in the mammal world," she read. "Five times larger than a human brain."

"That could generate a lot of energy, especially if stressed," Clair thought out loud.

"Theoretically anything is possible," Ted said.

"Buck, do you have any lab animals we can test?" Clair asked.

"Can we do that? Ethically, I mean," Buck asked.

Not one to be squeamish, he'd seen the medical breakthroughs resulting from animal testing, but testing practices had to be extensively reviewed by academic panels and government agencies before practical use.

Clair rejected Buck's concern. "If any of this is really happening there is nothing to debate. We can allege a Homeland Security threat and do just about anything," she said. "Let's set up for animal testing. Buck - you and I will prepare for protein-ligand interactions. Ted, you prepare for functional macromolecular experiments." Clair hadn't forgotten Hank was here or that he was in charge. She glanced in his direction and noted no dissent or even interest in what was happening. The information in the folder held his full attention.

It didn't take long to set up the biology lab for the experiment. Buck brought in white rats, cockroaches and crabs for testing. They prepared several syringes with a solution of nano-machines and saline, then injected nanos subcutaneously into the subjects.

The team determined that the alteration of the biological sample must have occurred quickly given the Navy cleanup of the initial disaster had been prompt. Dissection and research would begin two hours post-injection. The two-hour wait went by relatively quickly. Each researcher filled the time with sensory activities to organize thoughts and meet proprioceptive and vestibular needs.

The result of the experiment on the animal subjects demonstrated that the nanos remained active in each animal, proving these nanos would draw power from the electricity generated by even a small brain – for example, the cockroach. However, each organism remained unchanged by the nano-machines. Thus, this experiment did not explain the sample tissue, much less the creature swimming around in the Pacific.

Clair took Hank to an office with access to a VPN (Virtual Private Network) to search for research projects focused on nanos and biology. Virtual anonymity allowed them to dig deeper into scientific research sites for information on nano applications.

Buck and Ted were tasked with the write-up of the results, and because of the sensitivity of the research, they needed to clean the lab themselves. They returned unused rats to holding cages. Ted loaded crabs into a crate. He hadn't cleaned up after himself in years. He thought there might be cerebral satisfaction from the exercise, but was mistaken. It was just boring work. He postulated on the paper he would publish after this project was finished. Absentmindedly, he tripped over a cage of rats and dropped the tub of crabs he toted; crabs spilled out onto the lab floor. He watched while several crabs scurried away. Using the face piece from a hazmat suit as a scoop, and a long nozzle from the water table as a nudger, Ted corralled the scattered crabs back into a crate. One was injured beyond repair – one claw and a good portion of the carapace smashed – he left that one to sweep up later.

Having served their scientific purpose, Buck offered up a quick prayer to Saint Felix of Nola, the patron saint of spiders, and dumped the cockroaches into a bio-waste container. A vegan girl he'd dated in collage tried to find a patron saint of insects but could only find reference to Saint Felix. Legend told that Saint Felix had been protected by spiders and freed by an angel to help the sick. Since the insects used in research were routinely used for medical research, it had seemed an appropriate offering.

"Hey, who is the patron saint for crabs?" Buck mused out loud as he watched Ted approach the damaged crab with a broom. Ted chuckled and took a swipe at the smashed crab on the floor. He stopped mid-sweep; a long metallic filament extended from one of its broken limbs.

"Buck! Get over here!" Ted didn't move. He flipped on his cell phone camera and began recording. He couldn't believe his eyes. He amended his command to Buck. "Before you come, you better go get Hank and Clair, and don't worry I got my cell camera running. You're going to want to see all of this."

Clair and Hank huddled over one computer screen. They had arranged themselves in such a way that their bodies did not touch. Boldly Clair had chosen the only seat right in front of the screen while Hank contorted his lanky body to see the screen over her shoulder. Buck exploded into the room.

"Hey! We've got something!" he said and skidded to a stop near them. "Ted sent me; he wants you two." It was impossible not to notice the bizarre pose Hank had taken up.

Hank stood and the pain in his back eased as he unfolded from the jack-knifed position.

"I've linked to a study on nano construction and the protein keratin! I'll save it to my flash drive." Clair fished her flash drive out of her pocket.

Flash drive, Hank thought. "Information stays onsite until I release it,: he said. "You understand?"

"Yeah, right." Clair scoffed. She couldn't help but let some attitude show. His hijacking this project had chaffed at her for the past several hours, and since she'd been immersed in research she hadn't slipped back into employee mode. The computer flashed, signaling that the article had been uploaded. Deftly, Clair clicked and released the flash drive and secured it back into her pocket.

"I've got to get back," Buck said and bolted out of the room.

"Of course you'll have full disclosure of all information Hank. The study I uploaded is the only one we've seen that comes even close to what we're looking for." Clair stood and faced Hank. They were eye to eye. Hank didn't move, blocking her path. Seconds passed. For the one millionth time today, Clair tamped down her rage and lowered her eyes.

Hank took great pleasure in the power moment. His satisfaction all but dripped off him. He stepped aside. "After you, Clair." He sneered.

They returned to the biology lab and see that Ted has used his long nozzle to shuffle the injured crab into an empty tub. "I was afraid it might crawl away," he said.

They stared in disbelief; Nano regeneration was taking place in front of them. Hank knew the program. He had been part of the team that developed it. However, those nano's were designed to repair mechanical objects. These nano's were repairing biological material.

"I'm running out of space on my cell cam," Ted said.

"This is way beyond changing Keratin," Clair said. "This needs to be recorded." *Thank God I don't have to be the AV guy on this project,* she thought. "There are video-built-ins throughout this lab," she said. "I'll get them running."

"Do whatever, Clair. But it has to be secure," Hank said. He knew he needed to contact Brasco immediately.

The team stood by and recorded what was unfolding. Structural changes were taking place in the crab's exoskeleton. The damaged left claw was reconstructed, now heavy duty and longer. Nanos augmented the left side of the shell and the left legs to manage the new weight on that side. The crab was now too bulky for the tub he had originally used to contain it so Ted nudged it into a larger crate.

Several hours passed as they watched the methodical transformation. As one structure was enhanced, the supporting areas were also improved. The team assumed the internal workings of the crab were altered as well, but that could only be determined during necropsy.

After two hours without noticeable change to the exterior of the crab, they decided to put it into the lab's cold storage for the night. The nanos Hank developed would retreat into sleep mode when exposed to extreme temperatures. Hank set the thermometer at forty degrees and Ted and Buck carefully moved the crate into the unit.

"You two stay here throughout the night and monitor what happens," Hank directed Buck and Ted. "The sample sent to the lab was in stasis until we thawed it, so it is safe to assume these will go into stasis too."

He turned to Clair. "All other personnel will leave the premises. I will not have this project compromised because some well-meaning secretary walks in here with a pizza." They all knew he alluded to Sharon. "I'm going to secure myself in a computer lab down the hall for the next few hours." He said. "I see no reason for you to stay either. Go home.

Chapter 9

Nash Research facility boasted two fully furnished private sleeping quarters and a bunk room. The private rooms were small - ten by ten square with an extra-long twin bed, a four-drawer dresser, a desk, chair, and a small closet. The bunk room slept eight. Four bunks lined opposing walls with a dresser neatly placed between beds. Ted and Buck chose to sleep in the bunk room.

"Any wife, girlfriend, or whatever expecting you tonight?" Ted asked while he made up his bunk. It wasn't often researchers from different disciplines crossed paths in this facility. He and Buck had never met.

"Divorced for five years now. Women think I'm too much work – at least that's what all my exes say." Buck lay on his unmade bed with his eyes closed.

"Clair and I are friends," he continued. "She is going to my place to take care of my dog and chameleon." He peeked through a half-open eye at Ted and his almost-made bed, his own bedding neglected in a pile on the bunk next to him.

Ted surveyed his finished product. Bedding storage had provided several choices for bedclothes. He'd chosen the cotton sheets – not flannel- and a navy-blue lightweight comforter. The three pillows were balanced at the head of the bed. *Perfect*, he thought.

"I called my wife. We have a baby. This is the first time I've been away overnight since he was born," Ted said.

"Was she mad?" Buck asked. In his experience, when you called and told whomever that you weren't coming home – whoever was usually mad.

Before Ted could answer, his phone chirped; he had a text message.

"New Message From: Clair Hardin" lit up his screen. He clicked open the message.

"It's from Clair," he said. "She asked, 'Did u receive this?'"

Buck sat up. "Well, tell her 'yes you did,' right?"

Ted texted back 'yes.' The two men sat quietly. Ted stared at the screen. His screen saver, three-month-old baby Sean, stared back at him. Buck stared at Ted.

The phone chirped again. "New Message from: Clair Hardin." Ted was standing now. Buck walked over and stood next to him. He angled Ted's hand so they both could read the screen.

WTF is going on here???

Buck laughed. "I wondered when Clair's claws would come out," he said. "She held it together pretty well today considering . . . Anyway, what the fuck *is* going on here?" he asked. Ted was already texting back to Clair.

Theory: If there was a calf in close proximity to the mature whale, the calf may have been sheltered from the most intense heat and destruction. The injuries the calf sustained in the explosion would be substantial. Think of the stress level, i.e. the energy the brain created to deal with the pain. If it survived, and if the nanos encountered it . ..?????

After what we saw with the crab change today -- regeneration could have taken place.

He turned the phone for Buck to read. Buck's face indicated that he thought this was plausible.

"Send it and see what she says," Buck said.

Clair sat in her car a couple of blocks from the facility, crouched down, peering intently at her BlackBerry, waiting for anything from Ted. Her BlackBerry dinged as his text hit. Forgetting her cloak and dagger posture, she sat up straight and read his response. *Holy shit*, she thought.

Bambi with a twist, she texted back.

Clair knew mother whales and their calves experienced close maternal bonds. There would have been a sense of loss and a period of grieving for the young whale. She experienced an unexpected wave of sadness. During her career she'd spent days injecting serums into animals that could kill them. Often subjects were destroyed after the experiment. *It must be the mom and baby thing making me weepy*, she thought. Her phone dinged again.

Buck and I think Frankenstein is a better movie analogy, you know, science gone bad, death and destruction follows.

Ted sat on the floor, back against his bunk; Buck sprawled out on the bed watching the cell phone screen over Ted's shoulder.

Then that makes Hank the mad scientist, replied Clair.

Chapter 10

In a computer lab several doors down from the bunk room, Hank tapped into an encrypted channel and set up video chat with Brasco, and confirmed the samples were part of the original Project Nano. Florescent lights illuminating the lab washed out any color in Hank's already pasty face.

"You look like shit. Are you gonna be able to do this?" Brasco asked. Reading people was one of his talents. He hoped he'd gotten it right this time.

Hank bristled at the insult. "It's one o'clock in the morning and I've been dealing with that giant-pain-in-the-ass Clair since 9:00 am," he said. *I have a right to look like shit,* he thought. "And, I don't trust her."

"Well, you shouldn't," Brasco said. "I'm monitoring her cell phone right now and she and those guys in the lab are texting each other. You should have taken away their cells, Hank. There should be no communication outside that lab. Oh, and FYI – she just called you a mad scientist."

"What? I told them not to call anyone after they made their one phone call. Hang on, I'll go get the phones." He was seething.

"Stop!" Brasco shouted at his tablet. "I can block their cells. There will be no more texts tonight." Compared to what was ahead, he knew that jamming cell signals was relatively easy.

Hank plopped down again in the seat in front of the computer, ranting. "Mad scientist! She's just a pencil pusher – some no-name nerd who probably slept her way to Executive Director of this irrelevant lab! Mad scientist—why—why— I'm—published! What else did she say?"

Brasco noted that Hank didn't look pasty anymore. "Not much. They're trying to figure out what they're dealing with. If Clair realizes how significant this is, she'll want in."

"If what you've been telling me is true, there will be enough money to go around," Hank said.

"I said 'significant,' not profitable. There is a difference. Anyway, if she thinks there's an opportunity for career advancement, you bet she'll want in on it." Brasco hoped he wouldn't have to decode everything for Hank. He checked Clair's cell activity.

Hank changed the subject. "Did you find James yet?"

"About that, are you sure you want him on this project? There are plenty of other good scientists you don't have a wretched relationship with we could use" Brasco said, now looking at the file on Buck.

"No," Hank said. "Even when he fails it turns out to be genius. I have my reasons, Brasco. You promised." Over the past few years, his resentment toward James had grown to epic proportions. Hank was determined.

"Ok then, I'll get him." Brasco reassured him. "Get to your hotel; I'll be there in a couple of hours. I expect our company to arrive at 3:30 am sharp. Clair told her boyfriend not to expect her tonight. She's going to Buck's to take care of some critter and then she says she has some 'snooping' to do. She has nothing to snoop through, right Hank?" Brasco asked. Forgetting to take the phones from the goofs in the lab was a harmless mistake, Brasco reasoned. There were much more damaging things Hank could have overlooked.

Hank's rage shifted into full-blown paranoia. He MapQuested Buck's address as he spoke. "Nope," he said, and ended the call.

Brasco took the scenic Blue Ridge Parkway through Virginia to get to the mountainside inn where Hank was would be staying. The moonlight provided a stunning backdrop to the towering evergreens along the drive. *I should get up this way more often,* he thought as he soaked up the scents and sights of the Appalachian Mountains.

He arrived at the Inn at 2:30 am, parked in front of cottage seven and walked directly to cottage four. The door was unlocked. He stepped inside and shut and locked it behind him. He was pleasantly surprised to find the living area simply decorated – dark wood and earthy colors – cabin colors. He supposed he had expected a more feminine feel for something called a "cottage," like delft blue and white pine. This room had a masculine feel.

Hank sat sprawled in a leather recliner. A bottle of booze and several tumblers cluttered a small coffee table. He held a whiskey glass in his hand and scraped at the price tag on the bottom.

"Come on in," Hank said. "I got these glasses at the liquor store. This bottle of Bourbon here," he nodded to the booze on the table, "it's from the Hirsch Reserve. It cost three hundred dollars. The guy said, 'good thing we're so close to Pennsylvania.' That's where it's distilled – Schaeffer town, Pennsylvania. It's the most expensive Bourbon." Hank stuck his thumb in his mouth. He didn't have enough thumbnail to effectively remove the price sticker, and his thumb was rubbed raw.

Brasco stood in the entrance of the cabin, staring at Hank.

"Everything ok?" asked Hank.

"Do you think we're going to sit around and drink with these guys?" He hadn't believed Hank was such a neophyte.

"I couldn't care less who drinks this with me," Hank said. "I wanted to drink the best Bourbon, and I wanted to drink it out of a glass. Highball glasses come packaged in sets of four." He poured one glass of the expensive amber liquor.

"Ok, ok, pour me one too," Brasco said. He noticed sweat trickled down Hank's sideburn and snaked through a course patch of whisker stubble.

Brasco sat down in an Adirondack chair next to Hank. "Dude, you gotta change your shirt," Brasco said. "You're too sweaty. It's a tell, like you're doing something wrong." Brasco laughed; he hadn't sweat in years.

Hank poured a generous portion of expensive bourbon into a second glass and handed it over. The men angled their drinks toward each other in a silent salute.

"I've named the beast," Hank said quietly.

"What? Moby Dick Franken Whale?" Brasco said with a snort.

"No shithead! I've named it Titan, like the race of giants the Greek gods feared." He clenched and unclenched his empty fist.

Hank seemed a bit off, and Brasco did no want to agitate him further. "You know, that's actually a good name. I think I'll put that in the file." Brasco took out a pen from his pocket and wrote "TITAN" in large letters on the manila envelope he had with him.

Hank headed to the bedroom for clean clothes. That's when Brasco noticed dried mud on the back of Hank's shirt.

"The back of your shirt is muddy. Did you fall down?" he asked.

"Yeah. I fell down. Pour me another drink and one for yourself if you want. I've got to change this sweaty shirt." He looked at his watch. "It's 3:17. We'll have time for one more drink."

Brasco felt cold tentacles of doubt twisting into his consciousness. He'd waited years for an "opportunity" and this had looked like one. Several collaborators had come to mind when the piece of junk turned up, and Hank was a calculated risk. The file on Hank described him as an egocentric hypo-megalomaniac – a kind of low-key asshole; an expert in his field and filled with resentment. *Workable,* Brasco thought at the time.

A knock on the door interrupted the quiet.

"Company has arrived," Hank said, now presentable in a crisp white shirt, open at the collar. His face had been dried and his hair slicked neatly back from his forehead. He walked to the door and opened it.

The man at the door carried an oversized briefcase. In fact, the man coming in the door was oversized. *Looks like they sent muscle,* observed Brasco. Brasco himself was a little over average-sized – six feet tall and weighing in at two-ten.

He'd spent several years in the Special Forces. He joked with his mega-sized buddies that he may be small, but if he had to he could kill with his bare feet.

The newcomer did not acknowledge anyone and expertly stared at nothing. "I'm here for exchange," he said with a thick, Eastern European accent.

Brasco handed Hank the envelope with "TITAN" scrawled across the front; Hank turned and gave it to the european man, who then put the briefcase down.

The huge man turned to the door and waited. *How do you end a clandestine meeting where hundreds of thousands of dollars are exchanged?* Hank wondered. He considered shaking the man's hand.

Brasco jumped up and opened the door, "He's not going to leave any prints here," he explained.

Hank moved the briefcase to the coffee table. He carefully replaced the top to the Bourbon and placed the bottle on the small kitchen counter.

Brasco had experienced countless exchanges as a federal agent. This was different, he thought. This time he was not covertly buying or selling secrets for the good of God and country. He knew this exchange changed the trajectory of his life. Now set in motion, it could not be stopped.

Hank scratched at the price tag on the bottom of his glass with a butter knife.

Brasco knew from experience this juncture was where you lost your weakest link. There was real money now, but the deed was still to be done. A week link crumbles under the pressure of the task. Brasco chatted up his retirement plans with Hank, ideas for spending his fortune, shared his fantasies about boats, babes and beer. By the time he was ready to leave, he felt secure Hank was still on point.

"We'll meet up early at Nash Laboratories," Brasco said. "You let the remaining two researchers go. Clair will be furious, but I have a stellar letter of recommendation for her, and tell her I'll give it to the DOD personally. That should pacify her."

Hank downed a shot of bourbon and poured himself another.

"Go easy on that. I need you to be at the top of your game. Even with the recommendation, Clair's going to be pissy." Brasco took the suitcase and left.

Chapter II

Early the next morning, while Hank parked his car, he noticed two security guards leading a hysterical Sharon away from the Nash building. The police officer that stood sentry at the entrance alerted security of Hank's arrival. The lobby bustled with police. Brasco grabbed Hank as he entered and walked him through and out of the lobby – into the lab areas.

"Did you know that Clair Harding is dead?" Brasco hissed. Hank stared at him, speechless. Brasco continued, "Her car went off the road last night after feeding Buck's Iguana or something."

"It's a chameleon," Hank said.

"We've still got to go in there and remove Buck and Ted from this project," Brasco snapped, and stormed to the bunk room.

Hank stopped him. "Do you think they know about Clair?" he asked.

"Probably. It's been all over the news. Security just hauled some distraught woman away because of it. Let's get this done. You better hope you haven't screwed everything up."

They went directly to the bunk room and found the two researchers. Buck smoked a cigarette while Ted paced. The room was filled with smoke. A makeshift ashtray sat on the table. It was full. Empty coffee cups and crumpled snack wrappers littered the table.

"Isn't this place supposed to be smoke free?" asked Brasco. Both researchers ignored him.

"What the hell is going on?" demanded Ted. "Buck and I had no way to contact you. As far as we knew, you were dead in a ditch too. We've been here since yesterday. Somebody better tell us what is going on." Ted was terrified. Early in his career, he'd dismissed working for the military and decided to work in the private sector. The money was good and, except for the random eco-terrorist, a relatively safe gig.

"Do you think Clair's death had anything to do with what's in the deep freeze?" asked Buck. He and Ted had theorized several nefarious scenarios in the last few hours. If this project involved advanced weaponry – bio-weaponry – they knew bad guys wouldn't be far behind. He didn't wait for an answer. "I know I indicated I wanted to stay with the project, but it's taken a real ugly turn. I want out."

Without hesitation Ted agreed. "Me, too. This is too much drama for me. What do we have to sign to get out of this mess?"

Brasco had each man sign the same standard government confidentiality agreement signed by the other members of the team yesterday.

"This is what I recommend," Brasco said. "Bury Clair and then leave town. I don't care why – go on vacation, take a leave of absence. But disappear until things calm down; any questions?"

They both had a million, but knew better than to ask.

"You've been unusually quiet," Buck said to Hank. "You were technically her boss – our boss; I would'a thought you'd have something to say." It was a bold statement but Clair had been Buck's friend, and Hank had treated her badly.

Hank looked directly into Ted's eyes. "Ted, I have some advice for you. Sometimes what you're thinking up here," he tapped his forehead, "should never come out here," he tapped his lips.

Without losing eye contact, Ted uttered, "Asshole," and walked out.

Hank and Brasco waited a few minutes in silence, and then headed to the parking lot. "I've got to assemble a team and find James," Brasco told Hank. "You head to the lab in Colorado. I don't know how much time this will take and I don't want to waste what time we have."

"Am I supposed to get the pieces of Titan to Colorado?" Hank asked. He had no idea how to make that happen covertly.

"I'm already on it," replied Brasco. "As the original client, I contacted Nash Laboratories' board of directors before you arrived and told them they would receive the entire monetary amount they expected after my crew cleaned the place."

This is a swanky private lab. They're not used to researchers being killed." He added, " –accidently – and they were just as eager as Ted and Buck to get out of the contract."

The men reached their cars. Brasco turned to Hank. "You stick to research from now on. Do what you do best, and I'll handle the spy stuff. No more surprises. Clear?"

Hank flipped him off as he opened his car door and said, "Thanks for permission to just be me."

Chapter 12

Brasco loved his custom cherry-red Lincoln Navigator with its tinted windows and chrome-plated wheels. The interior boasted custom mahogany panels and leather upholstery, Bluetooth and sync-voice activation with a fourteen-speaker surround-sound audio system. He'd heard theories on why men drove big, obnoxious cars – they were compensating. Well, they were certainly right on his account – he was compensating for something. For the past thirty-five years, he'd held a job that required him to remain invisible. His car generated a lot of lusty looks from jealous losers and great conversation from grease monkeys. He was definitely not invisible when he drove his car. Activating his stereo system, he told it to play Josef Suk's Symphony No. 2. There was a five-hour drive ahead of him and he could relax listening to the sweeping works of this Czech composer.

It was a quarter past two in the afternoon when Brasco pulled into his condo's garage in DC. He had paid extra for a unit with inside access. Most people wanted inside access because they didn't want exposure to the weather when they brought in their groceries or came home from work. Brasco wanted it for security. He'd seen more than his share of slit throats and stabbings in a breezeway or portico and was a fanatic about his own personal safety. He punched an intricate code into his sophisticated security system and entered his home. Rich earth tones of moss green and nut brown provided a warm background for his mixture of mission-style furniture, antique Hoosier cabinets and humidors. His place was inviting and comfortable.

The answering machine read "Message Center Full." It begged to be answered as it flashed out its SOS but Brasco ignored the plea and headed into his office to retrieve the folder containing information on the original Nano Project. Melinda Davenport's file rested at the front of the dossier. Hank specified he wanted her on this new project.

Brasco worked around her several times and knew her to be very smart and adaptable. She'd be a hard one to control, but if they also brought in Tillman – and in the shape he was in – Brasco was certain Melinda Davenport could be managed. She was easy to find. Still contracted to the military, she currently worked on a research expedition in the Arctic Circle. He noted that she'd attached an electronic "Do Not Disturb" warning to her and the project, and he smiled. He was pretty certain there was no such protocol. She was on the research vessel The Shackleton.

Brasco slogged through a maze of bureaucrats in an attempt to reach her, impressed that she had managed to intimidate most administrators attached to her project – they did not want to disturb her. However, Brasco could be even more intimidating and finally reached the captain of the research vessel where Davenport worked.

Chapter 13

Hunkered down in a small, state-of-the-art research facility located on the lower decks of the ship, Melinda Davenport reviewed her latest findings on secondary aerosol gas to particle conversion in frigid temperatures. This ten-by-ten space had been her refuge for the past several months. Her previous two assignments had been huge collaborative projects. This independent assignment restored her individuality and renewed her commitment to creativity and innovation. It had been a particularly satisfying assignment. She thought it ingenious to add an authoritative "Do Not Disturb" warning on the title page to her electronic link to this project. No such directive existed in any military manual, but for some reason it worked for her. Without constant interruptions regarding timelines, budgets and other tedious tasks, she concentrated specifically on this cold climate mechanics project. Ahead of schedule, she looked forward to a holiday in the Netherlands.

A knock on the door interrupted her contentment. *Smug too soon*, she thought and arranged her face into an angry scowl. *This should scare anyone away.*

She opened the door. "What is it," she barked. The young seaman at the door was unimpressed with her irritated demeanor. *Hmm, this is new.* Usually, the crew was apologetic when they had to disturb her.

"Morning, Doc. There is a Lieutenant Brasco on the horn for you." The seaman waited for her response.

The "Do Not Disturb" would not fool Brasco, she thought. She remembered him to be the no-nonsense type, but also friendly. He worked special security or something on a previous and particularly disastrous military project. It had been her first big assignment and everyone involved had been close; such exciting research ended in an unexpected catastrophic incident. The feds closed that project and kicked the team to the curb quickly. She'd scrambled to find something else before word got out the project tanked.

She wondered what could he possibly want with her?

"Is he still on the horn? Waiting?" she asked.

"You know, Doc, when you don't screw your face up all mad-like, you're not half bad to look at," remarked the sailor. "And, yeah, he said he'd wait."

"Sailor, you been out to sea too long," Melinda remarked as she slipped on her boots and grabbed a coat. Before putting it on, she asked, "Do I need to go topside?"

"Yes, ma'am. You better grab a hat, too. It's blowing a gale up there."

Melinda reached the communication center quickly. She'd wanted to take her time, but the freezing temperatures and whipping winds caused her to forget to dawdle. She signaled the sailor at the radio to hold on a few minutes longer. Melinda evened out her breathing and took the mic. "Hello, John, does this need to be a secure conversation?"

"I've secured the line at this end. You'll need to secure your end," Brasco replied. He chuckled to himself; not many people called him John anymore and Melinda knew it.

She showed the cabin crew her federal ID badge. "OK boys, get out. I need to secure this room." The crew was somewhat surprised that their cranky "research girl" was also a federal agent. However, in this crew's experience, strange things can happen out at sea, and her being an agent wasn't the strangest.

"All clear," she said, and Brasco updated her on key events of the past several days. Melinda couldn't believe it – they were reinstating Project Nano.

"John, John," she interrupted. "Stop. My head is about to explode. I need to process this. What can you send to me ASAP? I can't listen to much more." Melinda sat down on the floor of the cabin. *Nano modified whales and crabs?* She felt faint. She'd heard if you felt faint, you should put your head between your legs. She was limber, but that remedy seemed near impossible in a down parka. She took several deep breaths.

"Melinda, are you still there?" asked Brasco. He heard her taking great gulps of air. "Christ, slow down; don't you know about relaxation breathing! I took you for a yoga girl."

"I'm 'research girl' here, and yes I know how to do relaxation breathing," she said. "But up here in the Arctic the oxygen is very thick. If you don't gulp it in, it takes forever to reach your brain."

She took a few long draws of breath through her nose.

"Can you set up a secure link to my computer and send me all you have on this project. I don't want to be days behind when I arrive."

I've got to think forward, Melinda thought.

"And when can you get me? You do realize that I'm in the middle of nowhere in mid-winter darkness; oh yeah, and we're in the middle of a snowstorm."

"I'll keep track of the weather," he said. "Winter darkness? Is that the opposite of midnight sun?" Brasco asked. "Anyway as soon as it's safe, I'll send a chopper for y–."

"You need to get a Cetacean specialist," Melinda interrupted.

"A what? Hank told me to get a marine biologist?" *Leave it to Davenport to say something unpredictable.*

"Hank and I are assembling a team." He ignored her request. "Are you sure you're secure out there?" Brasco needed to be certain there were no security risks. This project was too important.

"As I said before, I'm in the middle of nowhere in a never-ending snowstorm. This vessel is used exclusively for research, so there are security measures on top of security measures," Melinda explained. "Hey, John, don't you know, science is worth big money these days?" she quipped.

"So I understand," Brasco replied and disconnected communication. He looked at his notes; he circled and underlined "Cetacean Specialist." *Where would he find one of those?*

Chapter 14

Melinda scribbled "Do Not Disturb" on a piece of paper, added a skull and crossbones for emphasis, and taped it to her door. With just a few phone calls, she excused herself from her current project. A near complete research portfolio and a detailed outline would await her successor. Leaving this project resulted in forsaking any byline on the research. Of course, quitting a project at any time was toxic for a researcher's reputation. However, her reputation would more than survive if what Braso said was true.

She recalled all she had on Project Nano as she waited for Brasco to send her the report. Originally tasked with developing innovative ways to repair equipment, the Nano Project began as a government research project. The military's fascination with the Middle East generated billions of research dollars in arid climate repair.

Once the government got the bugs out of repairing military hardware damaged by sand, heat, and wind, a researcher named James Tillman pulled her and several others together to investigate the use of nano-machines in repairing underwater equipment. James was a "wunderkind," the kind of researcher that comes about very seldom. His research on robotics was stunning. Frequently, found a few steps behind James in the research, was Hank Hardin. The two worked closely on the project. Though obvious to others, James did not notice the acrimony developing between himself and Hank.

Melinda's laptop chimed; an e-mail from Brasco. The preliminary data suprised her. These nano-machines' functions far exceeded the prototypes she'd worked on. The research Brasco sent her hypothesized these nanos' could alter biological material. The original nano program was to fix broken hardware. She remembered the prototype nano's had the capacity to link with wireless computer technology. *Could that explain the change in the nanos' program?*

Still sitting in her small, nautical cabin, she turned her attention on the whale. *Should she even call it a whale?* The report contained a pixilated image of some variety of Cetacean. The file offered no information on biological material in relationship to nano material; but outlined the discovery of nano-enfused whale skin. This project needed a whale specialist. Whales lived in communities, had family units and communicated. If the hypotheses put forth by Nash Laboratories were correct, this transcended any ethical slippery slope.

Melinda stopped her thoughts from wandering to what the whale might be experiencing. Over the years, she managed to avoid projects requiring extensive animal research. However, during graduate studies she witnessed scores of them. She'd told herself that the ends justified the means, but couldn't look one of those animals in the eyes without sensing fear, hatred or loss. She supposed a marine biologist would be able to shed light on what the whale was experiencing and how to proceed humanely.

A break in the weather allowed a military helicopter to land and retrieve Melinda from The Shackleton. She packed light, one duffel bag and her laptop. She emerged from the interior of the ship and stopped to appreciate the beauty during the moment of rare Arctic light illuminating the horizon. Blues and greens waved and wobbled where the earth met the sky. This latitude was in its third week of darkness, and the last few days had been awash in a vibrant aurora borealis. Several times during the past few weeks, they'd experienced a humming and crackling in the air when the colors deepened into red and purple. Sailors called this the aurora guovssahas, or "the lights that can be heard." Taking time now to appreciate this breathtaking part of the world gave her pause to regret her time spent below deck, consumed by research. Dragging her attention away from the horizon, she struggled to take a few steps forward into the raging wind; a nearby sailor grabbed onto her petite frame and anchored her as she made her way to the chopper. She hoped to snag a window seat and take in the last bits of the ocean scape as they headed out. Inside she spotted three military types and who she guessed was another researcher sitting next to a window. The seat beside him was empty. Curiosity overcame natural beauty – she gave up her desire for a scenic view and plopped down next to him.

Making a wild guess she said, "Are you the marine biologist, or can I hope, a whale guy?"

He looked at her and said, "Maybe I'm military muscle."

Melinda shook her head. "Nope, you're traveling with a duffel bag and a laptop – you look like a researcher to me," she said, nodding to her own carry-ons.

He laughed. "OK, busted," said the man wearing a thick, woolen sweater and glasses. "I'm Dan Peterson, Whale Guy."

Melinda smiled. She introduced herself. "Alrighty then Dan Peterson Whale Guy. I'm Melinda Davenport, and for the last several weeks, aboard the Shackleton, I have been Research Girl."

Melinda explained to Dan that while she had spent the past several weeks in the Arctic, she hadn't taken the opportunity to enjoy the beauty surrounding her. She excused herself and moved to a window seat across the chopper. The sky was unusually clear and the scenery breathtaking. The robin's egg blue of the winter sky provided a stunning backdrop to the alabaster-white bergy bits and growlers – small and mid-sized icebergs jutting up from the dark-blue Arctic. Viewing the ocean icescape from above, in the helicopter, allowed her the extraordinary view of more than the tip of the iceberg.

This bird's-eye view gave her greater respect for those that navigated through this ocean. Many large icebergs jutted up through a pool of blue-green. The beauty of the turquoise water camouflaged the danger below – an ice mass ten times larger than what showed above the waterline.

The scenery couldn't hold her attention for very long; Project Nano kept crashing into her consciousness. She bounced back to the seat next to Dan.

"Why'd they pick you for this project?" she asked.

"I'm a Navy Seal and a marine biologist. I've worked several covert operations with Brasco," Dan explained. "Pirates are not the only danger on the water; bio-terrorism is a huge threat on the open sea."

"What we needed was a Cetacean specialist," Melinda complained aloud.

"Whales and Dolphins? Loved them as a kid," Dan said, "studied them as a grad student . . . provided groundbreaking insight into whale family and social structure, blah, blah, blah." Dan was also going to be cautious. Brasco provided sketchy information on the project and no information on Melinda Davenport, Research Girl. He didn't always trust Brasco. Nothing bad ever happened – the guy always ended up transparent, for the good of the country,– however, Dan's gut prompted him to be careful around Brasco's projects.

"Well," said Melinda, "we could waste a lot of time trying to figure out who knows what and how much, or we could just dive into the research I've been doing. I'm kind of stuck at this point." She smiled and continued, "I need a good whale guy to fill in some blanks." Dan and Melinda spent the next several hours reviewing her research.

Chapter 15

After three helicopter rides, a four-hour layover in the Chicago O'Hare airport USO waiting area, and two ground transport trips, Melinda and Dan arrived at a laboratory in Colorado. *Great*, thought Melinda, *it's too late to go directly to the workroom.* A fidgety young man, leaning from one foot to another, stood at the entrance of the facility. As Melinda got closer, she noticed he held two 8x10 color photos – one of her and one of Dan. The young man squinted at her photo.

"Long flight, huh? You guys look terrible! Melinda, right? I don't mean you look terrible. You just look, well, awful!" He looked closely at the glossy picture of her again, as if to make sure it really was Melinda. He finally shoved the photographs into the file he carried.

He turned to Dan. "I think you probably look awful, too." The young man gently placed his hand on the small of Melinda's back. "I am Moto -- your support staff. I must insist you both get some sleep."

Melinda started to protest, but before she could get a word out Moto cut her off. "Travel fatigue can be reversed within the first few days with adequate diet and rest," he said as he expertly steered the two researchers into the lab. 'You will sleep for three hours, then I have arranged bright light exposure to reset your circadian system; optimal timing is critical," he nattered on. "Using circadian science, I developed a spreadsheet of light exposure to assure re-entrainment progresses one timezone per day."

For the first time in years, Melinda worried that she looked terrible. She didn't think Dan looked terrible, but a more critical observation proved him to look disheveled, stubbly and kind of stinky. *I probably do look terrible*, she thought.

As if Dan read her mind, he said, "You don't look exactly terrible, just not as good as you did hours ago."

Moto tugged at her duffle bag.

"Thanks, Whale Guy," Melinda muttered, then yanked her duffle firmly back into her control and followed the peculiar man. They ended up in a pristine hallway with several doors lining the left wall. Each door was open, standing at attention as they walked past.

Moto chatted on about the rooms, "Guys-Guys, these rooms are all the same. Just pick one. Sorry Melinda, none with a bigger bathroom or large vanity for you to store your make-up! Ha!" Moto snorted as he barked out a one-syllable laugh. Melinda turned into the nearest room.

"I'll take this one," she said to Dan. "I guess I am pretty tired. See you later." Dan smiled and indicated he'd take the next room.

She closed her door and hoped she wasn't going to hate this Moto guy.

The room was ordinary. Quite like her last room, maybe bigger, with different art. This ten by twelve private dorm room featured pictures of local flora – yellow aspens, Engelmann spruce and pink moss – with the Latin genus and species typed neatly at the bottom of each framed poster. The desk was sufficient, she thought, and placed her laptop on it. She tossed her duffle onto the floor next to her bunk. Gingerly, she bounced a few times on the bed, testing the firmness. It seemed fine, however the pillow situation was a different story; one measly, flat-as-a-pancake pillow. She knew this would not do. An idea flashed in her head - *like a cartoon light bulb,* she mused – and she went to pilfer pillows from the empty rooms. Back in her space, she kicked off her shoes and fell into bed. Hoping to fall quickly to sleep, she willed her mind quiet.

She found Dan already in the lobby exactly three hours later. An extra hot shower and a brisk bout of teeth brushing helped revive Melinda. She wore a butter yellow J-Jill T-shirt and black yoga pants. Dan wore Gray lightweight sweatpants and a black T-shirt, and he wore them very well. *I am not doing this*, Melinda said firmly to herself. *I am not going to care about how he looks.*

Moto was the last to arrive. "Good morning!" he greeted them. "Are you ready for the long hours ahead of us?" He led them down a stairway to the lab.

At the door, Moto punched a code into the security panel. "Bio-scan please," the computer voice directed.

"Security will use both a numerical code and a bio-code. To access this research, a biometric template of either your iris pattern or voice recognition, along with a fingerprint is required," he said. "I've entered the fingerprints Brasco sent into the system; you can download your voice and iris patterns at another time."

Melinda and Dan took turns at the bio-scanner. They pressed their thumbs into the print sensor. The computer recognized them and allowed entrance into the laboratory.

Moto sat on a lab stool at the counter. "I am fully briefed on this project. I know what each researcher brings to the table. My job right now – today – is organization of information. Oh, I know, I know, it's not sexy, but it needs to be done. First, Dr. Hardin wants Dan to educate us on everything sperm whale. It's a good thing we are not twelve and snicker every time we say 'sperm' because this is a sperm whale. So we'll be saying it a lot, you know, 'sperm' . . . a lot." Moto stopped talking, folded his hand in front of him, and looked expectantly at Dan.

"From my perspective this is more a nano project than a Cetacean project," Dan stated. He pointedly left out the word "sperm."

"Good! Good observation, Dan." Moto's attitude jumped from chattering innkeeper to encouraging sensei. "But it's going to be a sperm whale project soon enough, and whatever we don't know about sperm whales you're going to teach us."

Melinda explored the lab, examining tools and greedily ferreting out all the built-ins, like video and recording equipment. She found stashes of specialty apparatus – operant conditioning chambers, spectrophotometers and calorimeters.

Moto interrupted her examination. "The larger, more sophisticated equipment is kept behind a panel," he explained.

She located the panel. It struck her as odd; there was very little evidence of nano research in the lab. In fact, there was very little evidence of any research in the lab. "When do I get to see the little buggers?" she asked.

"Soon enough. We need to finish our three-way with Dan first." He barked out what would become his trademark whoop at his double entendre. "I don't know much about sperm whales. I haven't had the time to do any research.' Again, Moto looked expectantly at Dan, who sat on the lab stool nearest him.

Dan began with an overview.

"Migratory patterns take this particular whale species into the deepest waters worldwide; generally between sixty degrees North and seventy degrees South on the parallel maps. Males tend to travel more pole-ward – to the south, further into the Antarctic. We see more shifts in patterns during the change of seasons, like increased movement of herds at the beginning of spring and summer, with returning patterns in the fall. However, out of any species of Cetaceans, this one has the most unpredictable migration." Dan waited for questions or comments; Moto surprised him.

"Well, this sperm whale followed what is considered to be the pattern of the North Pacific or Alaskan stock," Moto said, "and its pod is expected to spend its summer feeding in the Gulf of Alaska."

Melinda interrupted Moto.

"Wait a minute; I thought you didn't have a chance to do any research," Melinda said and looked accusatorily at Moto. An uncomfortable silence should have emanated from Moto's direction since she caught him in a lie, however the only ill feelings in the room came from her.

"Okay, okay," Moto said and raised his hands in mock surrender. "There is a set of World Book Encyclopedias and a Ping-Pong table in a rec room down the hall. The reference books are from the early 1970s; they are bound in a creamy faux-leather and the pages have gold edges, making them seem very valuable." Moto calmly steepled his fingers. "There are no Ping-Pong balls; I've looked. Anyway I did read through the sperm whale segment and discovered that for management purposes, sperm whale who migrate through US waters have been divided into five groups or stocks. Our whale seems to be of the Pacific or Alaskan stock." He stopped for only a moment and finished with, "Interestingly, in the 1970s we did not know what the spermaceti's purpose is. We do now, right?" He looked at Dan.

Dan listened to Moto's explanation with a measure of awe. His family owned a set of white, faux-leather World Books and he had spent many hours as a boy reading about the different scientific classifications of Cetacean. He actually remembered the passage Moto talked about – explaining the eventual division of the different suborders of whales by migratory groups. *Curiouser and curiouser,* Dan thought. He didn't sense a bad vibe from Moto, in fact he kind of liked him; he was just, well, odd. He decided to continue the Cetacean conversation.

"Ah, yes we do know that the acoustic lipids are required for the precise echo-location that the sperm whale and, say the bottle-nosed dolphin, may use. The viscosity of the wax, fats or oils, allows most toothed whales to distinguish between prey and non-prey in total darkness. In captive mammals, it can be trained to distinguish balls and toys of different sizes or shapes."

"Very good Dan!" Moto gushed. "Do we have any questions?" He looked at Melinda.

"Yeah, where's this rec room?" This facility looked like something from a science fiction movie; a set of reference books from the 70s seemed far-fetched.

"Ha!" Moto barked. "I'd be disappointed in you if you hadn't challenged me on my story Melinda. Let's head to the rec room. You can see the books; you can hydrate and get some light exposure, and I can tell you all about Massimisso Mulcrone.

Chapter 16

Brasco searched military archives for the location of James Tillman. Tillman's military contract ended years ago, but because of his work on several sensitive projects, he'd been tagged a person of interest. Tillman's file was easy to find and totally empty. The discovery of washed or cleaned files was a common occurrence in this line of work, but an empty file was a rarity. He rechecked the information on the file, and the security tag assigned to Tillman caught Brasco off guard. The additional three numbers attached to the researcher's social security number indicated that file information was accessible through the president of the United States solely. *This is, like, 007 clearance. Why give it to just a researcher?* He didn't waste time thinking about that; secondary team members were gathered in Colorado and he still needed Tillman.

Brasco returned to his red SUV and punched a code into his military issue "Com-Sis" or communications system. Luckily Brasco also sported the additional three numbers attached to his social and within minutes of making the phone call, had secured a noon meeting with President William Leslie.

This type of meeting does not take place in the oval office and parking is a bitch when you are not on any official entry list, Brasco lamented. He drove into the neighborhood near the White House where he'd have to park his SUV. It was a rough community; hijackings and hold-up were an ongoing problem. He parked several blocks away and walked. He entered the White House through the visitors entrance, paid his money and walked through to the Lincoln Bedroom. There, he studied a holographic image of the Gettysburg address displayed on a Victorian-style desk and waited for a secret service agent to retrieve him.

Right on time the agent appeared and escorted Brasco to a mid-sized conference room in the West Wing where he continued to wait for the president.

President William Leslie walked along a walled off hallway toward the secured conference room, his face barely concealed his disdain for this particular meeting. Never fond of Brasco or his type, Leslie thought Brasco and his covert projects were relics, vestiges of a clandestine operation he wanted retired; however he'd inherited the program and didn't engage in battles with his chiefs of staff over their inevitability.

Leslie entered the room and without preamble asked, "Why do you want to know where James Tillman is?"

Okay, no polite banter, thought Brasco. "The unidentified craft in the Pacific is a result of his failed Nano Project," he explained. "We need his expertise."

Brasco wondered if Leslie knew the craft was biological. Titan should be top-secret. This was a good opportunity to see if the security restrictions he put in place included the White House.

President Leslie sat at the conference table. He put a file folder in front of him and placed his hand over it. "James is needed on the Titan project?" Leslie's intense brown eyes looked for a hint of surprise from the spy. Brasco remained poker faced.

The president continued, "Why wasn't James your first call? He was the lead researcher on that project, after all." The president tapped his fingers on the file on the table. "James is significantly ill," he said. "He has been teaching at a small research outpost on a mountain in the Andes Mountains. His illness a direct result of military exposure. From what I understand, he won't survive for long in any climate in this hemisphere."

Brasco was unmoved. "Hardin developed an inhaler that should keep Tillman alive while he is working with us. Mr. President, I wouldn't be asking for him unless he was vital to this project. I, as well as anyone, know what this level of clearance means. Tillman is under your protection. If what we think is happening in the Pacific is true, our country needs your protection from Titan."

"You don't get the folder, Brasco, but you get Tillman." The president ripped the closure flap off the folder, hand-wrote the location of the research facility on it, and got up to leave.

"Look it Brasco, I don't trust you or your undercover operations," Leslie said, with no attempt to hide his contempt, " and I would like nothing better than to see you and your type held to the same standard of appropriateness that our traditional military is held to each and every day. However, something always comes up, and this week it is this . . . anthropogenic catastrophe." He tossed the scribbled note of Tillman's whereabouts on the conference table. "And yes, James is under my protection. Remember that."

"Thank you, Mr. President." Brasco remained standing and waited for the president to leave.

"Don't mention it, and I mean don't mention me or my complicity in hooking up James Tillman and Hank Hardin."

Brasco walked out of the White House with Tillman's location in his breast pocket. *That went well*, he thought facetiously. The former administration regarded Brasco and his type as heroes. Meetings with that particular president started with an expensive, hand-rolled, Gukha cigar, and ended with a hearty handshake and a heartfelt "Thank you for your service.

Chapter 17

James Tillman, dressed in a short-sleeved shirt and lightweight khaki pants, carefully prepared a tincture at his laboratory. The state of the art facility was located on the summit of the Aconcagua Mountain in Argentina. His staff consisted of graduate and undergraduate students interning at the research center. This project focused on hydroponics and cold climate plant growth. The team had several "hot houses" at different climate levels throughout the Argentinean Andes. Not one was a classic hot house with tropical temperatures. The temperatures ranged from, at their warmest, chilly to, at the coldest, just under freezing.

James had called the summit lab home for the past two years. The giant rock of a mountain range was not picturesque in a traditional sense; stark and scrappy for miles with dirty hardscrabble snow surrounding bare patches. However, over time, he'd learned to appreciate the barren beauty that kept him alive. His health tolerated this climate so he didn't venture far. He insisted his team use the Koppen climate classification system – a system that calculates temperature with precise accuracy with just pen and paper. Global climate change caused temperature fluctuation of several degrees even at this altitude. Using the Koppen system allowed him to anticipate temperature change and bivouac to colder areas when needed.

Today's group consisted of second year undergraduates here for their study-abroad semester. This program was one of the more affordable foreign internship

programs offered since there was little opportunity to spend additional money
during their stay at the summit.

James coached them through the preparation of the fertilizer solution used in the
hot houses.

"Students," James said while he worked on his blend, "You should not mix up
too big of a batch. A slip up in calculations and you've got a pretty powerful bomb."
The kid to his left, mixing the solution, hesitated a moment. "And the Sherpa fire
and bomb squad is a three day trek away – by camel. That being said, this solution
needs to be mixed and applied on site, at each hot house."

The young student next to him finished his mixture. "How do we know it's
right?" he asked. James stuck his finger in the solution and then tasted it. "Ahh,
that's some spicy fertilizer, kid – a little heavy on the nitrogen, but perfectly
acceptable."

The student looked horrified; another student piped in, "Hey James, is sipping
that shit what makes you impervious to the cold? If so, give me some on chips, cuz
it's pretty damn cold in here!" They all laughed. Everyone liked this program, and
they especially liked the very mysterious lead researcher Dr. James Tillman. If you
googled him, nothing popped. Physically, he looked like an underfed vampire and
was prone to sweat when temperatures reached above thirty-five degrees. Each
night he served very smooth, very cold Argentinian Vodka while he really listened
to the students as they talked and planned their futures.

James laughed with them, ignored the reference to his penchant for cold
weather, and passed around the vial of the fertilizer he'd made. "Everyone dip your
finger in the solution and have a taste. That is what it should taste like when
prepared correctly. A little more or less acidy is fine."

He looked at this team of young, geeky kids. "How many of you did any
physical training to prepare to come here?" A few raised their hands; one guy flexed
his muscles. "When traveling between hot houses, you have to pack light," he
reminded them.

Dillon, a graduate student in the middle of a yearlong appointment with James,
added, "The trip between each hot house is not a hike; it's a trek. Don't be fooled by

the cerebral work you're doing here. This can be physically grueling. Hopefully, you are all prepared for that particular part of our program."

Before anyone could respond, a young student burst into the laboratory. "James, you know that chopper that just came in? Well, it's not supplies – it's military and there's a butt-ugly guy looking for you." There were moans and groans regarding the lack of supplies. No one noticed the concern on James' face. *Someone looking for me?* he thought. *That's odd because no one should be able to find me.*

The helicopter pilot recognized the man walking toward the chopper. It was not often he dropped someone off on the frozen tundra in his short sleeves. This mission was similar to when he left this guy: pick up, drop off, and it never happened. The pilot turned to the military thug in the back and said, "Hey, we had this target before, remember?"

"I don't remember anything asshole," snarled the goon sent to escort the target.

James walked out of the lab. Immediately, he recognized the man coming at him as the guard that got him up here. Without missing a beat, he turned and started back to the lab. *There is a panic room there,* he thought. *If I can get there and . . .* Suddenly a sharp pain smacked his butt. He looked and the last thing he saw before he passed out was a dart dangling from his backside.

When he regained consciousness, James found himself in a heap at the back of the helicopter; handcuffed to a long bench. He rolled to a sitting position and looked around. An imposing six-foot frame, topped off with the ugliest face James had ever seen, sat guard over him. A buzz-cut, square head showcased a bulging forehead that capped bleached-blue eyes and a pendulous nose.

James rubbed his bum. "I figured if I ever saw you again, you'd be a pain in my ass," he said, "however, I wasn't aware it would be so literal."

The goon flipped him off and tossed a package into James' lap. "This is from Hank," he said. "He told me to tell you to trust him and use it." The brute settled back and stared at James.

Trusting Hank Hardin was the last thing James would ever do. He tore open the package and found an inhaler and thermometer. Scrawled across the inhaler were the words "VIRAL BUSTER – BREATHE DEEPLY."

James knew what the thermometer was for. He looked and the temperature was rising.

"Tell the pilot to turn off the heat!" barked James.

"Piss off!" replied the soldier.

James panicked. He looked down at the thermometer in one hand, noting it had inched up one degree, and the inhaler in his other. *Pick your poison*, he thought. He put the inhaler in his mouth, pressed the button and inhaled deeply.

Bitter bile rose and gathered in the back of his throat. James choked it back. He waited a few moments; for what, he didn't know. Nothing happened. Nothing at all. He checked the temperature on his thermometer – fifty-two degrees. He should have been sweating and shaking by now. He hadn't exposed himself to this type of heat in two years. Through trial and error at the summit he'd discovered that he functioned normally with the thin atmosphere of the Andes and a temperature of no more than forty-eight degrees. Anything else and symptoms would quickly reappear.

"Pilot!" shouted James. "Where are we headed?" He decided to ignore the goon. And, it seemed, the goon had decided to ignore him.

"Ultimately, Colorado; two stops in between to refuel. You are not authorized to leave the chopper," replied the pilot.

"What if I have to go to the bathroom," James asked.

The pilot nodded to a bucket. "There's the head, sir," He replied.

Chapter 18

In Colorado, Dan and Melinda followed Moto to the rec room in silence. The recreation room sat in the middle of the giant research facility. Designed in the tradition of great rooms of the 1990s, or great halls of medieval times, this room featured a vaulted ceiling, different recreational game tables, a kitchenette and a small study area with all-purpose furniture and a bookcase. This communal area aimed to be the crossroad of the facility where people could relax and refuel.

Moto ushered the two into the room. Melinda was underwhelmed. What she saw was a classic cafeteria/ recreation area, similar to common areas on a dorm floor or an employee-friendly office building. A couple of twelve-foot Formica tables hosted an assortment of brightly colored plastic chairs in one corner of the room. A large panel TV hung on a wall and comfortable looking furniture enticed people to gather and sit for the shared experience of a movie or TV show. Discretely scattered throughout the room were smart chairs, with individual audio and video equipment, available for those seeking a solitary experience.

Artfully angled against another wall were Ping-Pong, pool and chess tables. The chess tables sat in a noise-reducing cubicle, intended to muffle the raucous repartee at the other game tables.

A quick cooker and a toaster oven sat in competing corners on the wall dedicated to satisfying hunger. Confetti-colored counter tops, a double sink and a full-size stainless steel refrigerator promised to meet any mealtime requirements.

Melinda walked directly to the low, pressed board bookcase located in the reading area. She noted a hodgepodge of 1990 hard covers – Grisham, Follett and Clancy and science fiction classics from Brin, Ismonov, and Arthur C. Clark. An impressive assortment of prominent authors from the 2010s – Loper, Novack, Holt, Gray Kaye and Buckson – created an eclectic feel to the group. Showcased in the center of the shelving, numbered spines queued up in numerical order, was a complete set of old World Books Encyclopedia.

Dan picked up WXYZ. "I noticed the last time I was at my Mom and Dad's house my set had yellowed; did you clean these up?" Dan ran his hand over the nubby, vanilla, fake leather cover.

"Yes! I did! These were quite dingy, and they smelled kinda bad. They still smell bad — smell them." Moto sniffed his own R volume and waived it under Dan's nose. "I just wiped them down with wet wipes and—voilà! – they came clean. Check out inside volume A," Moto said to Melinda. "There is a sticker that says 'this complete set of World Book Encyclopedias XIX edition belongs to' and space to write a name. Well, Gretchen Greenwood carefully wrote her name and the year 1970."

Moto watched as Melinda found the volume. "I looked her up you know," he said. "She earned her doctorate in forensic anthropology and physical anthropology."

Melinda opened the cover, and there, in perfect penmanship, was the tightly written signature. Seeing these books reminded her that, several years ago, she'd left a set of engineering books by Henry Pitroski at a lab where she'd worked a long-term project. Unable to part with her early reference books, Melinda had lugged them around for years, only to abandon them to a similar shelf like this one in a research laboratory in Phoenix.

Quiet surrounded the three as each thumbed through the dated reference book they held.

The intercom system cracked, and a male voice interrupted the silence.

"Where is everyone? Motto? Are my researchers here? Tillman is about thirty minutes out."

"That is Dr. Hardin, project manager. We need to get to him."

"I am here to help you and the team," Moto said to Melinda. "I can be the 'great organizer' or the 'ultimate finder,' whatever you need me to be. I have an exceptional reputation in the field." He smiled expectantly at her.

She looked at this odd young man, with his copper-colored hair, pale skin and black eyes. She sensed something genuine about him.

"You never did tell us the 'real story of Massimo Mulcrone.'" Melinda smiled back at Motto, then turned a definitive glare to the intercom. "But first I've got to find out why James is 'thirty minutes out' from a project that should be his!

Chapter 19

The pilot announced the approach to their final destination. As the helicopter moved closer, James noted a mixed conifer forest peppered with quaking Aspen trees and a not-so-distant mountain range framing the mid-sized research compound. His escort made no movement to leave the aircraft, but James stood to leave as soon as wheels hit dirt. Outside the aircraft, the hum and rustle of quivering leaves supported the idea they'd landed in Colorado. He shaded his eyes and adjusted to the natural light while he scanned the area.

At the front of the building, the hazy outline of two men manifested; he recognized one. Years of fantasizing what he would do when confronting Hank again raced through his head. In the early months of exile, he'd played out this scene. Today there was no plan. James walked straight to Hank and socked him squarely in the nose. The other man laughed.

"Hank said there might be some resistance from you," the other man said. "I bet he's wishing for some of that 'resistance' right now." Brasco stepped away from Hank's dripping nose. "I'm John Brasco, Naval Intelligence."

James ignored Brasco along with the pain searing through his knuckles from its collision with Hank's nose.

Hank's attempt to appear unruffled proved futile since his nose poured blood like a running faucet. His ears rang and he saw stars.

"And here I was going to offer you a nice, hot cup of coffee," he said and did his best to sneer as he pinched the bridge of his nose. "Why are you angry? You're alive aren't you? I had to work blind on a cure." Forced to stop talking, he coughed, gagged and spit out blood that oozed down the back of his throat.

James' normal pallor erupted a ruddy pink. He moved closer to Hank and hissed, "If it wasn't for you, there would be no need for a cure." James' spittle splashed across Hank's face.

He turned to Brasco and said, in obvious disregard for Hank, "You must be in charge. I don't trust that I'll be alive for very long so order Hemorrhaging Hank here to turn over all research on that nasal spray."

Brasco watched the exchange with a mix of amusement and concern; the clichéd chest thumping and childish verbal barbs between the two rivals bordered on the absurd, however Hank's inability to see the futility of James' attitude was a concern. Hank needed to get control of his ego if he was going to be an effective leader of the research team. Brasco decided to get right to the point.

"The Nano Project has taken an unexpected turn. We need your help." That changed James' focus. Brasco produced a folder from behind his back and handed it over. The file was slim; James calmed himself, opened it and read its contents.

"All information gathered indicates that nano-machines have altered the sperm whale in the photos," Hank explained. "Whether they are specifically the nano-machines lost in the explosion several years back is one of the questions this assembled team will answer."

"Where's the evidence?" James asked Brasco. The information and file photos were unbelievable.

" A piece was recovered from a military conflict and analyzed. Preliminary data show the nanos to carry the marker of our project," Hank replied.

Concern creased James' face. "How badly damaged?" he asked.

Hank started to answer him, gagged and spit out a clot of blood from his nosebleed. Brasco answered. "The whale/craft survived combat but two military crafts were destroyed. We've been approved a very small window of time to capture this thing or it will be destroyed."

"Who else do we have working on this?" James asked, again he addressed Brasco.

Hank answered. "I'm in charge of the project, James. Melinda Davenport is on board, along with Dan some-thing-or-other, a Cetacean specialist."

James rejected Hank's comment and spoke directly to Brasco. "How many people have this intel?"

Hank moved and stood between James and Brasco. "You can't ignore me and be on this project," he said. "You're going to have to decide. I put this project above whatever happened between us in the past. I want you on this project, but I don't need you."

Exhausted, James rubbed the back of his neck. While in the helicopter, he'd slept with one eye on the military beast. Also, he'd been fairly certain he'd die from his virus before reaching the states; any thoughts and dreams during the flight were tormented with elements of death. However, he hadn't died. In fact, he felt better than he had in a very long time. He turned to address Hank. "Who else knows?" he asked. Hank carefully arranged his face and masked the self-satisfaction he felt.

"Just a handful of researchers from a private lab that's been paid substantially for their silence," answered Hank. Clair's murder briefly crossed his mind.

Brasco added, "Of course, select members of the intelligence community are also aware."

James walked away from the two men toward the facility in the distance. "I want in on the project," he said to no one in particular. "I'll be a good team player but I don't trust you Hardin. And Brasco, I don't think I trust you either."

The two men stayed outside while James entered the building. The smart lab would alert Moto of a visitor and he would see that James settled into his quarters.

Hank reached up and gingerly touched his swollen nose, wondering if ice or steak would stop the throbbing.

Brasco stared critically at Hank's swelling nose. "You're going to have at least one black eye."

"The cretin thinks I tried to kill him," Hank said, arrogance dripping off his words in tandem with the blood dripping from his nose.

"Is he going to live — at least as long as we need him?" Brasco asked.

"He's lived this long, so he'll survive." His swelling nasal membrane pushed against his vocal cords, producing an adenoidal whine.

"The spray I developed was effective on the nanos I tested – the ones affecting James," Hank said. He coughed and hawked up bloody phlegm. He added a sardonic tone to the stuffy whine caused by his swollen nose. "I was worried the nanos had mutated – like the ones that transmogrified the whale – so it was a risk, but it worked. And we don't *need* James, I want him here for–"

"I know what you want, just be sure you can do your job!" Brasco interrupted.

Both men followed the path to the lab; Brasco positioned himself smack in the middle of the walkway, which allowed little room for Hank. Hank silently limped along beside him, one foot on the pebbled path and the other in the spongy moss that lined the trail. Brasco pulled up short and forced Hank to stop too close to him.

Brasco turned and pushed his face even closer to Hank.

"And, don't try to intimidate or impress me," he snarled. "You would be surprised by my broad scope of knowledge. Transmogrify! Now you call your Titan a monster?" Brasco flicked Hank's swollen nose with one hand and opened the door with the other.

Chapter 20

A tactical team of stealth submarines, using combined acoustic and fluid cloaking, monitored the leviathan's movement. The US military restricted all air and water space within a hundred-mile circumference of the threat. While the special squadron awaited orders, it emitted infrasound, employing long wavelength noise in the water.

The waters turned hypnotizing; nanos fine-tuned the buoyancy of their vessel. They struggled to ignore the spellbinding clatter. Titan hung twenty-five meters below the surface. At that depth the water density muffled the buzz that threatened to bewitch him.

The nanos monitored the cloaked submarines lurking in the distance.

Titan sorted through the noise and listened for his family's coda. He kept his family a safe distance from the enemy that lay in wait. Thoughts of his clan and their activities filled his mind. He envisioned one particularly boastful friend herding a school of mackerel toward their pod. He pictured her pridefully slapping her tail on the water in delight as her family feasted. He knew a certain pock-faced elder, her massive head white with scars, would scold such arrogance.

Titan vowed never to expose his pod to danger again. The brutal retaliation Titan had executed against several ill-fated submarines had ended quickly. Clearly, the danger was after him. He knew it hid close by.

Safety of the biological fleet/family is critical.

Periodically, Titan edged closer to the shadowy threat that hovered in the distance, while nanos scrutinized counter maneuvers, watching for any threat.

The nanos no longer adjusted for emotional state – nano and temperament functioned as one. The joint awareness understood his ability to focus on attackers and destroy them.

Titan examined the past several months. Nothing added up, but everything made sense. Though he had been undoubtedly injured several times during the previous attacks, there were no visible wounds. Memory of familiar faces and places differed from the vistas and visages he'd encountered since his return to the pod. However, there was no doubt he was with his family.

Indisputably his body was the least fragile of his pod, but he tired easily at the surface. His vision was imprecise. None the less, when he focused hatred onto an object, he destroyed it. He had done it, and now danger stayed away. As long as he heard his pod, he had no reason to attack. The unnatural hum vibrating throughout the water numbed him. He continued to listen to his pod, and if they fell silent, he would attack again.

Chapter 21

James vibrated with anger as he entered the building. He clenched his hands and teeth. In the entryway, he stopped, speechless. It had taken the strength of Hercules to stuff down his anger and his pride long enough to agree to work with Hank, but it was erupting again. *This situation is ludicrous*, James thought; *me working with – no for Hank!*

Moto arrived and assessed his charge, who practically glowed with anger. He shepherded James to his bunk in silence. Once there, Moto suggested James take a shower while he prepare a small meal.

"I know just what you need. Something my mother prepared for me when I was muddled." Without touching him, Moto gently shooed the still mute James toward the bathroom. Calmed by the guidance, James turned toward the offbeat little man and smiled. Unable to pull together a sentence, James managed to burble, "Who? . . . What?"

Moto picked up the backpack James had dropped on the floor and put it on a dresser.

"Who? Why, I am Moto. As for 'what' – first you shower and you eat and then we go to the lab where research is being done!"

Moto scurried to the pantry, where he knew there was a Panini maker. He would make a grilled cheese sandwich and prepare a can of tomato soup – comfort food.

He rushed around the kitchen hunting down ingredients for the simple sandwich. He remembered seeing an herb garden around back of the facility, and welcomed the walk to gather basil for soup. He slowed his pace and took a deep cleansing breath. James swirled with chaos and Moto reacted to it. James' aura had more than a tinge of sad, Moto noted and briefly wondered why. There was no time for reflection; Moto collected several large leaves of Italian basil and returned to the kitchen at a more metered pace.

Chapter 22

In the lab, Melinda studied Crabbo – that was what she called the nano-transformed crab.

After reviewing the information provided by Nash Laboratories on the spider crab and its transformation, Dan and Melinda developed a plan for their initial research. They asked Moto for a large basin to house the mutated crab and an assortment of decapods to create a simple vivarium. He delivered a large aluminum tub and two more spider crabs.

"I purchased pet-quality hermit crabs with delightfully decorated shells," he said, gently dropping several into the tub.

The nano-altered crustacean was in a cold-induced coma. They retrieved it from cold storage and placed it into the tub to awaken. Melinda's work with the initial nanos and the information she'd garnered from the Virginia Labs' research enabled her to calculate how and when the sample would awaken or more accurately, come back on-line.

Dan had never thought about crabs once in his career and needed simple biological data on the species. The two researchers set up shop next to each other; Melinda worked with a tablet and a laptop while Dan needed only a laptop and skittles. He discovered two things: one, crabs were simple and boring creatures, and two, he really liked sitting next to Melinda while doing research. She was very communal about it. If a particularly colorful image popped on his screen, she scooted herself closer to him and oohed and ahhed over it, lamenting each time on how lackluster her own research looked compared to his.

It was impossible for him to reciprocate because her research was tedious. Melinda's search on nano technology provided little more visual stimuli than an occasional blueprint or an uninspiring complex design.

The clacking of shells bumping into other shells from the tub pulled them away from their screens. They moved their research closer to the tub to study the awakening crab as it bounced around in a drowsy condition.

"Look Melinda, the left legs and claw show signs of epibiotic snarling organisms – but the right side does not!" Dan marveled at the creature. He slowly paced around the tub, referencing each visible difference. "The left carapace is dressed in debris and small invertebrates; however the right mutated carapace is unadorned." He made his way around the tub and stood next to Melinda. They stared at the crab as it calmly groomed its eyestalks.

The complex changes to the crab fascinated Melinda.. The carapace, or shell, on the right side of the crab was denser, which made sense since several of the right legs and the right claw were also thicker and longer. This was no mechanical prototype, this was a live creature enhanced by the nanos.

At a glance, all parts of Crabbo appeared operational. In fact, it behaved quite crab-like. However, they did observed new functions. When Melinda kicked the tub threateningly, instead of retreating, its posture became aggressive. Dan suggested they "attack" one of the other crabs in the container and note any reaction from Crabbo. Melinda searched the lab and found nine-inch surgical tweezers. She poked at a nearby hermit crab, sheathed in a shell painted with a bright-pink peace sign. Crabbo remained uninterested, tapping three of its mutated walking legs on the bottom of the tub.

"Poke at Crabbo," Dan recommended. Without much thought, Melinda turned the tweezers on the mutated crab. With lightning speed, its reinforced claw telescoped outward, menacingly snapping its pincer. Dan's reaction was swift. He grabbed Melinda around the waist, yanked her backwards, and they tumbled to the floor. James and Moto walked in to see Melinda sitting on Dan's lap.

"No funding for a conference table?" kidded James.

"What's going on?" Moto surveyed the scene. The nano crab appeared agitated, its right claw extended and flailing about the tank like something from a cartoon.

"What the hell?" said Melinda. The attack had happened so suddenly she questioned whether she'd perceived it correctly.

"That thing would have snapped off your arm!" Dan said, as he carefully inched them back and away from the thrashing claw.

Moto helped her stand and gently pried the tweezers from her clenched fist.

Dan stood. "We're going to have to kill that thing in the Pacific," he said

Moto stared warily at the mutated crab. "I am sure Dr. Hardin will advise us as to the next steps," he said.

The crab continued to wave its protracted cheliped at Melinda while the attached chela, or claw, snapped out an angry refrain. The four unaffected walking legs dangled just above the floor of the container and tread air. The crab emanated a nasty odor similar to expensive, stinky cheese. The assortment of non-altered crabs clustered as far away from the mutant as possible. Moto addressed Dan, but did not take his eyes off the angry crab. "Can we all safely step away from the container?"

Dan estimated the distance the expanded merus could cover. "I think we're at a safe distance now. If we stay away, it should forget we're here. Crabs are pretty stupid – and so we're we Melinda. We should have been more careful." Melinda nodded in agreement. Dan never should have recommended her to poke at it and she should have refused when he said it.

Melinda backed away from the container. She was as eager to get away from Crabbo as she was to analyze what had just happened. "We can talk over here." She pointed to a round conference table in the far corner of the lab.

James followed her. He surprised himself by noticing her hair was different. He noted a clippie-thing secured her long hair behind her head. He remembered she had worn it loose and it had overwhelmed her delicate face. Her whiskey-colored eyes still startled him as they met his. "Long time no see," he said and immediately regretted the sophomoric greeting.

Jeez, he looks like death warmed over, Melinda thought. "I did look for you after the dust settled from the original Nano Project," she explained. "Everyone just disappeared."

The government agency in charge of their contract -- *Navy*, she remembered -- bullied all contractors off the project. Hints and insinuations, dropped by government representatives, swept through the research community that the disaster was a career-ending failure. Everyone opted out of his or her contracts fast. Consensus was that the farther away from the Nano Project they landed, the better.

Hank entered the lab. His appearance on a good day went way beyond bookish, putting him solidly into the nerd category. Today, two very black eyes hovered over his brilliantly bruised nose. He looked pathetic.

"What the hell happened to you?" Dan said. "You look like you've been in a fight!". There was no obvious security system or any security guards. "What is the security protocol here" he asked.

"Are we in some kind of danger here?" Melinda asked. "Why were you in a fight?" She looked pointedly at James..

"We are working in one of the most secure facilities in the US. Do not be fooled by the lack of obvious security trappings – this smart structure is state-of-the-art, top-secret secure." Moto reassured the team.

'I'll take no questions regarding my appearance," Hank said. He carefully circumnavigated the crab container in an attempt to join the team.

"Then why don't you just disappear," James said. He did not try to hide his contempt.

Hank ignored the sarcasm. "I watched what unfolded here just now with that crab on a remote feed. We need to gather data so we can move ahead," turning to Dan he said, " I think we're a long way from making any decisions as to what the outcome for Titan will be." He knew these researchers would not have input into the outcome for the whale.

"Who's Titan?" Moto and the team said in unison.

Hank shifted uneasily. On an impulse, he'd named the nano-whale Titan. Having said it out loud to his learned peers, he felt foolish.

"Military handle given to the creature," Hank lied. He strutted around the lab, his hands clasped behind his back, detailing next steps. "Moto will brief us on all military movement. These two," he momentarily released a hand to wave toward Melinda and Dan, "have focused on the research non-stop since arriving. Therefore Dan will follow up with the parallel between Titan behavior and sperm whale behavior." Hank swaggered around the perimeter of the lab, picking up beakers, flasks and cylinders. He examined each as if it were a rare or strange specimen.

"Melinda can brief you on these current nanos," he continued, "and lastly, if needed, James can provide perspective from the original Nano Project. I will continue to monitor your progress from my office." Hank indicated Moto should begin his intel.

Eager to examine the new nanos, James sat through the briefing, hoping it would be just that – brief. He respected the data in Melinda's report but it was clearly observations and conjecture. He enjoyed her performance; she enlivened tedious material with simple hand gestures or the arch of an eyebrow. It was clear Dan had strong feelings regarding the impact of the nanos on the mammal. Moto's report regarding the navel skirmish and the damage the creature was capable of, was noteworthy. However, it was James' experience that the military would harvest the scientific outcomes and discard opinions, assumptions and forecasts.

Melinda interrupted his thoughts. "James, if you don't have any questions, let's examine the new nanos." They edged toward the tub containing Crabbo, petite Melinda boldly leading the procession.

"Hank would like us to come up with a way to tranquilize this Titan creature," she whispered.

Close behind them, Dan quietly added, "I don't think that's a sound idea. We ought to put this thing out of its misery."

"What does Hank think he's going to do? Capture it? Put it in some ocean mammal Guantanamo?" James joked. He didn't want to think about the whale. He wanted to get his hands on the nanos and discover how they'd evolved.

"I think your interpretation is far too close for comfort," grumbled Dan. He knew these techie-type scientists couldn't care less about research animals. Experimental or theoretical, animal research usually ended badly for the animal. The number one reason he left research was that no one cared about the test subjects, only the outcome. Currently, he put his expertise to a practical use as a consultant to the military on bio-terrorism.

"Look, is your bleeding heart going to make a comment at every step of this project?" James asked. Dan gave him a look that indicated yes.

"With the insight Dan has provided on sperm whale intelligence, I'm inclined to agree with him," said Melinda. "At this point, the only ethical thing to do is to destroy Titan. We don't know if the nanos will be destroyed, too," she added.

Melinda paused, still a safe distance from Crabbo's container; she turned her attention and comments to the crab. "From what I've observed of this crab, even with its minimal brain capacity it can manage to do some pretty frightening things."

She had not convinced James of anything. Actually, when she thought about it, she'd provided no scientific purpose behind destroying it. Comparing intelligence of the two mutated creatures did not provide measurables.

She chided herself --- not very scientific. "Hank's right," she said. "We need to gather more data before we make any decisions." She returned her attention to the crab container.

Crabbo raucously rambled around with the other crabs. They knocked noisily into each other as they congregated in one corner. The three spider crabs (including Crabbo) appeared fidgety and tapped their walking legs, while the hermit crabs dragged their painted shells from one side of the tub to the other.

Melinda turned to James. "I know you could spend years studying Crabbo, but I've observed it, and as interesting as it is, I think our time is better used studying the pieces of cetacean skin recovered a few days ago. These pieces of skin have active nanos working within the biology."

Queued up behind Melinda, the three researchers stared at the mutated crab. Dan stood between James and Melinda; his athletic frame concealed her from James' view. James craned his neck carefully around Dan's expansive shoulders to answer Melinda.

"Just get me to a microscope and some of the new nanos. I don't care what biology they're using as a host. I don't want to be a whiner, but I still haven't examined them yet."

Hank kept his eyes firmly on the mutated crab. "The only way I would examine that thing," he said and nodded his head to Crabbo, "is if it was segmented and pinned to a slide."

"It didn't take long this time for your chicken-shit attitude to rise to the surface," James said.

"There are nanos stored in a refrigerator unit. We can head there," Moto interjected.

The team headed to cold storage in silence; a reprieve from the clatter of clacking shells and scratching claws. Moto filled the quiet with informative chatter.

"This particular lab is surprisingly sizable. There are two levels below grade, as well as the two levels above ground. Yes, yes, there are two levels above ground!" Moto assured no one and everyone, since nobody had questioned him. He continued, "The levels are split, so we're in a split-level laboratory...a portmanteau of sorts," he finished, very proud of himself.

"A suitcase?" questioned Dan. He had been considering how to quit this project and this last bit of badinage caught him off guard.

Moto barked out his trademark laugh, "No, No! A portmanteau can also be—"

James interrupted, "A combination or multiple – a term commonly used in computer programming, "finished James, equally proud of himself.

When they reached the elevator, Hank distanced himself from the team. Moto punched in the code that summoned the elevator. The three researchers and Moto waited in quiet harmony.

Chapter 23

The skin samples were stored in a cold room in the sub-basement two levels below grade. This working space was long and narrow. A stainless-steel counter stretched down the center of the room. Conveniently placed along its length were sinks, microscopes and other all-purpose laboratory equipment. The flat walls were baked enamel with a satin finish, and the recessed lighting delivered a soft, steady illumination over the work surface. This room was perfect for cellular biology research.

"Hank asked that I leave you here and join him elsewhere. If you need additional items, you can contact me through the intercom system." Moto nodded to the simple wall communication panel. "Melinda did some research here earlier; she can direct you to the envoi-suits. I am required to remind you to observe OSHA's Permissible Exposure Limits Protocol." Moto eyed his team for a hint or tell of hesitation at using the protective gear; sensing none, he turned and left.

James was in awe of this laboratory. Though proud of the functional lab in the Andes he'd cobbled together through trading, borrowing and outright thievery, today he would occupy an actual environmental room designed for research and development. He would not have to worry about room temperature flux, refrigeration quality or avalanches.

James pulled on a blue environmental suit designed to moderate human temperature. The lightweight gear allowed one's own body heat to circulate to maintain body temperature. Melinda surprised him by leaving her face uncovered and her hands bare. He cocked his eyebrow in concern; she took time to explain.

"The first researchers who worked on the samples used minimal caution, except the biologists – and you know how they can be." She winked at Dan acknowledging her flippant remark. He rolled his eyes in response. "Anyway, your hands may get cold so just rub 'em together, or if you have to, you can warm up with the heat lamp in the chemical hygiene area adjacent to this room."

Once dressed, Melinda punched in the security code on the door panel, and with a slight popping noise and a blast of cold air, the door opened. A sealed container sat on the aluminum lab table.

James looked into the see-through container. "When was this specimen gathered?" he asked. Despite being in an airtight or dry case, it appeared moist and glistening.

"Good question," Melinda replied. "It's a piece of what was recovered several days ago, and, yeah, it looks like we just pulled it from the water." She ducked down, opened the panel under the lab table and hoisted another container up next to the dry case. "This tub is filled with water and another piece of the recovered specimen," she said.

James peered into the wet container. The sample looked exactly like the specimen in the dry container.

"Dan and I examined these two specimens several hours ago. Microscopic examination indicated the nanos provide whatever the specimen needs to remain healthy." Melinda paced back and forth next to the table with the crates, as she tutored James on the discovery.

"For example, the water in the wet container started out as a simple saline solution. If you were to examine the water now, it would prove to have the composition of seawater. We don't even have to control the water temperature! When we examined it at the microscopic level, we discovered the nanos replicated microprocessor controls and temperature recorders to monitor internal and external conditions." She stopped to let the information soak in; Dan used the space for further explanation.

"I monkeyed around with water and ambient temperatures and the nanos consistently adjusted to a healthy level for the specimen," he said.

She turned and pointed to the dry container. "This specimen is really remarkable. There is a critical need for water for this sample to stay viable so the nanos have developed a process to leach water out of the fat cells. They are reconfiguring at the cellular level and producing whatever is needed – water, nutrients, etcetera."

James was speechless; Melinda's voice existed somewhere in the distance. His heartbeat pounded in his stomach. The information on these nanos crashed into his brain and collided with the data on his original Nano Project. Never in his wildest dreams had he imagined his nanos would have this capacity. Granted, they had been the smartest designed to date; however future forecasting never indicated this level of independent functioning.

"You are describing a Cybernetic organism – nano technology working in harmony within the whale biology." James needed to reframe what she'd said to clearly articulate what was created.

Dan watched as James internalized the information. Color leeched from his face, and black pupil's dilated as James realized the significance of what was being said. He also recognized the trepidation that crept in as James' color returned. Recognize it; hell Dan experienced it himself several hours ago when he and Melinda examined the sample.

"Destroying Titan may not even be possible," Dan interrupted. "I've wracked my mind to discover how we could get close enough to deal with this thing at all, then the Crabbo attack on Melinda brought any ideas I had to a screeching halt," he said.

James looked at Dan blankly. "This cannot have happened," is all he said.

Dan's practical experience working with the military against global bio-terror helped him through this "unbelieving stage" James was experiencing. They did not have time to coax James into accepting what was happening.

"James, think of the process this way; we are way past Plato and his theory that the world is round, way past Pythagoras and his mathematical calculations equaling a rounded earth. Melinda and I are Magellan and we have just discovered the world is round."

"Our research," Melinda said, "Dan's and my research proves without a doubt the nanos – *your* nanos – are working with the biology of a sperm whale.

"We don't have time for you to theorize the progression from your prototype to – whatever is happening. You've got to believe it and move on," Dan said.

The analogy worked. James got it. "What next?" he asked.

Disturbed by the Crabbo attack, Dan shared his newest concern. "The way I see it, Crabbo has a very simple cerebral cortex, and it was extremely aggressive when threatened. This cetacean has a very large and complex mammalian brain. I think we've seen a very specific, very dangerous pattern of behavior from him in the pacific," he concluded.

This declaration was so off-topic that James and Melinda just stared.

"I think Titan is systematically attacking subs because he perceives them as a threat," Dan explained.

"Then we need a way to capture and analyze the whale before the military destroys it," James said. If what Dan assumed regarding the whale's behavior was correct, then the military would certainly destroy it.

Dan's expression screamed he didn't agree.

Melinda positioned herself across from the two men. She watched them square up to debate their agendas. James earned her respect as a thoughtful and intelligent researcher during their collaboration on the initial Nano Project. Now, she admired his desire to examine and utilize the new technology.

Her work with Dan these past few days provided her with a new appreciation of cetaceans, sperm whales in particular. The men expressed objectives that were too polar to bring together quickly. She needed to move them forward.

"Doctors, we can't start our research with outcomes," Melinda began. "In fact, Dan and I have good data on what is happening to the wet and dry specimens; we need to move forward in the direction of determining what we can use to have any affect on Titan. We need to research medication to tranquilize or euthanize him *and* weaponry useful to stun or destroy him."

Melinda stopped and waited to see how they would react. She respected both men. Hell, she'd had a pretty good crush on James when she worked with him years ago, and she was in the middle of a pretty good crush on Dan right now. *After this project, I've got to see a shrink*, she thought.

Both men regarded her with respect. As they'd squared off to support their own beliefs, they had deviated from the scientific process.

James was the first to reply, "Right, Right. We need to move forward on the task at hand: how to contain this Titan in the Pacific."

Relieved James was first to concede their standoff, Dan let his shoulders drop and took a calming breath. As the odd-man-out biologist among the engineers, he was prepared to butt heads with them regarding conclusions. At least now, they agreed to study together.

"I can examine the effects of different medications on the biology of the specimen," Dan said. "One phone call and Moto can produce nearly anything we can think of."

He walked to the intercom to call Moto. As interesting as the dry sample was, the target was underwater. He needed a water bath big enough for several hydrated sample pieces. He also voiced that they should move to a warm laboratory with suitable space for all areas of research. He wanted them together.

The three settled into a simple diagnostic lab. As much as Melinda wanted to work with Dan, a better use of her time was to work on the nanos. "I'll work with James. We'll find something to Block the nanos," she said with confidence.

Dan mulled over the samples. "I'm going to start by soaking a dry sample in saline solution – similar to sea water," he said.

Melinda smiled at Dan in agreement while she set the area up for computer research. James adjusted the chair he would occupy for the next several hours. He moved it up and down several times, intermittently sitting, leaning back and turning on the seat, maneuvering the chair into the perfect position. After finally finding the perfect height, back tensile, and twirling capability, he sighed and scooted up to the computer screen. Melinda cocked an eyebrow curiously at him.

He shrugged sheepishly. "We didn't have adjustable chairs at my last project. I'm excited not to hunch," he said.

Dan had watched James' delighted maneuvering of the simple chair. The candid statement made him smile.

"Yes, do what you think is best for the biology of this experiment," James finally agreed. "Melinda and I will review my research on the original nanos." He gracefully swung around in his chair and joined Melinda, who was already totally engrossed in the data on her computer screen.

Chapter 24

Melinda and James tackled the challenge of neutralizing the nanos. He'd originally designed the nanos to withstand electrical overload. Built with sophisticated circuit breakers, they had the capacity to reroute if they encountered a barrier.

The prototype nanos were "team players," meaning the more nanos there were, the more effective they would be.

Data showed that nanos saturated the skin sample.

Melinda moved from her computer station and circled the stainless-steel water table. She chewed her lip and stared at the piece of flesh soaking in the salt water, willing a plan to come to mind. Dan prepared the area for collection of basic data on water, climate change and composition.

"Maybe we can shock them," Melinda said. "Moto, get me a pair of jumper cables and a battery charger!" She turned to the group. "Rubber boots and gloves for everyone," she said, as if she was ordering a round of drinks for the gang.

James swung his chair around and faced Melinda. He appeared exasperated. Melinda waved him off as he began to argue. "I know, I know . . . your design included circuit breakers, but we're going to shock the sample from the outside, your breakers are for internal wire overload." She crouched down and examined the water table.

"The electrical conductivity of stainless steel is relatively poor." She slide under the table like a mechanic checking the break system. "I wish this was aluminum," she grumbled.

Moto returned with all the requested items and heard her desire. "This particular water table has a fairly low fraction of nickel; it may prove to be better than expected," he said.

Melinda grabbed up a pair of boots and gloves and looked expectantly at the others.

"Why do I have to wear these?" Dan asked. Deep into promising research on sedatives, he was hesitant to take time out of his research. "I could just take my research out of the lab and wait until the experiment is over."

"I can't predict what the nanos will do when they experience the shock," explained Melinda. "Hopefully we'll discover a window of time when they are inactive, and I want all brains on deck."

Already into gloves and boots, she and James examined the battery charger. James attached the clamps to the terminals and Moto signaled a clumsy gloved thumbs up, indicating they were securely attached. James started to walk to the wet container. "Do you think they know I'm coming?" he voiced, slowing down a bit.

"I don't think so," replied Dan, now wearing boots and gloves. "At least we haven't evidenced anything like that," he quantified.

"We're pretty lucky this isn't plastic," James noted, his voice hushed. He gently clipped the cables to the side of the container.

There was no reaction from the nano-infused skin.

Melinda skillfully managed to edge out Moto at the rheostat of the charger. "How much juice should I send?" she asked.

"Crank it up pretty good," James said. "The original nanos are set to withstand a pretty substantial shock."

Melinda set the charger on high. "Ready?" she asked. There were nods, and she flipped the switch to on. The reaction was immediate. They heard a loud pop as the electrical current was pushed back into the charger. Acrid smoke drifted up from the charger as fluid oozed from burst seams. Water flew from the container and the air crackled with electrical current. The water surrounding the flesh roiled, and droplets danced against the sides of the water table. Melinda felt her hair stand on end.

The hunk of whale flesh sat in the container, ominously still.

The team fell silent. Dan finally spoke. "I feel like that cop from the movie Jaws, you know, the one who said 'We're going to need a bigger boat.'

Chapter 25

The three cleaned up in silence. A small area of the lab was affected, some water on the floor and battery acid slowly chewing its way through the ceramic tile on the floor. The pungent smoke, a bitter reminder of the experiment, hung above them. Melinda gathered the boots and gloves and placed them orderly against the wall.

Moto left and returned, wearing neoprene gloves and apron, with protective goggles perched at the top of his forehead. He used a neutralizing acid absorber to clean any corrosives from the floor. Dan grabbed a mop and bucket from the storage room and quietly wiped at an insignificant wet spot.

James sat, his swivel chair tilted as far back as it would go, his eyes closed against the inevitable. "This isn't primarily a nano project, is it Dan?" James said.

Dan leaned on his mop, thoughtfully. "Nope; as I see it we have to figure out how to stop the whale." He placed the mop against the wall, next to the boots. He walked over to his research area and flipped open his laptop.

James rolled over to the computer. Dan moved slightly, opening up a space for James in front of the screen. Dan clicked expertly through several tabs and settled on a medical site.

"There are more than a few different tranquilizing agents we can use against Titan and sufficient data supporting several models that keep him alive," Dan revealed.

James' sagging silhouette perked when he heard they might be able to keep Titan alive. Encouraged by James sudden show of interest, Dan continued.

"This sort of procedure is done frequently at aquariums and places like Sea World," he clarified.

"What we don't have is data on the Novo Cetus, or mutated whale. For example, how much does it weigh? We see that Crabbo's weight increased significantly with the addition of the nano-altered exoskeleton. In parallel – this Titan is huge. The skeletal structure must have changed significantly to support the creature in the pacific. He clicked through several other tabs and landed on a picture of Crabbo. Dan leaned in to the screen and questioned, "What damage and repair has been done here that we cannot see?"

Melinda listened and nodded her head in agreement. She and Moto pulled up close and paid careful attention. Moto's eyebrows furrowed with determined concentration. His eyes popped wide.

"Gretchen Greenwood!" he blurted. Three confused faces stared at him.

"The forensic anthropologist," he explained. "She would have made use of the more than adequate digital imaging lab here. We have ultrasonometers, x-ray bone densitometers, and I've even seen a mandibulometer and other forensic equipment," he finished, obviously proud of himself.

Dan took advantage of Moto's satisfied silence and said, "I think what he said was that we could use that digital equipment to see what changes took place inside Crabbo. We can determine bone density, body proportion and may even get a three-dimensional representation of any organ reconstruction."

"Do we have a Spectral Doppler? I don't suppose you can get your hands on a Japanese hand-held MRI?" Dan rushed his questions together.

"Whoa," James interrupted. "I thought hand-helds were only in the concept stage?" The possibility of internal examination of Crabbo excited him, but micro-machines were his passion.

Dan pinched the bridge of his nose and shut his eyes tightly against the memory of his last encounter with that particular piece of equipment.

"I was on assignment last year in Kabul," he said. "A guy I was working with used one to discover a microchip hidden in a terrorist's shoulder joint." Dan shuddered. "Even with the MRI image, it was pretty messy to extract."

Melinda made a very disgusted face. "Alrighty then . . . We're way off topic now. . . Moto how long do you need to get everything together?"

"Why don't you three take time and have lunch," he said, as he calculated the time it would take to locate and prepare for the trial. "You can structure the experiment while I prepare an arena for the examination to take place."

Grumblings of empty stomachs exceeded grumbles of rebellion; they reluctantly agreed and headed for the rec room in search of food.

Chapter 26

m oto sat cross-legged on the cement floor of the laboratory's garage, Stanley Pro-Mobile Tool Chest next to him. He busied himself deconstructing a twenty-eight-liter Cole-Parmer Digital Water Bath. Removing the shaker platform proved easy, however extracting the water tank from the casing that housed the temperature controls, timers and alarms turned out to be extremely difficult. Screwdrivers, ratchets and wrenches were no match for the water-proof design.

The impenetrable construction finally surrendered to several whacks from a tire iron.

Moto trotted from laboratory to laboratory collecting different ultrasound machinery. Along the way, he filled his leather apron with interesting bits and pieces. He used a bi-metal hole saw and aquarium sealant to securely attach medical equipment strategically inside the tub. The addition of artfully stacked beakers, ampules, and flasks filled with colored water created a vibrant and textured habitat. As an afterthought, Moto scattered an assortment of colorful paperclips, pen tops and small sponges for Crabbo to use as trimming. He stepped back and reflected on the twelve by six foot artificial tide pool. Pleased with the effect, he left to scavenge a forklift.

He returned piloting a small drum carrier transporting Crabbo and his tub mates in the old habitat to the new glass tide pool. With a shout out to Saint Albert the

Great, one of the patron saints of scientists, for an uneventful transfer – he dumped the inhabitants into the water bath. As expected, the mutated claw slashed out toward the drum carrier, violently gnashing at the air. A putrid odor, released when the crab was distressed, bloomed from the container. Moto shifted the drum carrier to reverse and it beeped its telltale warning. In the rear-view mirror, he caught sight of James' lanky figure with the other two scientists close behind.

Melinda trotted over to the artificial environment. "It's breathtaking!" Her eyes swept over the colorful habitat. She tugged at Dan and urged him to look at the pool.

"Moto used lab instruments to add conturing to the bottom. See, hermit crabs have already taken up residence on top of one," she said.

Dan observed three hermit crabs, housed in psychedelic shells, lounging on a spectrophotometer.

"How on earth did you accomplish this so quickly?" he asked, surprised at the thoughtful effort.

Moto sat inside the cab of the drum carrier. "You will find I am very succinct and organized," he said and backed the drum carrier out of the laboratory while the others discussed their responsibilities in the upcoming experiment.

Each researcher reviewed his or her role for the test. Dan would start the ultrasound remotely and then monitor the biology in the container, while Melinda narrated and recorded the images delivered to her computer screen. Lack of sufficient data on the mutated crab along with the crab's history of aggression raised safety concerns. Therefore, James was tasked to stand by with a Telescopic Stunning Baton in case things went south. He positioned himself at the ready and waited for Dan to start the ultrasound equipment.

Melinda settled in front of her laptop and said, "Just to confirm worst case scenario – if Crabbo goes bonkers in the tub and starts – I don't know – throwing hermit crabs at James, he will stun him with that police poll, right guys?" She sat far away from the action and felt out of control.

James stood by awkwardly with the stunning baton. Initially, he thought it exciting to be the badass of the experiment, but now he felt asinine standing by the colorful habitat as Crabbo worked to attach a pink sponge to his shell.

"We've poked at it several times and so far there's just the protracting claw and the rotten smell," James reminded her. "However, I'm armed and ready." He jiggled the poll slightly as evidence.

Melinda looked at James and thought he didn't look very ready; he seemed self-conscious as he stood with the stunning rod limply directed at Crabbo.

"James, that mutant has easily sliced off the tip of every broom, mop and shovel handle we've poked in there!" she said. "Your job is to keep everyone safe, so firm up that grip on your rod and be ready for anything!"

Moto entered the room, heard Melinda's reprimand, and barked out his signature "Ha! That's funny – right? What she said lends itself to two meanings, a double-entendre." He looked to Dan and James for confirmation and got it as the two gestured rudely.

Irritated with all of them, she pulled her auburn hair into a tight pony and sighed.

"Can we just start?" she said.

James straightened into position while the others readied themselves for the experiment. "Okay then, let's do it on three," he said.

"On three, or on go? Like, 'one, two, three, go'?" asked Dan. He hated team synchronization; anything could go wrong.

"On three," repeated James. "One – Two – Three!"

James flipped a switch and a droning buzz filled the room as 250,000 volts of electricity hummed inside the baton. Dan turned on the imaging equipment. Crabbo conveniently wandered in front of the ultrasound machine, plopped down, grabbed an eyestalk with his left cheliped and began to pick it clean.

"Jeez, Louise!" Melinda said, awestruck by what was unfolding. She quickly regained her composure and narrated her observations.

"We should be calling her Crabbette. She has a U-shaped telson. It looks like one half of her structure has been rebuilt, internally as well as externally." She flipped to a section of the biology book she was using as a reference.

She leaned in closer to the computer screen. She held a stylus and tapped it on the screen, causing the image to enlarge. "The hepatopancreas has been rebuilt. I bet that is where the smell is coming from. An oddly formed sac is attached to the stomach; that sac is not in any of the crab anatomy we looked at during lunch."

She moved her stylis around her computer screen, placed it on a particular image and zoomed in. "The ovaries have been rebuilt. Do you think she could reproduce?" She looked over to James as if he would answer her. He scowled and nodded her back to the task at hand.

She turned her attention to the screen. "Right—ok–one set of gills has been mutated. They appear much thicker, not 'feather like,' and the mutated set is pinker than the other set. Dan, I can't seem to locate the heart, but I'd venture to guess that it hasn't been altered, and the rest of the stomach seems to be untouched." At this point, Crabbo scurried out of view and began scrabbling through the sand, looking for food.

Dan turned off the ultrasound machine. "There is so much research we could be doing on her right here, right now," he said. "Her trans-mutated biology is groundbreaking. We could get funding for years to study her."

James powered down the Stunning Baton and couldn't help but notice the longing in Dan's voice. Leaning on the baton James looked wistfully at the aberration cleaning its eye-stalks.

Moto recognized the disappointment and recognition that this was not the time for studying the crab.

"This feels like a once in a lifetime opportunity," he said, validating their feelings. "But we are committed to another once in a lifetime project and Titan is our focus, not mutant her biology," he reminded them gently. "Let's put this little lady in stasis until the Titan project is concluded."

Melinda absentmindedly chewed on her fingernails as she watched Crabbette carefully attach a paperclip to her carpas. "I don't think we have to put her on ice," she said. "She's pretty harmless. The nanos will take care of the water quality. We should monitor how long they can sustain osmoregulation."

Dan sat at his laptop and concentrated on an image of Titan. "This experiment went great, but how does this translate into finding information on what to do with him," he said, pointing to the screen.

Melinda joined him at the computer. "Did you know the military remains cloaked and that Hank provided them the static frequency for cloaking that Titan hasn't figured out – yet." She turned to James. "Do you know anything about this static?" she said.

"Let's not bring Hank and his research to our table just yet," James replied.

"What research?" both Dan and Melinda asked.

"Let's not waste time on Hank and his bullshit." James tried to be evasive. He felt his comment should satisfy them for now.

Melinda wanted to argue; something was bubbling just below the surface between James and Hank.

Wrapped up in the research, Dan studied the data on Titan and pulled up a photo for closer examination. He zoomed in and focused on the eyes.

"Externally, these appear all wrong," he said and waved the others over to his computer to take a look aqt the military footage of Titan. "In the still photos, they look protuberant or 'bugged-out.' When I run the film footage we have in slow motion and zoom in on the eyes, they appear to function independently." The team concentrated on some of the best footage available.

He has chameleon's eyes!" James said, as he watched the eyes turn in different directions.

"Finally, something new! Can we use it to our advantage?" Melinda asked.

"Vision is interpretive," Dan replied, taking the time to explain visual perception. "Meaning our brain has to have something to reference things to. For example, even when you taste, smell and touch an apple, if you can't see it you won't necessarily recognize it," Dan said as he mentally reviewed any information he had on the visual system.

"And then there are optical illusions," he continued. He opened a new tab and searched for a particular image.

"Look at this." Dan showed them an illustration. "What do you see – a woman gazing into a mirror – or a skull?"

"At first, I saw the woman and the mirror," Melinda said. "But when I looked for a skull – I found one!"

James mumbled something about not seeing the skull, pushed his way closer to the screen and squinted his eyes in an attempt to find it.

Dan moved away from the computer. "Maybe we can create a visual deception." He faced Melinda. "You know, make it think we're something we're not."

"Like camouflage or something – to get closer to it?" she responded.

Dan paced the large garage to the far wall and back to the water bath. He peered into the water at Crabbette; she stared back with one eye while the other watched a bright purple hermit crab burrow under a pile of glass beakers.

"What are we going to mimic?" he asked no one and everyone. "How close to perfect do we have to make it? And *where* the hell will we make it?"

"I will have to bring Dr. Hardin and Lt. Brasco in at this point," Moto said, looking at James. "I foresee the need for more materials than I can scavenge."

"Whatever." James tried to act dismissive, but only achieved snide. "You call in our handlers."

"What do you mean 'handlers'?" asked Melinda.

"I mean, we can't do anything of substance without clearing it with Hardin or Brasco," James said as he walked out of the lab. He hated to include Hank in any research, but right now they had a direction and momentum. If they needed Hank for authorizations, so be it.

Melinda hadn't considered this. She'd worked government contracts before and actually felt more in control today because of the team's organic approach to their work. "We're not being handled, are we, Dan?" She looked at Dan, who was still staring into the artificial tide pool.

"I've been working for the government for a long time, so it doesn't feel like handling, but, yeah, I guess we are."

Chapter 27

While the team worked in the garage, Hank power-walked along a well-groomed path in town. Mentally he evaluated his posture: *chest raised and shoulders relaxed – check; arms bent slightly – check; hands cupped, not clenched – check; and small but fast steps, rolling from heel to toe – check.* He envisioned himself as quite the skillful walker, envied by other novice pacers. Regrettably, the path was surprisingly deserted today so he could not compare his smart style against others.

He focused on a conversation he'd had with Moto a few hours ago. The team needed complex underwater equipment to carry out their newest research. Their ideas were brilliant yet dangerous since there was no conclusive data on Titan's vision. Furthermore, no matter how scientifically sound the outcomes hashed out, this project started with an assumption and that could be, at the least, problematic and, at the most, dangerous.

A familiar voice interrupted his musings. "Dr. Hardin, I need an update on our project." Hank turned and faced a man dressed in loose, black exercising gear. Long hair fell in stringy dreads that seeped out from under a wildly colored do-rag. The addition of aviator sunglasses helped obscure his facial features. The jogger's oversized windbreaker fell just below his waistband.

Concealing – what – a dagger or gun? Hank wondered.

"I thought communication was through Brasco," Hank complained. He uncocked his arms and let them fall limply at his sides. Anxious around the cloak and dagger stuff, his eyes darted to the path behind the jogger.

The intruder moved in closer, and Hank's ego-inflated chest of just moments ago sunk away from the physical confrontation, but his feet held their ground.

"We talk to you when we want to, we've paid for the privilege," he said, his speech slow; his accent thick. "I ask again, what is the progress on our project?" The jogger did not move.

The physical intimidation worked and Hank took a step back. "My researchers are moving ahead. We still have complete government support. No one suspects anything. You need to be patient." A line of sweat formed along Hank's upper lip.

With a gloved thumb, the jogger gently wiped away the sweat. "You are correct to be anxious, my friend." He lifted his windbreaker, revealing a gun and a nasty looking knife tucked into his waistband.

Hank stumbled farther backwards. His eyes swept to the left and then right. *Where are the people – runners, bikers, dog walkers?*

As if reading Hank's mind, the jogger responded. "You American runners – or whatever it is that you do – always do what is right; like you wear the right shoes for your sport, you wear the right clothes for the weather, you have the right equipment." He nodded toward Hank's Spibelt, cinched at his waist. "And if I drape official yellow tape blocking the trailhead that says "do not cross' I can count on you Americans to do the right thing." He finished speaking and leaned way left and then way right, stretching his oblique muscles.

Jesus, he's referring to crime scene tape. I hope this is not going to be a crime scene, Hank thought. "I'm moving my research to Seattle tonight. If our experiment succeeds, I expect to be in the water within the next few days." His body trembled but his voice did not expose the extent of his fear.

"We can be patient, if necessary. This time you have given us reason to be patient." The jogger turned and sprinted away.

Hank let his body slump. He unclenched his hands and took some deep breaths. He wondered how long he'd have before runners returned to the trail. He needed to contact Brasco. He opened his Spibelt, retrieved his cell phone and a few watermelon jellybeans. Hoping the sour beans would relieve his dry mouth, he popped a few in and was grateful when his mouth exploded with saliva. He leaned heavily on a nearby pine and dialed up Brasco.

"Some spy just accosted me in the park!" he hissed into the phone.

"Are you okay? Do you need an ambulance?" Brasco was driving fast on the interstate; he looked for a place to pull over.

"No! But I'm looking for a men's room. He scared the shit out of me." After exhaling heavily, his breathing became more regular.

Brasco relaxed and continued driving at a more reasonable speed. "I guarantee if they had 'accosted you,' you would need an ambulance. What exactly happened?"

"They want information. I told them to be patient. I also reminded him that all communication was to be filtered through you," Hank fussed. He didn't want some hoodlum to materialize and intimidate him again.

"Maybe you didn't realize this but these people don't play by any rules. So if they want to talk to you, they will talk to you." Brasco wondered if Hardin was as naïve as he sounded. He hoped not; the guy needed to be on the ball from here on out. There was too much at stake.

"I guess he just caught me off guard," Hank replied. "I don't need people jumping out from behind trees to talk to me."

"Well, I hate to disappoint you, but they are not going to make an appointment with your secretary so get used to it. Someone will just turn up, and you had better have information for them each and every time. Moving on, what is the progress on Titan?" Brasco might as well get an update, especially if someone had approached Hank looking for information.

"I'm moving the team to the Pacific Coast. The Center for Marine Biodiversity and Conservation has several research stations there. Moto is securing one now. The team has momentum and as good a theory as any. I will be transferring them tomorrow morning," Hank reported.

The telltale rustle of prairie grass as runners veered off path to pass interrupted the quiet. He checked his state-of-the-art Polar Heart Rate Monitor Watch, relieved to see normal beats per minute displayed – down markedly from a moment ago.

"The plan is to disguise a small sub as an ocean sunfish and try to get close to Titan with ultrasound equipment. I'll be at the research station too; I'll call you from there." Hank was ready to get going. Hikers, dogs and runners filed past. He pressed "end call" and returned the phone to his pack.

Brasco recognized the hollow sound of a dead phone line. *Sunfish?* The word brought him back forty years to fishing with his grandpa on Little York Lake in upstate New York. Every evening they caught shiny silver sunfish – with bright orange underbellies and vivid red spots where their ears should be –then fried them up in a cast iron skillet. They used hotdogs or bread balls as bait because his grandma wouldn't eat one if it had just swallowed a worm. He imagined a thirty-foot punkin-seed sunny swimming up next to Titan. He hoped this would work.

Chapter 28

The transfer of the team from Colorado to Washington started out on a small military plane. Everyone used the six-hour flight to do research. Dan worked exclusively on the design for the Mola mola, or ocean sunfish. Moto connected him to Thingamajigs, a special effects studio in Seattle. They would outfit a small surveillance submarine with a fabricated "Mola suit," turning it into the large ocean sunfish.

The two-man submarine measured out at just over eleven feet in length. For this decoy to pass as a credible ocean sunfish, the "Mola suit" could only add three feet to the silhouette of the sub – a tight fit, but the costume crew assured Dan they could do it. Dan and the mechanical art crew at Thingamagigs decided on fleshy pink with silver polka dots for the skin and scale color. The dots were designed shiner than traditional Mola mola dots to match the reflective tinting used to cover the portholes. This would camouflage any ultrasound equipment that peeked out through some of the dots. They equipped the tail end, or clavus, with mucus ejectors. Mola mola's were famous for expelling slimy mucus from the base of their dorsal and anal fins when threatened. Moto concocted a thick secretion with dual purpose: to distort the mechanical noise produced by the sub and, as an exit strategy, to distract Titan.

Melinda and James tracked down the ultrasound machines in Seattle on the internet. The project needed machines that function at a frequency far different from those used by cetacean in echolocation. Data gathered by Passive Acoustic Monitoring (PAM) indicated that sperm whales operated at a mid to high frequency – thirty-five to fifty-five kilohertz. Medical ultrasounds used at least ten megahertz Melinda researched ultrasound equipment appropriate for the task, and James converted the kilohertz into megahertz. They found five machines right for the assignment. Finished with their task, they turned their attention to Dan's project.

"How's that Mola sub coming along?" James asked. Pictures of the disguised craft looked like the head half of a fish crimped off just behind the dorsal and anal fins.

Dan welcomed the break from watching the design team and answered. "We've decided on a waterproof, poly-foam fabric design because it can be textured and colored to mirror a Mola mola. Also, it won't add much weight to the sub – it's the same fabric used in some sport mascot outfits," he explained. "Anyway, I weigh about 240 pounds – and you James, you're all skin and bones, Moto figured you at about 185 pounds, right?" James nodded. "Our additional weight needs to cap out at 700 pounds; we figure with the mucus, equipment and us, it will be close." He turned his laptop toward them. "Thinamajigs arranged a live-feed video so I can monitor their progress – no audio though – they don't want a 'backseat designer.' Come over and take a look."

The two-man sub was a streamlined design rather than a diving bell. A creature designer attached fleshy pink side panels with cutouts around the mucus ejector and ultrasound sites. The scalloped rear-end was a flawless copy of images of a Mola mola clavus. A wiry guy perched atop the costumed sub attached the five-foot dorsal fin, and a young woman sewed silvery polka dots onto the side panels. Interior creature designers measured portholes for tinted glass.

"Wow! These guys are great, that is really looking like a Mola mola! I thought special effects were all green screen and CGI nowadays," Melinda said.

Her genuine reaction pleased Dan. He'd been looking at it so carefully it had begun to look cartoonish. "Don't even mention CGI to this art crew. They consider computer generated images just smoke and mirrors. We are using mechanical artists.

They produce actual objects." Dan had received a curt tutorial on the difference between Computer Generated Images and character or monster building. He turned to James to get his reaction, but had a reaction of his own.

"You don't look so good," he commented.

Chapter 29

James needed to talk to Hank. After using the inhaler, he'd felt fine for the first seventy-two hours, but in the last few hours, he'd been sweating. He knew the shakes were next.

Shocked by James' appearance, Melinda grabbed his arm and pulled him into a nearby seat. "Sit down! Do you need anything? I think you need water – I'll get some water." She ran to the galley, snatched several water bottles out of the refrigerator, ran back and handed him an opened bottle. She stood there, drinking her own water and staring at him, her brow scrunched with concern.

"Do you think it was something you ate? I hope it's not anything you ate. We all ate the same thing, right Dan?" Melinda hated getting sick. Dan came around, stood next to her and stared at James.

James drew in a long calming breath. He was going to have to tell them what was happening. He exhaled slowly and closed his eyes. "I need to talk to Hank. He didn't stop his research on my nanos after the accident; he developed an antivirus to the infection I have." He kept his eyes closed and pressed the water bottle onto his neck in an effort to cool a pulse point.

"I test positive for nanos."

"What exactly do you mean by that?" Dan asked. He was pretty good at figuring things out, but he knew what he was figuring couldn't possibly be true.

"He developed an inhaler that allows me to function at warmer, external temperatures – like this." James lifted his trembling arm and made a sweeping gesture.

"I don't give a damn about your curative inhaler; I want to know if we've been exposed to some kind of new nano bacterium!" Dan said, enraged. Over the years, he had worked with scores of deadly organisms and had been painstakingly cautious.

Melinda took an involuntary step back. As an engineer, she hadn't worked much around contagions.

Dan turned to Melinda. "Were you aware of James' exposure?"

"No! I'm just as shocked as you," she said and directed her attention towards James. "And I'm thinking that Hank had something to do with your exposure. That's why you're so confrontational with him," she speculated aloud. "And I thought it was because he was in charge of your project."

At this point, Dan stood aggressively occupying the space between the others and the cockpit. "Calm down, Dan," James said. "Exposure to my virus is through ingestion or intravenous. There is no airborne or other danger." His voice was still strong because he was in the slight, or physiological phase, of the tremor. The temperature in the cabin needed to be much cooler or he would quickly move into the pathological stage, where talking or walking would become almost impossible because of the tremors. It would take hours to recover if he reached that level.

"Please, someone turn down the heat and turn up the air conditioning on this airplane," he begged. "We need to bring the external temperature to around forty-two degrees, then I'll tell you all you want to know."

Dan got the air conditioning cranked up, while Melinda encased James in cold water bottles. She turbaned a wet towel around his head. Satisfied with her result, she confronted James.

"What the hell is going on?" she demanded. When Melinda had calked James in water bottles, Dan had retreated angrily to his laptop to continue to monitor the construction of the Mola suit, but now he looked accusingly at James for his answer.

James carefully recounted the events that had forever changed his life.

"Hank and I spent a lot of time theorizing the medical benefits of our nano technology. We often lamented that not only did we feel stuck in this Department Of Defense contract, but it would take years to get approval for animal trials." The cold cocoon Melinda had created worked and the tremors and sweating stopped. James' hunched shoulders relaxed and he unfurled his clenched fists. Reassured that the virus had stabilized, he continued. "Hank agreed to be the one to ingest the nanos. We had reliable data proving the majority of nanos would be eliminated within hours." His voice rose, as if to convince everyone of their good sense. "Anyway, Hank would ingest the nanos and I would take samples – blood and tissue. We had unfettered access to sophisticated research and imaging equipment," he explained.

"I would also have an emetic, and we would flush his system within the hour." He stopped. The cold nest that had comforted him moments before did nothing to shelter him from his reality.

"So what happened?" Melinda demanded. Under no circumstances had she seen Hank as the kind of researcher to take risks. In fact, she remembered Hank as meticulous in following all safety protocol.

James stared at the table tray locked in the upright position in front of him. Emotionless, he recalled the chain of events.

"Hank said he got there early, put the Kup 'o Koffee on my desk and went to take a piss; and while he was off pissing, I got there and thought 'oh, good someone brought in coffee' and I drank it. Besides all that cream and sugar, there were ten cc's of nanos stirred into that Kup 'o Koffee. The effect was immediate – all my organs went into overdrive – heart rate, blood pressure, even body temperature. Every negative symptom we theorized occurred immediately. I hoped I could send the nanos into stasis by bringing the ambient temperature down, so I hightailed it to a cold lab. Hank returned and waited for me, and waited, and waited. About an hour went by before he checked on the Kup 'o Koffee and figured out what had happened. He found me in a cold lab – freezing, alive and angry."

Halfway through the story, Melinda moved to the bank of seats in front of James. She knelt in the middle and peeked between the seats as James droned out the story. She remembered the Lab's fascination with "Kluck Kluck Koffee." They all drank the scientifically engineered hot or cold coffees, some sweet concoctions and others bitter brews.

"What about the emetic, did you use it?" she asked.

"It was too late. By the time Hank want back to retrieve it, the nanos were already bound to my DNA. The rest is just complicated, Melinda. I'm a top secret research project that has been shelved for the last few years." He closed his eyes, indicating there would be no more talking for now.

Dan didn't let him leave it at that. "Any more secrets, Dr. Moreau?"

James visibly cringed at the reference to the mad doctor, and Melinda looked at Dan, oozing with disapproval.

Dan defended himself. "It's going to be James and me in the Mola sub. There has to be trust."

"Well, don't trust Hank," James said. "He's still working on the nanos. I don't know why I was brought into this. He could easily run this project without me."

The pilot announced they would land soon. Dan turned his attention back to the progress on the Mola suit while Melinda replaced some of the water bottles, surrounding James with colder ones. She buckled herself in next to him. "This is really bad, James – really bad," she said.

Chapter 30

Moto picked up the trio at the Seiku airport in a Lincoln Super Stretch limousine. He collected the team and their meager belongings (a backpack and laptop each) and traveled the Strait of Juan de Fuca highway to a research station near Orzette, Washington.

The three researchers huddled together on a bench seat, snuggled under a tacky blue blanket, featuring a garish white stallion, they'd picked up at a roadside stand. The air-conditioner blasted and all vents pointed at the uncovered James as he lounged on the opposite bench.

Moto read from the "Explore Washington!" booklet he'd picked up at the stand. "... And there is a nice footbridge in Clallam's downtown that goes over Clallam River and brings you to the beach, where eagles, osprey, and other birds can usually be seen. From there, you can walk to the Slip Point Lighthouse and enjoy the low-tide marine life." He looked to James for reflection or remark; getting none, he closed the book. It was apparent no one was paying him much attention. Melinda dozed and Dan still monitored the progress of the Mola on his tablet.

"When we reach the Orzette Ranger Station, we will use one of their vehicles to get us to our lab," Moto said.

James shifted and sat upright. "Will Hank be there?" he asked. Melinda opened one eye in interest, and Dan watched Moto, curious of his answer.

"Yes, he is waiting for us" Moto replied.

The rest of the trip passed by in silence interrupted only by heavy sighs of restless nappers, and periodic oohs and ahs as they watched the Mola suit's progress.

They traveled along the Hoko River, speeding toward the pacific coast; the researchers took little time to appreciate the ruggedly beautiful landscape they passed through. For the last leg of their journey they transferred into an All-Terrain Denali and bounced and jangled along the dirt road that led to the research station.

Chapter 31

They arrived at the lab in the post-dawn gloom particular to this overcast region. Moto shut off the ignition and turned to James, who was riding shotgun. "I called ahead and had them set the temperature at forty-two degrees," he said. "Dr. Hardin is waiting for you – us – will that be ok?"

The question revealed Moto's concern with more than just the temperature.

Alert and anxious, James responded, "I've put off dealing with Hank's duplicity so far – I just want the inhaler."

The team exited the ATV and executed several stretches and bends to relieve the kinks developed from hours of sitting. James hunched against the cool dampness of the morning fog as they walked into the laboratory. Hank met them in the lobby and handed the inhaler to James.

"How much of this stuff do you have?" James asked after sucking a large dose from the inhaler.

James' posture relaxed like an addict after a fix.

"Enough," Hank answered. "You'll need to take a hit from the inhaler more often than we first thought. Stress must accelerate your body's absorption rate. Are you keeping a log – recording times and symptoms?"

Dan and Melinda watched the exchange. They couldn't help noticing the indifference Hank showed to James' condition. Dan's pissy attitude toward James after his nano virus confession now shifted to Hank. "James told us what a stellar team member you are," he spat. "We're really excited to be working with you, right Melinda?"

Melinda was furious. Hank's blunder with the coffee was at the very least careless, and his lack of empathy now was reprehensible. She'd scrutinized Jame's story about the conveniently placed cup of nano-coffee and his subsequent drinking of the science experiment. There was no way Hank accidentally left it on James' desk. She'd worked with Hank and knew how cautious he was.

"I listened to James' rendition of how he became infected with the nano virus," Hank said. "How convenient to play me the villain when it was he who was the reckless one."

"How the hell did you listen to what James told us?" Dan asked. "That conversation took place in the airplane."

Moto cleared his throat and stepped physically into the conversation. "The airplane you arrived in was fully outfitted with audio and visual surveillance equipment. There were disclosure notices in the galley and both bathrooms."

"Bathrooms?" Dan and Melinda exclaimed in unison.

Melinda slumped into a nearby chair, worn out. *This situation is pathetic,* she thought. *They should destroy the whale, but we are all too interested in those fucking nanos to kill it.* She looked at James for some reaction to either Hank's twisted interpretation or Moto's disclosure, but he was preoccupied with checking his heart rate and pulse. Dan's wrinkled brow showed obvious concern for her; Moto's features were composed and unreadable.

The lull in the conversation drew James' attention away from his health issues. From the look on Melinda's face, he could tell that she needed him to respond to Hank.

"Hank's pathetic attempt at revisionism is laughable," James told Melinda. Seated, he matched her posture in an epic slump of his own.

"Are you going to be alright?" she asked. "If you're not going to be alright, I will walk off this project." She stared at James. He still had two fingers on his wrist pulse point. "If you cannot work under these circumstances," she looked pointedly at Hank then returned her gaze to James, "I will follow you out the door. Do you understand?"

James was acutely aware of what was going on. The moment he found out this was going to be a nano project, he'd envisioned himself the lead researcher. Finding out he was working for Hank stuck in his craw. Now, Melinda offered leadership to him. He glanced at Dan, who gave him a "that would work for me" look and a slight nod; Moto remained poker-faced. He turned to Hank, who met him with a practiced sneer.

"Well, well, it looks like you've been picked as team captain – again – congratulations! I could care less your pecking order," Hank hissed. "Ultimately you all will have to listen to me."

Hank turned to Moto. "Keep me informed of the progress on the Mola suit. When it's ready, I'll get Brasco to coordinate the time of the Mola Operation with the Navy." Hank retreated down a hallway.

Moto led the team on a tour of the private facility. It housed several research labs, cabins, suites, and dormitories, along with a dining hall and lecture rooms.

They chose a suite of rooms as their home base. Four ten-by-twelve rooms surrounded a shared living space. Dan and Melinda took rooms that shared a bathroom.

"You will have two hours to rest," Moto said. "During that time, I will take the mucus I made to Thingamajigs. We will meet up in the dining hall." He left.

James dropped his duffel on the bed. Too keyed up to lie down or even sit, he did some wall push-ups and popped as many joints as he could, then did some deep breathing. This calmed his body but did nothing to slow down his racing thoughts.

Melinda and Dan would defer to him on the project now, and he would decide whether they killed or contained Titan.

His biggest question – how did the nanos infecting Titan mutate? Then he allowed himself the awful thought, would his own nanos mutate? No, his nanos were unprogrammed, he reminded himself. He was an epigenetics expert, meaning he studied the quantum science that studies how things outside the DNA sequence, like environmental and energetic effects, influence the evolution of biological systems. Over the last few years he'd had the opportunity to experiment on his own DNA-laced nanos and not one trial reanimated them. Would epigenetic theories affect Titan, he wondered. An unproductive contemplation he concluded, since the Mola sub would not be collecting any tissue samples. He learned in graduate school that it was a waste of time to postulate on things that you wished you could do or things that you were not tasked to do. He successfully napped for the remaining quiet time imposed by Moto. He woke up, executed one last wall push-up, splashed some cold water on his face and trotted to the dining area.

Seated, James watched as Melinda and Dan entered the dining hall. Both had obviously changed clothes, and they still looked damp from showering; *alone or together*, he wondered. With Hank's fondness for surveillance, he hoped that wherever they showered – they did it fully clothed.

James thought he detected a blush from Melinda as she nodded her greeting. Sheepishly, he glanced at his own rumpled day-old clothing. *It's no wonder I don't get the girl*, he reflected.

Dan placed his laptop on the table and plugged it into a common port. The projector screen over the counter blinked to life. An invitation from Thingamajigs to join the online meeting flashed onto the display.

"I've set up for our web conference with the creature people," Dan said. "They've outfitted the sub with the Mola suit and want us to look one last time before they pack it and transport it." He clicked through the windows, searching for the screen with the Mola sub.

The audio kicked in before the visuals and a disembodied voice broadcast clearly through the dining hall. "We're close to wrapping up this Men in Black job," a voice boomed. "Chris and Jen get over here before agents X, Y and Z show up in virtual reality."

The screen flickered, and the Mola sub materialized. Two twenty-somethings rushed into the screen and scooted to a stop next to a beefy guy wearing a paint-spattered apron. "Dr. Peterson, are we connected?" he said into a microphone. "We have no visuals here, just audio. I need confirmation from your end. . . Dr.

Peterson?" He tapped the mic and the researchers winced at the resonating clunks that echoed through the dining hall.

"Yes, Dickey, we're here," Dan replied. "The Mola sub looks great! Give us one last tour."

Dickey handed the microphone to Jen for description. "You provided quite a bit of imagery for us to choose from when we were designing this," she said. "This pinkish color is a common color for the largest Mola mola. Larger polka dots are uncommon, so we limited the largest silver dots to just the ports for the mucus ejectors. The shape and positioning of eyes are perfect to conceal camera equipment." The screen filled with the image of a dark, glassy eye as big as a dinner plate.

The camera zoomed out as Dickey grabbed the microphone. "We can fill you in on how to work this thing from the inside. Is anyone coming here for a lesson?" Dickey asked. Dan checked the time. It was close to eight o'clock in the morning. He looked to James – his project – his call.

"This is Dr. Tillman," James said. "We're scheduled to have this Mola sub in the water at four pm today. Dr. Mulcrone – Moto – is on his way to you with the mucus. You will arm the Mola sub with the mucus at your location. Then Moto and Chris will bring the Mola sub to the deployment site where we will receive our tutorial," he rattled off. "Make sure all the ejector buttons and ultrasound knobs inside the sub are simply marked – I'd hate to think I was zooming in on something and accidentally squirt out snot," he added, half-jokingly.

Dan ended the conversation. "Give our thanks to all your crew at Thingamajigs, Dickey. You've done an outstanding job in a ridiculous amount of time. Since our lab is not connected visually, Moto brought the neutralizer pen and will use it on you guys when he gets there." Dan added the comment about the memory eraser from Men in Black to bust Dickey's balls. Dickey laughed at the reference and said no one ever wore sunglasses in Seattle so they were all probably screwed. The screen went dark.

Chapter 32

The research lab where the team worked was a two-hour ride from the Mola sub launch site. Hank worked with the Navy to coordinate their responsibility to the plan; to provide a small transport vessel would carry the team and the Mola sub to within five miles of Titan.

The researchers used the time before their transport to the launch to customize an M1 Underwater Defense Gun and its ammunition. If they needed a last stand for survival, they planned to shoot a highly toxic venom-dart into Titan. They did not share information on their last stand for survival with Hank.

Thingamajigs provided a thorough tutorial on the operation of the Mola sub. Now all five members of the project huddled in the small galley of the transport vessel.

"Dan, I wouldn't depend on that tranq you've got stashed in the Mola sub for anything. Without comprehensive data on Titan's weight and fat ratios, you cannot be sure of the outcome. There is a good chance it will just piss Titan off," Hank said.

Dan glared at Moto, who sighed. "I did not share the 'last stand' plan with Dr. Hardin," Moto reassured Dan.

Hank laughed. "There are no secrets in a mini-sub. Another one of my guys swept it to see if it was seaworthy after all the modifications made," he said. "I also had him check for any unusual contraband."

"Again, I'm overwhelmed by your astonishing lack of confidence in this team Hardin," Dan said, barely hiding his contempt.

Hank ignored the sarcasm. "I needed to make sure that giant sunfish of yours would work. Besides, the tranq wasn't even hidden." He allowed the tranq to remain on board. He was confident if Dan and James needed to use it, it would be the last thing they did, thus leaving only one loose end to deal with.

"For once, can't you just keep your shit to yourself, Hank," Melinda said. "This is inherently dangerous and thus, serious. So, unless you have something helpful to say, keep your mouth shut." Hank's sweep of their vessel was shifty, she thought, but boasting that the tranq was probably useless was despicable.

Dan, James and Melinda used the remainder of the trip to ignore Hank. There was no mention of Titan, Crabbo or mutant nanos either. Having traveled to exotic locations around the world for work, they took this time to compare notes.

"Nothing is more desolate than the desert," Dan said. "Sand for miles, dune after dune after dune."

"I'd enjoy the vastness of it," countered Melinda. "The cramped quarters of a research vessel during an ice storm are the pits. Recycled air, and nothing but 'Meals Ready to Eat' for days."

James listened to the playful banter of whose experience was more miserable. He didn't care to join into that conversation. His time in the Andes these past few years had been lonely. The stark beauty of the boundless tundra belayed the fact that he was a prisoner to a very small research facility. The conversation stopped when the captain announced their arrival and was awaiting instruction. It was showtime and Hank had the good sense to stay silent.

"Last one in the sub is a rotten egg," joked Dan and ran toward the Mola sub; James trotted after him.

"Never issue a challenge you can't win!" James said and picked up speed. They reached the sub at the same time and pushed at each other in good-humor.

"Boys, boys, there's only one way to enter. Sorry, Dan, but you're the rotten egg by default," Melinda said. "Your computer access is on the left, so James has to get in first." Melinda jogged after them, encouraged at the pretense of courage.

James slipped easily into his seat and gave Dan a smug, I'm-the-winner face. Dan glided into position. "I'm more in the front seat than you are, so I get to be captain," joked Dan.

Melinda could not maintain the careless repartee. "You guys be careful out there, okay?" She was very scared; she noticed she was literally wringing her hands. This was the Mola's virgin voyage. They had no time for even a simulated run. James gave her a thumbs up and Dan winked at her as he shut the portal. Melinda ran in earnest to the secure computer Moto had set up for her to monitor the Mola sub's progress.

The navy amped up the audio static cloak surrounding Titan and lowered the Mola sub into the water. Intelligence reported that Titan hung upside down two-hundred feet below the surface.

The plan called for the navy to deploy an unmanned rubber craft at a predetermined time to lure Titan's attention away from the Mola sub. During this time, the researchers would float their vessel in, get ultrasound images, and then get the hell out of dodge. The mission relied on the assumption that Titan would focus his attention on this rubber craft - not on the extra-large Mola mola swimming innocuously by. Big assumption.

Chapter 33

Titan hung deep below the surface. A toxic clamor permeated the water; he balanced at a depth where the sound tormented him less. He was still engaged in a standoff with the enemy that floated at the surface. If the enemy moved closer, Titan leveled out and matched its advance, inch for inch. When it backed down, so did he. Every so often, his biology felt the unique rhythmic sequence of clicks that identified his pod. Comforted, by their cadence, he remained at guard.

Chapter 34

In the Mola sub, Dan cut the engine, letting them drift toward Titan. At one-hundred meters from the target, they turned on the ultrasound machine. "Are you picking up images Melinda?" asked Dan.

"Yes, the equipment is working fine – continue in radio silence," Melinda replied quickly and quietly. She was cross – again. When she arrived at her computer, Hank sat in *her* seat. It was *her* job to monitor the project. She dragged a heavy chair without casters over to the computer screen, gave Hank's wheelie chair a strong boot out of the way, and shoved her chair firmly in front of the computer. Undeterred, Hank scooted in next to her.

Aboard the Mola sub, Dan and James continued in silence. Thingamajigs had reworked the Mola sub's coolant system to maintain temperatures between forty and fifty degrees.

Dan checked the interior temperature gauge; it read a crisp forty-five degrees. That hadn't stopped beads of nervous sweat from gathering at his hairline. He glanced at James, who gave him the thumbs up. *Good*, Dan thought, *he seems healthy enough.*

Drifting limited Dan's power to navigate, but with effort, he turned the Mola sub, and Titan came into full view.

"Jesus Christ," whispered Dan. Suspended, head down; was the colossal sperm whale. It was all of twenty meters in length. The front section – or head – was massive. The eyes were large and perfectly placed. The lower jaw pivot was located farther back than a typical sperm whale jaw, and its hinge turned up slightly at the corners affecting a maniacal grin. Unnaturally long flippers hugged its sides; unmistakable weaponry jutted out from their tips. The heightened dorsal was knobby and knuckled from the dorsal hump backwards to the fluke or tail. A velvety sheath, void of scaring, replaced typical prune-textured skin; Dan squinted as the sun glistened off the burnished metal woven into the hide.

The right corner of Melinda's computer flashed a message: *The navy deployed the Combat Rubber Raiding Craft topside.* She watched the Mola sub move closer to Titan and willed him to focus his attention on the decoy.

Titan identified the Mola as the large sunfish wobbled into view. He checked data available on the approaching fish. *The Mola mola or Ocean Sun Fish is the largest boney fish in the world, typically weighing one ton. The largest Mola mola ever found was 6,000 pounds. These fish typically grow up to eleven feet and can be as long as they are high.*

Harmless, Titan concluded and continued to hang in the water.

It is a work of art, James marveled. Titan's balance of biology and technology was breathtaking. It shone brightly, suspended in the sapphire blue of the ocean. Dan elbowed James, interrupting his thoughts; Dan pointed to his own eyes, and then nodded towards Titan. James looked specifically at the eyes. They telescoped outward and one was turned toward the Mola. Clearly, they were being examined.

Titan observed the creature drifting toward him. He noted this rosy-colored sunfish was particularly large with a rare speckled pattern. Titan sensed activity above him. He identified a small, rubber raft. The nanos would not let him disregard anything completely, so Titan kept one eye on the peculiarly patterned Mola mola and turned the other eye to the surface.

James worried about the exit strategy. The team had spent little time on it in comparison to the research plan. In theory, Dan would steer the Mola away from Titan after they acquired ultrasound images taken from different angles; they had hoped to drift or maneuver completely around Titan to get several angles. Currently they drifted within forty yards of the hanging leviathan. The telescoping eye glared at them, unmoving. James would not risk further examination by Titan. He waved his hand under his throat, indicating the mission was at an end. The extraordinary piece of art he'd admired earlier now looked menacing. He readied himself to pull the nobs labeled "snot" to eject the mucus.

Melinda worried. Titan did not show as much interest in the decoy as they'd expected. The mission depended on his attention to the navy's over-inflated rubber raft while the Mola sub gathered data. She turned to Hank, who was closely monitoring what was unfolding. Hank spoke before she could, "Titan is not buying into your decoy. As I see it, he can keep one eye on the decoy, and one eye on your boys."

Damn! She thought. *We didn't consider the chameleon effect the eyes had when we developed our exit strategy!*

"Think! What can we do to give them a few more minutes to get away?" she said. The Mola sub was too close to Titan.

Hank turned up the volume on the static emitted from the raft. "I outfitted the decoy rubber raft with underwater speakers so, if needed, I could add a 'pots and pans' effect—"

She interrupted. "Pots and pans effect?"

Hank explained, "Like if you want to distract an angry bear, you bang on pots and pans. Anyway, I've added some Pink Floyd, Dark Side of the Moon. Let's see if Titan is a fan of heavy metal."

Dan and James focused intently on Titan's eyes – particularly the one following them. Dan managed to remain calm and maneuver the Mola in a predictable pattern. The static streamed into the water changed; Dan noticed it was louder and had a head-banging band mixed in. As soon as Dan observed Titan's eye shift to the surface, he gunned the engine and James ejected the mucus. Neither scientist looked back.

A change in the sound drew Titan's attention away from the Mola mola. Music now blared along with the muddy static that permeated the water. Titan focused his weaponry on the vessel buzzing noisily around on the water. He calculated it would take a small energy burst to destroy the vessel. He locked on his target and fired. At the same time, Titan noted the Mola mola skittering away in a cloud of mucus. Aware weapon deployment was fear provoking, he assumed the blast had scared the Ocean sunfish away. The nanos noted a mechanical noise around the Mola mola; they filed this information for further analysis, along with a sample of the mucus.

Melinda and Hank watched the Mola sub skitter away from Titan from the computer room. "I'm going to download a copy of what was transmitted," Hank said. He produced a flash drive and connected it to Melinda's computer.

"You're such a jerk," hissed Melinda. "The project is over, but they're not out of danger!"

Hank ignored Melinda, again. "If Titan is going to do harm, we can't do much to protect them from here. In fact, I'd recommend we beat it out of here pretty fast." Hank pocketed the flash drive, and turned to leave. "I'm leaving by chopper ASAP. I'll meet you at the lab. I'll be working with the team from this point on."

Melinda returned topside and waited anxiously for them to return. She asked the boatswain for a pair of binoculars and scanned the ocean for the camouflaged mini-sub. Two hundred yards out, she caught glimpse of the disguised sub as sunlight bounced off one of the reflective polka dots.

As the Mola sub drew closer, the gorgeous construction captivated Melinda; the fabricated suit fit snugly over the mini-sub. The head and back showed pale pink fading to a metallic blush on the clavus and underbelly. Silvery polka dots peppered the image. With its crimped off fish tail, it looked like a giant – although beautiful – fish head swimming toward her.

Melinda waited for them to emerge from the Mola. The stress that had built up during her scan of Titan melted away when Dan and James materialized. She laughed and hugged them hard as soon as their feet hit the deck. The men looked at each other, confused.

"I was so worried about you guys!" Melinda burbled. "That was pretty intense when the eye ball thingy extended out toward you."

"Eye-ball-thingy? Is that a scientific term?" teased James. Melinda gave him a punch and then another hug.

"Okay, Melinda, chill out. We're fine," Dan said, startled by the niggling feeling of jealously. He smiled at James and winked at Melinda. "Let's head back and analyze the data. I can't wait to see what we've got." He wrapped his arm decisively around Melinda.

She relaxed easily into his embrace and signaled to the captain to take them back. "Hank hightailed it back to the lab as soon as your data hit his flash drive," she said. "He says he's working with us from now on." She looked at James. To her surprise, he didn't explode.

"That's convenient," James said. "I thought I was going to have to hunt him down." He stopped before he disappeared through the hatch leading below deck. "I'm feeling nauseous," he said. "I'm going to take a shot from my inhaler, and then lie down."

James lay on a bunk, spent. Seeing Titan had been sobering. It was just as much biology as technology. The entire experience had been a revelation. As they scuttled the Mola sub back to the transport, he reflected on his own situation. He and Titan were not very different. Both were organic and infected by nanos. His nanos banged aimlessly around in his cells – unprogrammed and without purpose. Titan's nanos were programmed to rebuild – and rebuild they did, creating a cybernetic creature. He sucked hard on the inhaler and his nausea subsided. He turned the device in his grasp and carefully inspected it.

What if they modified his inhaler and used it against Titan? James hadn't questioned Hank about the "cure." Truth be told, he was more than a little afraid it was some toxic remedy that would eventually need a cure itself. Confronting Hank and getting the data on the inhaler was the first item on his to-do list when they returned to the lab.

Back on deck Dan and Melinda finished a satisfying kiss. It was a brilliant day, and the ship's wake trailed a fan of sparkles. They marveled at the Exocoetidae – fish with wings – which hurdled across the wake looking like flying embers as the sun reflected off their silvery sides.

"What did it all look like from up here?" Dan asked Melinda about her observations of the Mola experiment.

Melinda snuggled in closer and sighed. "Terrifying" she said.

"That's what I thought," Dan agreed and dipped his head for another kiss.

Chapter 35

Back at the laboratory, Hank reviewed the data on the flash drive. The image quality was perfect. There was no mistaking biology and technology plaited as one. This type of accidental invention was unheard of in the U.S. Biomimetic scientists had researched combining organic material, like calcium and iron, with synthetic material for decades. Years of quantum biology research, and three billion years of evolution, upstaged by a freak accident.

Hank's thoughts bounced to the contract he and Brasco had with a very wealthy, very secret buyer from the Balkans, promising to deliver Titan alive. He concentrated on the data collected reporting Titan's size and approximate weight. He would to send this data to Brasco. With any luck, Brasco would send the statistics to the right people, and the right people would be satisfied with the information, and there would be no more visits from creepy joggers. The incident in the park left Hank in a state of full-blown paranoia. Everyone looked nefarious and dangerous.

The reason he'd left the transport so suddenly was because the sailors on board began to look sinister. His delusions considered any one of them an operative put there to ambush him.

Initially bewitched by the money, the consequence of his and Brasco's dance with the devil had eluded him. He almost wished he'd never gotten involved with Brasco but he was too far in to go back.

He pressed the heels of both hands into his temples, attempting to squeeze Brasco and bad guys from his thoughts. *I've got to pull myself together before the team returns,* Hank told himself. He opened a bottle of water to drink, and stared dejectedly at the unopened cup-o-chili mac sitting menacingly on the corner of the desk. Accustomed to a balanced, organic diet, his gut moaned in protest. These days, he only ate packaged food and never bought groceries in the same place twice. *Keep your eye on the prize,* Hank reminded himself. *Soon I'll be living in Tahiti, eating lobster and drinking any damn thing I want.*

The team walked in and disrupted Hank's depressive wallowing.

James cut right to the chase as soon as he saw Hank. "We're going to need the research you used to create the inhaler and then we're going to deactivate the nanos in Titan with it."

Brilliant, thought Hank, "I can access my data here, in the computer lab," he said.

"Good," James said. "Initially, you and Melinda can work on your data. Dan and I are going to review the Mola mola's findings and see what we can learn from the inside of Titan. Any questions?" he asked. Melinda and Dan shook their heads.

"Sounds like a plan," Hank said, and walked out of the lab.

Chapter 36

Melinda paced as she reviewed Hank's data on the inhaler. *It is so simple*, she thought. She finished her initial review and stopped pacing.

"So his inhaler is just a Faraday Cage and a HERF mechanism?" she said.

"Yep, it works like an EMP Shock Generator. However, I designed this electromagnetic pulse to neutralize the effect the nanos have on the biology of the subject," Hank explained. "The result turned out to be short term and the subject has to employ the inhaler as needed."

It really was amazing how uncomplicated the mechanism was. Survivalists, preppers and security fanatics had been designing personal EMP mechanisms for years. Traditional devises disrupt all electronics around a person, thus allowing that person to travel under the radar. Melinda had no desire to travel on an airplane with a nut wearing one, but security cloak and dagger use was commonplace.

"Why the non-traditional application -- the inhaler?" Melinda asked. "James could easily wear it like a beeper. Then he wouldn't have to re-expose himself when the effects wear off."

"I had to give it to him on a chopper ride," Hank explained.

Melinda's eyes widened and her jaw dropped in shock as she realized the danger Hank had put James in, expecting him to use the inhaler efficiently on a helicopter.

As if Hank had read her mind, "Calm down," he said. "I knew James had experience with an inhaler; I'd seen him use one when we were in the tropics."

Melinda pieced together the research protocol Hank must have used and it was unthinkable. "In your research, how big was your biggest subject?" she demanded.

"I don't know, how big you think James is?" Hank said.

"You keep proving yourself to be the biggest asshole!" Melinda raged. "You put James on a helicopter with a souped up EMP; gave him an experimental inhaler that had not been properly trialed and provided some bush-league instructions on how to use it!" Melinda was furious. Hank could have killed James several different ways that first day – helicopter crash, stroke, and system Block or over-load – the catalog of catastrophic effects was extensive.

"Look, Melinda, my trials proved harmless to the host," he explained, tired of her aggravated attitude. "I was very close to locating James and inviting him to be part of my research. And I'm sure he would have accepted. Also, nothing bad happened. Send my name in to be sanctioned by some monitoring committee, or have me investigated by 60 Minutes, but let's move on. James has." It was easy to brush off this particular Melinda rant since he'd lost his battle with ethics long ago.

"I can't work with you," she said, and stormed off.

Chapter 37

The inside of Titan was fascinating. Titan's internal structure was essentially submarine. Initially, the team had assumed the nanos repaired a damaged whale and then added modified weaponry. However, these images left no doubt in the researchers minds that the nanos created something altogether different.

"Zoom into the command center," James directed. "There's something there I can't identify."

"I'll try. I'm not sure what we'll lose in clarity if I do that." Dan saw what James was referring to. A section of the Com Center looked decidedly different from a typical console. He enlarged the area. Shockingly, the image showed a very damaged sperm whale calf wired into the command center of the vessel.

"I'm going to describe what I'm seeing. Is the recorder on?" Dan asked. James indicated it was and Dan began to narrate.

"The communication center appears to be remarkable. Obvious are tattered pectoral fins and a damaged tail or fluke; also visible is the complete head of a Physeter macrocephalus, or sperm whale calf." He zoomed in close.

"Size indicates it to be in its first or second season. Obvious is wiring originating from the head and connecting to -- what looks like a computer board. No movement from the calf has been noted." He turned to James. "Did you mark the time when we identified this?" he asked.

"Yes, it's been just over four minutes," he replied.

Dan returned to his description. "The skin appears to be healthy and moist – like the samples in the freezer. Wait – I detect movement where the diaphragm should be." There were several moments of complete silence.

"The calf is breathing."

What the hell is going on?" James had assumed Titan was just a souped-up whale carcass.

"It all makes sense," Dan replied. He turned away from the screen, the image too disturbing.

"What makes sense? None of this makes sense!" shouted James.

"It makes sense why the vessel followed typical whale patterns and stayed with a pod . . . Titan followed migratory patterns. He is a whale – and a vessel." It was easier for Dan to understand. For the perspective of a cetacean expert, the story of a mutated whale hull traveling with a pod of sperm whales had not made sense. The sperm whales would not have allowed it. With the calf wired into the system, mirror neurons would have facilitated Titan's integration into the pod.

James stared at the broken body of the calf, wires sprouting from fabricated ports in its head; every so often, and ever so slightly, its diaphragm rose and fell as air was pumped into lungs.

"I never programmed the nanos to do this. I designed them to use the material on hand to repair mechanics. I was involved in every step of their development. They were not designed to do this!"

"But they did, and there is no doubt now what's going on," replied Dan. "Is there any way these aren't your nanos?"

Like any good techie, he made sure his nanos were discretely marked. Always a fan of the homonym – and a proud Mechanical Engineer -- he'd imprinted the identifier "Trust ME" on the housing protecting the delicate interworking's of his nanos.

"I marked them. They are easily identifiable. I will double-check," James said and turned to leave the computer lab. He literally ran into a tearful Melinda.

James pulled her close. "What's wrong?" he asked. *This feels great*, he thought as he stroked her long, tawny hair. In a hurry to retrieve her from James' embrace, Dan jumped up, his chair tipped over and crashed to the floor.

Melinda hiccuped and looked over to Dan. "We can't work with Hank. He's such a boob," she said. Dan went over to them. James smiled and carefully handed Melinda over to Dan.

"He was a boob yesterday and we decided to work with him," Dan said softly. "What's changed?"

Melinda didn't seem to notice she had been passed on to Dan. "He tried to kill James," she said.

James' head snapped up. "How do you figure that?" he asked. Since Hank had agreed to share his data, James almost thought kindly of him. But Melinda had been working with Hank, reviewing his data. "Was there mention of my murder in his research?"

Melinda breathed in deeply. "Well, no. But he could have killed you! And he would have been held accountable for murder – if there had been a way to catch him. Anyway, he still wants to capture the thing alive and it scares me." Watching Titan in real time had been frightening.

James looked at Dan and rolled his eyes. Pointing to himself, he silently jerked his head to one side, indicating he wanted to leave.

"Well, I'm scared, too," agreed Dan. "And hungry and tired. Let's see what we can scare up in the way of food. James, do you want to eat, or. . ." He didn't have the opportunity to finish his sentence.

James was out the door and said, "I'm going to have a little chat with Hank."

Dan led them to the small kitchen in the facility. He walked Melinda over to the table and gently sat her down. He checked the refrigerator for what was quick and available; he didn't think it a good idea to leave James and Hank alone together for very long.

"There are eggs, toaster waffles, orange juice, and milk. What do you want?" He hoped she wouldn't say eggs.

"Eggs sound great!" She peeked over at him. He was studying the contents of the refrigerator intently. He hadn't shaved and probably hadn't showered either, but in her opinion, he looked fantastic. His hair stuck up in several directions. He was always running his hands through it, like maybe the gesture would pull extra knowledge from his brain. His clothes were rumpled and had scores of salt stains from standing on the deck. She was sure he smelled like salt and sweat.

Okay, he thought. *I did give her the option.* "I can fry up a couple for you and for me. Toast and juice?" He turned to her for an answer and was struck by how vulnerable she looked. He was always surprised at how petite she was. Her personality was so large, her confidence so solid, she presented herself as a much more substantial woman. However, right now she looked like a waif. Her rumpled clothes seemed too big. Usually she kept her hair scraped back from her face and secured into a neat ponytail; now most of it escaped the simple black band that now sagged, just below her right ear. She had twirled the escapees on one side of her head into tight dreadlocks. Bright hazel eyes that regularly darted between him and James – challenging them to come up with answers – stared out at him red-rimmed and swollen. J*esus*, he thought, *she was even wringing her hands.*

She noticed him staring at her. "I know. I should take a shower. I'm a mess." She shoved several dreads behind her ear.

"You look spectacular. Don't move. I'll make us some breakfast." Dan turned back to the refrigerator and rummaged for the food they needed.

Chapter 38

Since his exasperation with Melinda's tantrum exceeded his paranoia, Hank mustered up enough courage to walk out of the building. Surveillance inside the lab was extensive, and he needed a secure location to call Brasco to let him know that it was getting tense at the lab. He knew Melinda had run off to convince the other team members to walk away from the project. From the start, Dan made it clear his first choice was to destroy Titan, would his second choice be to leave? James' torment over his own infected biology tied him to Titan. Hank counted on him to stay with the project until the end.

A stand of Norfolk pine trees in the distance looked safe; he trotted over, leaned against a rough, gray-barked tree and dialed up Brasco.

"Hey, how's everything going?" Brasco asked. He'd realized from an earlier conversation that Hank was cracking up, seeing assassins around every corner. Brasco needed to keep Hank calm for just a little while longer.

"It's pretty tense here. Melinda's lost it, and I'm worried that she's going to convince the others to bail on the project," Hank said, pushing against the jagged shards of bark until they bit into his shoulder. He wished he still smoked; his nerves were frayed.

"Forget about Melinda. Her status as a bitch is legendary," Brasco lied. He'd known Melinda for years and her reputation was of a confident and principled scientist. He knew working for Hank had to be torture for her. Brasco considered himself a good judge of character and he bet she wouldn't endanger her reputation by leaving – not without Dan and James backing her up. "What is your sense of James?" Brasco asked. "His involvement is crucial."

Hank ignored Brasco's question. "She just ran off to tattle on me. She found my use of James as the first human trial with the inhaler unethical. . . Anyway, I thought I'd call you and give you a heads' up in case one of them contacts you. To answer your question, I'm not sure what James will do – if he's honest with himself, me handing him the inhaler without extensive trials is not too far out of his own wheelhouse, however I did neglect to let him know first – he could be upset about that. I'm assuming James is searching for me as we speak." Hank was annoyed, *while he was here, dealing with pissy scientists and scary terrorists, where the hell was Brasco?*

"Where the hell are you, anyway?" Hank voiced.

Brasco tamped down the urge to say it was none of his fucking business. He knew he had to keep him calm.

"I'm with U.S. military brass," Brasco explained, "trying to convince them not to blow Titan out of the water. I'm doing everything I can to protect our investment. I'm counting on you to do the same." Brasco asked Hank if he'd made any arrangements for his future.

"If you mean have I set up the new identity, yes," reported Hank. "I've opened an offshore account with the seed money you gave me, and my new self has been traveling in Europe for the last few weeks." Several months ago, Brasco provided him with a well-defined identity and instructed him to have his new identity buy train tickets and make dinner reservations several times before he needed to become this new person. "Any red flags?" Hank asked.

"Nothing so far, if any come up, I will deal with it – we're almost at the end of this. You need to hold it together. Can I count on you?" Brasco asked.

"Yes, yes. I'm going back into the lab now," Hank said. "I'm pretty sure James will be in this to the end. What should we do about Dan?" he asked rhetorically.

Brasco answered as if it were a logistical question. "We could be done with him, but I think he'll hang around as long as Melinda does. The end game still plays out as planned." They'd discussed it once and decisions had been made. Nothing had changed. The researchers were a liability once the project was over.

"I'm hanging up now," said Hank and disconnected the call.

Chapter 39

He returned to the computer lab to find James waiting for him. To pass the time, James had reviewed the inhaler research and discovered how Melinda thought Hank tried to kill him.

"It was pretty gutsy of you to give me that inhaler on the chopper. How'd you know I wouldn't spray the thing into the air first, before I inhaled it?" James said. He wasn't angry. He knew Hank had taken a calculated risk, one he might have taken.

"It was a risk, but I crossed my fingers and sent it on its way," Hank said. "If you sprayed it in the air, the chopper would have lost power and crashed in the Andes – nothing gained, nothing lost." Hank needled James. He knew him well enough to know that he would work harder on the project if he hated Hank.

It worked. James *was* angry. "Melinda was right – you are a fucked-up boob. I'll see this project through so I can take credit for Titan's nanos. Then I'll take credit for the inhaler research." James turned to leave the computer lab. "We need supplies to create a big enough parabolic reflector and HERF generator," James instructed Brasco. "You know the drill, ASAP." James walked out. *Well, he is certainly pissed*, Hank thought. Everything was going as planned.

Chapter 40

Moto delivered the materials needed to create a reflector and the EMP generator. Hank did his best to stay abreast of everything. This was particularly difficult because the three researchers ignored him.

James and Melinda took on the task of designing the generator.

Dan reviewed recent footage of Titan. He speculated that the static aimed at Titan kept it in a hypnotic state. However, as they had witnessed from the Mola sub, Titan was able to emerge from this haze and become dangerous. Based on the footage, navy inel and the information gathered from the Mola expedition, Dan would extrapolate the voltage and frequency needed for the pulse to deactivate Titan.

For the past several hours, the team had static pumped into the room that caged the nano-altered crab. "How's Crabbette doing?" Dan asked. Moto reported the crab exhibited the same dazed behavior as Titan.

Melinda added her discovery to the conversation. "She's walking around, licking her eye stalks, ignoring everything in her environment, even food. But if I crumple up a sheet of paper and toss it at her, she attacks it with her mutant claw."

"Are we ready to pulse her?" Moto asked.

"We're just about to do that now," Melinda said. "When I asked Brasco for a personal EMP with a Faraday box he delivered it quicker than Domino's delivers pizza. He must be more covert than I ever imagined," *and I've known him for years*, she thought. "Do you have a watch," she asked Dan.

"Yeah I do. If I have calculated Crabbette's EMP voltage correctly, I can extrapolate the correct voltage for Titan." Dan said, "I hope we don't hurt the little fella." Dan had grown fond of the mutant crab.

"You mean little Bella," Melinda corrected, "and I hope not too. I kinda like her – when she's not trying to snap my face off."

Hank snorted.

"Drop dead Hank," Melinda said without looking up from her preparation for the pulse trial. James and Dan chuckled.

"These personal EMPs are designed to be clipped onto your belt, like a beeper. Whoever wears it should just switch it on and walk up to her. Who wants to do the honors?" Melinda had no desire to zap her.

"I do," volunteered Hank.

Melinda ignored him. "Actually, I don't think James should do it, we don't want to fool with his electrical cocktail. You should stay very far away," she said to James. She turned to Dan. "So how 'bout you?"

"Sure, I'm game," Dan agreed. "What's the plan if I only piss her off? Did anyone ask Brasco for a dart gun?" He looked pointedly at Hank.

"Don't worry. If she becomes agitated, I'll rescue you," Hank said with a sneer. "I've got on my good pair of 'crab stompin' shoes." Hank lunged and stomped at an imaginary crab on the floor.

"Boob," Melinda muttered with contempt.

The trial went off without a hitch. The EMP incapacitated the nanos. The parts of the crab unaffected by the nanos were functional; eye stalks followed Dan's movement, and she skittered away as he approached, dragging her redesigned claw behind her. They experienced nothing aggressive.

"Gadzooks! I think we've done it!" joked Dan.

Hank poked at her with the end of a broomstick. Crabbette tried desperately to get away.

"Okay, Okay! We get it! She's defenseless! Let's leave her alone now!" Melinda watched as Crabbette dragged herself clumsily in the opposite direction of the thrusting broom handle.

Dan walked toward Melinda, wanting to comfort her. "I know you're sad for our little Crabbette," Dan said, "but she won't remember any of this five minutes from now."

Melinda would not be consoled. "She'll forget, but what about Titan?" she said. "We objectify him – refer to him as "it" in an attempt to skirt any moral issues looming over this project.

"However, you're the one who identified him as an imbedded pod member in all the field research films we viewed. You acknowledge a pod is a family group," she continued. "You explained the basis of sperm whale social structure – the matraline where mothers and calves travel together for decades. We've lamented this creature's probable evolution, its mother's death and the monsterfacation of the calf. Have you thought about his reaction to the pulse? What about him?" she finished ferociously.

"You're preaching to the choir, sister," barked Dan. "I've been concerned since the inception of this project that we were heading down a very slippery ethical slope. This whale will be chillingly aware of what is happening to him after the pulse. Based on my observations, there is not enough whale biology left in Titan's structure for him to skitter away like Crabbette did." Dan and Melinda looked to James, willing him to offer some reassurance.

James barely listened to their tirade. Stunned by what had happened to the crab, he turned to Hank, "if we turn up the frequency of my inhaler, what will happen to me— – my biology?" A very unscientific image of himself falling to the ground, in a paralyzed heap, crossed his mind.

"Nothing." Hank said, "First of all, your nanos – unlike Titan's nanos – have not mutated. Second, your nanos are not programmed. Your immune system just goes berserk when the nanos are active. Fever, chills, vomiting. A sort of allergic reaction."

"I know my symptoms," James interrupted. "I reviewed your research on my viral infection and the research seemed to stop once you perfected the inhaler, is that true?" James worried Hank could incapacitate him at any time.

"Yes. I was trying to locate you so I could begin human trials," Hank said. He did not want James to delve too deeply into what he had been doing these past few years. Several shady scientific groups wanted information on the original Nano Project and had approached him after the initial disaster. Brasco followed the trail of one such group to Hank. "When this Titan thing came up and Brasco said he could get you on my project, I assumed I would continue with the inhaler research once you came on board."

Melinda scowled at him, arms akimbo. "And now this is our project and our research. We get to decide what direction to take this in once we've taken care of Titan." There were so many implications for this type of technology, she thought. When this was over, the three of them would hash out what direction they would take their research.

"You'll have to figure that out with Brasco," Hank interjected. "You're under a military contract now and, as you know, they have jurisdiction over anything here." He knew he should have just agreed with her. But he was tired of her constant haranguing.

Melinda looked like she was going to start up again. James cut in. "We need to focus on what's going on here right now. Dan, have you come up with your estimate for the EMP yet?"

"I've got some numbers," Dan said. "I asked Melinda to poke around the Internet to see what she can learn about EMPs. We are going to have to generate an EMP as well as high frequency static. The reflector is a big project, but Moto is working with Thingamajigs. I think it's time to sit down and map this out." Dan was out of his element. Hank's research and development data on the inhaler proved invaluable. He needed Hank on this part of the project now and he was sure he was going to get resistance from at least Melinda.

"Let's get out of here for an hour or so," Melinda said. "You, me and James. Let's just get out and get a burger." Melinda felt like an actor in a Federico Fellini movie. The boundary between reality and fantasy was becoming blurry.

"Even as a vegan, I'm game for that adventure. James?" Dan turned to James, who was still staring at the immobile Crabbo.

No, thought James. *I'm not game for that. I want to keep working and get this thing finished.* Before he could voice his opinion, Hank cut in. "Brasco can't keep the military at bay for very long. Going out to lunch seems frivolous to me."

That decided it for James. "I'll go. We need some fresh air anyway." He turned to Hank. "Tell Brasco we'll be ready tomorrow morning – afternoon at the latest." He turned and walked out the door. Melinda and Dan followed.

"I already ate," Hank said to no one in particular.

Chapter 41

Hank stayed back with all the research data and no task. He reviewed Melinda's data, intent on discovering details he could use to override Titan's current navigation system, which would allow him to maneuver Titan. At this point, there was a good deal of information on the mutant nanos. It was no wonder to him why Melinda wanted it to be clear that this was her data. The military applications for these mutant nanos were endless, not to mention the medical and environmental possibilities. He experienced a fleeting image of the consequences if any of this fell into the wrong hands but it was too late for that kind of thinking; however, he thought Brasco may have sold the project too cheaply.

The mechanism they devised to deactivate Titan would be portable, easy enough for him to get his hands on when needed. The information Melinda gathered finished downloading onto his flash drive; he headed out of the lab and toward the cluster of pine trees for another conversation. He needed to tell Brasco the three musketeers thought they'd be ready as soon as tomorrow.

Chapter 42

The three drove to a small bar and grill up the road from the lab. The tavern's marque boasted the best beer-batter recipe in the northwest. Once inside they saw a few locals at the bar and a couple playing pool. The Mariners game was on a small TV set tucked up in a corner of the bar. Melinda led them to a window booth. "I like this," she said as she plopped onto the bench.

Soothed by the laid-back surroundings, James slid into the booth opposite Melinda. It had been a long time since he'd rubbed elbows with locals from anywhere. He recognized the tinny sound of music piped through a jukebox and breathed in the faint scent of pine cleaner. He hadn't felt this normal in years. "This was a great idea, Mel." He cocked a crooked grin at her. He hadn't called her Mel this entire project.

"You know, I can't call her 'Mel,'" Dan said to James as he scooted in next to her in the booth. "It reminds me of a guy – the greasy cook from the old sitcom *Alice*, or Mel Brooks – short and annoying."

Dan placed his arm protectively on the back of the booth behind Melinda. His special forces training made him check the room for all possible exits. *The locals look harmless enough,* Dan thought, *but you never know. ..* When briefing him, Brasco described this project as purely scientific; however, this project sweat trouble. Hank still held decision-making control here, and he was one startle away from a nervous breakdown. The team's organic approach to leadership – Melinda as pro-tem leader with James having veto power – provided enough structure to get them this far into the project, but crazy Hank's expertise on James' nanos was crucial in neutralizing Titan.

"Nobody calls me Mel anymore," said Melinda. "Let's get some menus." She snuggled into Dan's arm and smiled. She wasn't a snuggler by nature, or a whiner, but she'd done quite a bit of both the past several days. There was a desperate quality to this project and she could not keep a tight lid on her emotions. Calm enveloped her as Dan gave her shoulder a deliberate squeeze. *I could get used to snuggling*, she thought.

James and Melinda ordered burgers, and Dan ordered every fried vegetable on the menu. Without any dissent, they decided that they would order one pitcher of beer.

The beer arrived and Dan poured each of them a glass. There was nothing to celebrate, nothing to say cheers over. Dan lifted his glass. "Well, I suppose we could say 'to us'?" They nodded, tipped their glasses toward each other in tribute, and drank.

Dan hated to spoil the quiet contentment but there were difficult decisions to be made.

"I need Hank's expertise to come up with the frequencies and voltage for the EMP and HERF we're going to deploy," Dan said.

"Why?" Melinda bristled. "We all agreed he was a boob. We don't need him." Melinda wouldn't acknowledge Hank in the room, much less consult with him regarding research.

"Maybe you don't need him, but I do," Dan replied. "I've held my own in the physics of this project, but at this point I'm uncomfortable with the instability at the Lagrangian departure point calculations. I'm in over my head and Hank can help us with these equations."

"You don't know that," Melinda barked, easing away from Dan. "You don't have any idea what James and I have discovered. You haven't even been working with us." Melinda's irritation of moments ago, vanished in response to the betrayal she felt. She and James had worked non-stop with the pieces of mutant whale skin. They had made huge strides in making sense of the program running within it.

"I don't think Dan was saying we aren't doing our part," James said. He looked around nervously to see if anyone had heard her. "What I understood him to be saying is that he needs help with the weaponry needed to neutralize Titan." James had hoped Dan was more of a physics whiz than he confessed to be. He'd known from the start that if Dan could not calculate the frequencies for the HERF and the effective voltage needed for the EMP, they'd have to involve Hank more. "Wasn't there something in Hank's research to use?"

"I understand his research at a very elementary level," Dan said. "The nanos infecting Titan are exceedingly different than the ones infecting you. Hank can help facilitate the leap from your nanos to the mutant ones. He has already thought along the lines of static and EMPs. We don't need to re-invent the wheel; we don't have time." Dan knew Melinda didn't trust Hank. Hell, if he thought about it, he didn't either; but they needed Hank now, trustworthy or not.

The waitress appeared with their food, imposing a moment of reflection as they waited in silence for her to pass it around. A heavy uncertainty replaced the light, happy mood from a few moments before.

"Let's just decide and be done with it," surrendered Melinda. "I want to finish this job. I've never felt such a sense of apprehension on a project before." Melinda was not superstitious. As a researcher, she relied on facts to form her clinical opinions, even for the direction she took in life. But this project oozed with anxiety.

"We can't trust him, not at all," James said. Like Melinda, he'd sensed their light energy turn dark.

Dan left that statement alone. He wasn't asking anyone to trust Hank. His shoulders dropped a fraction of an inch, and he took a much needed lungful of air. With Hank on board, he knew they'd finish this thing soon. He wanted to say more, but knew enough not to. "Okay then, let's eat," was all he said.

Chapter 43

Huddled in the pine grove, Hank called Brasco to discuss the equipment. "I've worked around these personal EMPs," Brasco said. "They're dangerous if a nutbag gets a hold of one. When Davenport asked for one, I got a little nervous."

Hank snorted with satisfaction. "Now you know how I feel," he said. *Except I'm more than a little nervous these days,* he thought. "Just make sure any of *our* equipment is outfitted to withstand an EMP blast. As soon as I know the voltage and frequency, I'll let you know. James said we'll be ready within the next thirty-six hours. I've worked on a devise that will temporarily stun anyone within a twenty-foot radius of me, so I can secure and move Titan. Don't worry about me, I'm protected. Is there anyone else on board with me needing protection?"

"Hank, do what you've got to do, but you're the only researcher returning from this project." Brasco was tired of Hank's inability to verbalize that scenario. The plan was set; this project ended with the kidnapping and delivery of Titan and the death of the three researchers.

Chapter 44

The researchers finished their meal in harmony. Dan popped the last greasy mushroom into his mouth. "Let's roll."

Melinda stayed seated, unwilling to begin the final phase of the project.

"I know you guys think I'm 'the crazy bitch' when it comes to Hank, but he is psycho," Melinda said in an effort to put her behavior in perspective.

She turned to James. "Be honest – his giving you the inhaler in a helicopter without any instructions, except some pathetic reference to Alice in Wonderland, was lunacy. If you two think we need Hank's expertise from this point on, ok – but I won't change our majority rule. We've been a superior team from the beginning." Now she felt claustrophobic in the booth and gently shoved at Dan so she could get out. They walked to the car in silence.

Moto greeted them in front of the lab, waving enthusiastically as they drove up.

"How did you like Chicco's?" he asked as they got out of the car. "They have the best smoked salmon, Cheech smokes it himself – he has a smoker behind the bar."

"How did you know where we were?" James asked.

"You drive north, you go to Sandy's; you drive south, you go to Chicco's. I called Chicco's first and asked if there were three strangers eating there; they said yes and I knew where you were!" explained Moto.

Whether by accident or design, Moto's chatty greeting shifted the mood from ominous to curious.

"I'm going to see if I can gather some sperm whale coda we can use to divert Titan's attention if we need to," Dan said. Using this as a carrot to distract Titan in an emergency was dicey; however Dan wanted to prepare for anything. Following this vein, he planned to fine tune the toxin to kill Titan and for this, he needed to work independently. "The rest of you need to work on the frequency and voltage for the EMP and HERF." He walked away, deliberately separating himself from the others. "I finally get to use my whale guy expertise."

Dan stumbled upon Hank working at his laptop in the lobby. "I'm sitting this inning out," Dan said. Hank looked blankly at him. "It's time for departure-point calculations; you're up," Dan said.

Hank hated sports analogies. It always took him a minute to get them. Dan ignored his confusion, and continued, "The others are headed to the tech lab. They're expecting you. I'm going to be in the biology lab."

Hank closed his laptop and hurried to the tech lab. He'd anticipated their need for him. He'd purposely moved some of his research around, making his calculations hard to follow. He stopped at the doorway and listened while James brought Moto up to speed on the research.

"We have learned these mutant nanos work as a team. Each has a job – and in synchronicity are successful," James said. "Like my original nano design, there is no overlap in knowledge. Each nano's program is limited to a function. Originally designed with an inactive serial port, these mutant nanos developed an elaborate boot-loader that allows them to upload new code without the use of external hardware. We can find no process for program editing – makes sense since these are military minded. One thing we discovered was that these mutant nanos rely heavily on the internet for information; when something goes haywire, the nanos go to the internet."

"We believe the glitch in the system is that there is no process for determining malformed data – like the input from an angry sperm whale," Melinda added.

"Previously, I worked with researchers studying Event Related Potentials," Moto said. Melinda raised an eyebrow, indicating she'd be interested in further information.

"ERPs provide data about how the brain normally processes information and how this processing may go awry in neurological and psychiatric disorders. Within the ERP context, we can deduce the computer programs Titan is running are heavily influenced by higher brain processes -- like memory, beliefs and experience – these cognitive biases could be interpreted as malformed data." Moto stopped. "I guess I am not immune to the yearning and regret of the research I wish I could do." As a distraction, he opened a nearby drawer and reorganized the medical instruments contained within.

James noticed Hank at the back of the room. "How did you get an EMP without causing the geomagnetic field to heave?" he asked.

"I was able to extend the rise time. I needed my blast to be compressed," Hank explained, "and that extended the rise time and eliminated the heave signal."

"Since we will implement the blast underwater, do we need to take into consideration the rate that water conducts electricity?" Melinda asked.

"No," Hank answered. "Our pulse will be in the water for seconds. I have two main concerns: one, we may not knock the nanos out completely, and two, if we do knock them out, we have no data as to when they will go back on line."

Moto scrolled through the data developed by James and Melinda.

"If we disrupt the internet during our attack, it won't matter if the nanos come back on line," Moto said.

"Right!" Melinda said. "The pulse and the static frequency we blast at Titan may only fry some nano wiring. We cannot predict system failure, but we can predict chaos at the most intricate electrical level! These nanos will scramble for data to evaluate where electrons may have traveled along magnetic field lines. Data that cannot be retrieved without Internet access!"

Hating to make eye contact, but knowing it was unavoidable, she turned to Hank. "Is shutting down the internet feasible?"

"I'll call Brasco." Hank walked out of the room.

Chapter 45

Brasco had spent the past several days in intense negotiation with the U.S. military. Given Titan had not displayed any active threats, he was able to keep military action to observation and containment. He juggled constant communication with the consortium that bought Titan, requests from the research team and Hank's frantic phone calls. In the past, this intensity of negotiation energized him, but the outcome directly benefited him this time and his body throbbed from stress fatigue. The pressure showed; usually neat in appearance, today he looked wrinkled and messy. His phone rang and it took him a moment to recall whose number appeared on screen.

"What took you so long?" Hank said, annoyed.

Brasco ignored the tone. "How's it going? Are we on schedule?"

"What do you mean 'we'?" Hank said, thinking he'd reported in on a regular basis. It was time to hold Brasco accountable for his time. "What the hell have you been doing?" Hank demanded.

"I have been, and will continue to try to keep the military from blasting our investment out of the water," Brasco said, weary of Hank's petulance. "Look it, Hank, I don't have the energy to play ball with you right now so what do you want?"

Sports analogies again, thought Hank.

Brasco continued, "We're almost to the end of this. Stay focused – why did you call?"

"They've figured out how to knock out the nanos," he said. "We need you to Block the Internet around Titan for at least half an hour."

"You want me to what?" Brasco said. *Who did they think he was?*

"You probably know Al Gore didn't he invent the Internet? Get a hold of him, or that Zuckerberg kid," Hank said, half joking. "You expected the impossible from the researchers; it's time for you to pull a rabbit out of your ass."

Brasco took some of his own advice and focused. Actually, he was part of a covert operation that had disrupted the internet over Afghanistan to isolate Bin Laden after 9/11. The internet was down for several hours and intel suggested there was the capability of disrupting it for several days.

"I don't know if I can actually do that," Brasco said. "But we do have the capacity. The problem we've had in the past is that we cannot guarantee the scope of the disruption. Will you need any internet access during your attack?"

"No we won't," replied Hank. "Look, we've designed a devise that will carry out the attack. Our spectrum analyzer indicates that the EMP we employ will be surprisingly marginal. These nanos are extremely fragile when exposed to electrical or frequency bursts. We should be ready to go any time now."

"Good," said Brasco. "Tell your team I have Captain Gil Rogers of the *USS Edison* at the ready for you. Rogers and his crew survived one of Titan's attacks. He will skipper your submarine escort. A word of warning, Rogers is hell-bent on destroying Titan."

"How many people are going to be on this sub?" Hank asked. The body count for this project seemed to be climbing.

"Skeleton crew. Their job is to get you close to Titan alive," Brasco replied. "Once you and the Mola sub are off-loaded, Rogers will retreat to a safe distance – if there is one. I'm assuming you will deploy your weapon at Titan from the Mola sub?"

"James and Dan will be in the Mola sub. They will deploy from there," Hank said. "Once Titan is subdued, we can do pretty much anything." Deploying the

EMP and HERF weapon from the Mola sub seemed like a good idea for several reasons; the main one was that if the plan didn't work, Titan would go after the sub.

Brasco would contact Hank when he solved the Internet problem.

Chapter 46

James used silver mesh in the construction of the Faraday cage. This cage was surprisingly small, about the size of a tissue box. It would encapsulate the custom-built Flux Compression Generator, a twelve-volt battery and an inner pipe leading to an outer pipe. Once detonated, the magnetic field would compress and generate a focused pulse of electromagnetic energy through the outer pipe at Titan. This simple weapon could be fired only once, thus the frequency and voltage of the pulse needed to be exact.

Using a variety of measurement systems and frequency ranges from zero hertz to megahertz, Hank extrapolated the frequency for the EMP to use against Titan.

They counted on Brasco shutting down the internet, but Hank also concentrated on exactly how to target the internet host server surrounding Titan. He researched block proxies and regional IP addresses, but worried over the nanos' circumventing the block. He was relieved when Brasco delivered a High Energy Radio Frequency (HERF) gun to the lab. They would use this to direct a high-power radio signal in the vicinity of the internet server. Melinda's research on Crabbettes nanos proved that these mutant nanos had very limited ability to reform into a workable unit once disconnected from the internet.

Dan studied the sonic weaponry Titan had employed when attacking the submarines. The recorded vertical magnetic signals during Titan's attack verified its

weaponry to be echo-location on steroids. Dan created three parabolic reflectors –
or sonic shields; one to protect the Mola sub, one for Hank and Melinda's sub, and
one for the submarine escort. These reflectors would warp any sonic missile Titan
directed at them.

Now that she had the pulse frequency data, Melinda prepared to arm the non-
nuclear electromagnetic pulse weapon. She needed to be clearheaded so she took a
cat-nap on an aluminum counter in the back of the lab while the others worked.
After waking, her hands were steady as she finished wrapping the armed box in
Mylar.

They were ready; now they needed a time for deployment.

"It's about two a.m.," James said. "I think we should get some sleep and be
ready by eight a.m." James thought none of them would be able to sleep except
Melinda, who it seemed, could sleep anywhere.

Dan nodded in agreement. "Tell Brasco we'll need transportation at oh-eight-
hundred hours.

Chapter 47

It was a sunny morning by Seattle standards, and Hank, James and Dan were lounging in Adirondack chairs, pretending to relax in the morning sun, when the limousine arrived. Melinda had used her time in an extra-long, extra-hot shower; her hair was still damp when she stepped outside. She trotted past them and headed toward the limo. Once there, she squatted down and checked each crate's inventory list, nodding her head in satisfaction as she mentally ticked off their contents. Someone in the limo popped the trunk.

Dan stood up and walked toward the limousine. "Don't you think we should see who is driving before we put our work into the back? For all we know, it could be Boris and Natasha!" he said.

James agreed and rapped on the driver's window. The darkened window motored down revealing the goon who'd plucked him from the Andes.

"You and I got to stop meeting like this," James said, unnerved. *Who is this guy?* he thought. The thug's ugly mug disappeared as the window slid shut. James shook off his nerves. "It sure as hell ain't Natasha – but I know this guy – it's Brasco's pet goon."

Hank stood by while the others packed personal belongings into the limousine. Each parabolic reflector measured twice the size of a TV satellite dish; those crates were large. Moto loaded them into the back of the pickup truck he would drive to the drop site.

Gil Rogers waited for them in the limousine. As the researchers settled in, he introduced himself. "My crew and I will transport you to the mark. I'd like to know what you've discovered before we confront it."

"We can't talk to you without clearance," Dan said. Schooled in military protocol, Rogers' assumption that the researchers would just start sharing information surprised him.

Captain Rogers handed James a manila envelope. "Here are my clearance documents. We're less than a half day from deployment, right?" Rogers said, annoyed by Dan's jump to procedure. "I have a crew I'm duty-bound to protect, and I've been ordered to protect you, so forgive me if I'm moving too fast for you. I went head-to-head with that monster, and with the luck of Saint Elmo I survived. I won't be on the wrong side of the sail this time." Rogers continued, "You've given it this fancy name 'Titan,' and it may resemble a whale, but there is nothing to indicate it is using any functions other than military attack intelligence. I want any information you have so I can defend my ship, my crew and you," Rogers finished.

James scanned the contents of the envelope and said, "He is who he says he is. Captain Rogers battled Titan."

Rogers continued talking, focusing his eyes on James. "I understand you've been in the water with the beast," Gil said, refusing to call it Titan. "I've watched and re-watched the attacks on the three submarines, and I believe it cannot produce two consecutive lethal blasts. That's why my sub survived," Rogers explained. "*The George Washington* fired first; the beast returned fire and sank her. Military protocol calls for deadly force after an attack and the monster beat me to it. There was no hesitation before it blasted my sub. It's pure military."

Dan felt the anxiety in the limousine rise during Captain Rogers' diatribe. Dan knew Melinda and James had never worked combat or covert during a military contract. *We've got to keep calm*, he thought. *I've got to shut this guy down.*

"Thanks for the intel, Gil," Dan said. "However, our focus is on the science of this project. You just get us there safely. After the operation, you and I can swap stories."

Captain Rogers bristled at the putdown. "Respectfully, sir, I don't need to swap stories," he said. "I'm saying I'm not confident we can kill it once we get close enough."

"We're not going to kill Titan. We will immobilize and then contain him," explained Melinda.

Gil's head snapped toward her. "You've got to be kidding! Have any of you seen the attack?" *Are these guys crazy?*

"Check with Brasco if you need confirmation on the outcome of this project," Hank said, ignoring Gil's gaping mouth. "All you need to do is get us close and then get the hell out of there." He turned to Dan. "When we get to Gil's sub, check the Mola sub one last time before it's loaded."

They reached their destination. James flipped off the driver as he got out of the limo. Melinda had followed behind James and saw the gesture. She shot him a questioning look.

"It's our thing," James explained, remembering his insolent flip so many days ago. He went to the back to get his gear.

Captain Rogers stopped James before he got to the trunk. "You look reasonable so listen up: I will call Brasco, and if he confirms your harebrained scheme, I will drop you off and then get the hell out of there. I have no wish to lose one more man to that devil," he said.

James laughed. "He thinks I look reasonable." Melinda started laughing too.

Anxiety laughter, thought Dan. *This is never good.* He and Hank exchanged wearied glances.

"You guys got to pull it together," Hank said and thought, *Christ, none of them were under the pressure he was.*

Dan turned to the team. "After I've secured the Mola sub, I'm going to make peace with Captain Rogers. The sonic shield we developed should provide protection to his crew; it will be a more than adequate peace offering," he said.

He turned to address Melinda. "You install a reflector on the Mola sub and whatever submersible that you and Hank will use." He winked; she gave him a weak smile and thumbs up.

Chapter 48

Dan caught up with Captain Rogers at the main control room located in the middle of the submarine. It was a large, well-lit room; controls for the sub's vital operations whirred and beeped around them. In the center of the room, two navigation or plotting tables were positioned alongside the two periscopes. At the forward corner of the room were the seats of the control station. A very young helmsman occupied one seat, his job, to maneuver and steer. Another equally young planesman operated the diving planes and controlled the depth, and the third seat hosted a female diving officer who supervised their every action. A fourth chair for the Chief of the Watch faced the Ballast Control Panel; this officer maintained the buoyancy and trim of the submarine when submerged. Navigational equipment and a Global Positioning System completed the port side of the room.

A row of consoles on the starboard side of the sub controlled the weapons of the boat. Five seats held five navy officers queued up in front of the panels. The aft-most console housed the "fire" button. If the prerequisites for firing were met, the red button launched a torpedo or Tomahawk missile. Captain Rogers positioned himself in front of a flat-screen monitor streaming real-time image of the leviathan hanging vertical in the water.

Dan shuddered as his mind flashed an image of a very different looking command center – a severely damaged whale calf with wires and cables snaking throughout its ravaged remains, synchronizing it to whatever the nanos devised to operate the vessel.

"Now that it exists, do you think an organic vessel will ever replace this?" Dan thought aloud, as he stared at the monitor.

"I don't know what you've observed regarding the monster we're hunting, but my crew is trained to make split-second decisions based on many factors, including human casualty," Gil said. "That," Gil nodded toward Titan, "attacked without consideration. Clearly, its function is to destroy. I hope the United States never approaches combat in that manner."

Not wanting to make an enemy of the captain, Dan didn't pursue any argument; hell, when he thought about it, he was closer to agreeing with Rogers than his own team.

"Gil, I've brought a piece of equipment that you're going to be interested in," Dan said. "We can install it into the passive sonar system of the sub and it will protect you from the brunt of the sonic weaponry used by Titan; we're installing them on our small submersibles now."

That got Gil's attention. The damage to the sub and the casualties had been the result of sonic wavelengths. "Has this been approved for use?" he asked.

Tricky question, Dan thought, and replied, "I can say that I have tested this particular device and can guarantee it will work – but it has not been approved for military use." Brasco had been unable to get military approval for any modifications to a U.S. submarine.

"Sonar is located below deck. Lt. Robinson will take you there," Gil said without hesitation. "We'll need every advantage to survive your science experiment." Gil dismissed them with a nod of his head.

Chapter 49

A large school of anchovy surrounded the submarine. Splotches of white dotted the blue sky and water as gulls rotated in and out of the sea. James and Melinda barely noted the slow-motion feeding frenzy as they made short work of unloading their crates alongside the Mola sub. The Faraday cage lay next to the HERF gun. The silvery box looked unremarkable next to the weapon. "This is a surprisingly paltry amount of equipment compared to the enormity of the task," Melinda said as she looked around at the meager display. "So much has happened; there should be more than this." She poked at the equipment with her toe.

"There is," said James as he reached into his duffel bag. He handed her a set of expensive-looking earplugs. "These are for you. Moto got them for us from the nearest Air Force base. These are used by gas-passers on aircraft carriers," he explained.

"Gas passers?" questioned Melinda.

James clarified, "Guys who fuel jets on aircraft carriers are called gas passers. They use these specially designed ear plugs that mute engine noises."

"I would have thought they wore headsets?" she said, as she tried one in her ear.

"Some do, these are new technology. They relieve air pressure. Go ahead, put them both in, and then squeeze your nose shut and blow, like you're clearing your ears after swimming – like this," James said and pinched his nose and tightly closed his eyes exaggerating a deep breath and blow. Melinda followed suit. There was a distinct 'pop' as the pressure inside her head equalized. "Amazing. Are there enough for everybody?" she asked.

"I don't think so," James said as he counted out the earplugs. "Moto gave me fifteen pair of these and is ashore rounding up all of the Active Noise Controle headphones he can get his hands on."

"Who should we give these to?" He asked. "My report says there are thirty-five submariners on board."

"Well, we all should have something," Melinda said. She recalled reports of eye-exploding trauma caused by the sonic blasts, and shuddered. "Get one to Hank and give the rest to the Captain. It's for him to decide.

Chapter 50

Without leaving the control room, Gil reached Brasco on the horn. He inserted an earpiece in a display of confidentiality; however he expected his end of the conversation to enlighten his crew. He led with the assumption that an educated team was an effective team.

Without discourse, Gill began as soon as Brasco answered. "Am I to understand that our absurd mission here is to contain the target – not destroy it?" He noted with pride that his command crew's reaction to this news was imperceptible.

Brasco confirmed and added that if Gil refused, he'd have him court-martialed for failing to follow a direct order. The crew watched the flush-red anger rise from their commander's collar toward his forehead.

"I have no intention of dodging my duties," Gil said. "We'll drop your team off at the designated spot, and we'll monitor their safety. But if it looks like it's going bad, I'm getting my crew out." Gil was certain that there wasn't a military court in the country that would convict him if he left these madmen.

He snatched the earpiece off his head and clenched it tightly in his fist. He needed to address his crew. They'd prepared to confront this Titan for several days; this was completely unexpected. These researchers gave him no indication they'd perfected anything that would stop Titan. *Hell,* he thought, *the equipment they planned to take on the mission could fit in his six-year-old daughter's suitcase.*

Gil grabbed the microphone and readied himself to address his crew. "We've been above water too long. I thought I'd taken in too much oxygen – heard it wrong -- when I was told that this would be a 'drop and retreat' mission; however our orders are just that." Again, Gil admired the lack of traceable reaction from his crew. "So let's drop these oxygen thieves off, watch their demise and get ourselves back underwater," he finished. He could hear the whoops and cheers coming from all quarters.

Chapter 51

In the sonar room, Hank learned Titan's coordinates from the submariner tracking the whale. He'd tried to read the monitor himself, but the blue light used to illuminate the room muddled his vision. Leaving the sonar room, he headed for the boat's head to transmit the coordinates to Brasco.

Brasco texted Hank that after boarding Titan, they had one hour to secure the area before a private refrigerator vessel, the *Brodovi* showed up. Once there, the *Brodovi* staff would take control. Hank would then stay with the *Brodovi* and be off-loaded at a pre-determined location.

Hank panicked. He'd been so caught up in the research these past few days he'd ignored his exit strategy. He left the cramped bathroom and made his way to the submarine's Ward Room where he slid into an empty booth. He leaned against the stiff, red naugahyde bench and closed his eyes. Above the booth's flecked gray and red laminate table, he appeared relaxed, but under the table, his left leg bounced up and down in a fever pitch. He calmed himself by noting each inhale and exhale he took. Surprisingly, securing Titan did not bother him – he'd replayed those events in his head so many times, it was as if it was already done. However, the uncertainty of traveling with the buyer, then off-loading in the Philippines sent him into a panic.

Chapter 52

Titan hung in the water, allowing the empty space to swaddle him. The piped-in static vibrated through his spermaceti and, like the murmur of a cheap window fan, this stream of white noise relaxed him. Recently more vessels had gathered on the surface. They presented no threat. He scrutinized any ocean creatures that ventured close. Research on the mucus produced by a Mola mola that passed by a short time ago proved it to be synthetic. The synthetic mucus was harmless, however it was unwise tactically to disregard it altogether.

He carefully cataloged swimmers as they floated around. Today he noted a large, flat halibut drifted up and passed by, a school of albacore tuna followed scores of anchovy, and a steady stream of jellyfish that floated lazily along the current. Nothing out of the ordinary. He listened for his pod's familiar coda, and in the distance, he heard the playful clicks of his sister, Enapay. Titan continued to keep away, and as a result, he kept his pod safe.

Chapter 53

Dan and James stood next to the Mola dressed in wet suits. Dan's compact, muscular build accentuated James' tall, gaunt frame – a visual characterization of hale and frail. James held the Faraday cage. He would detonate it when they were within range.

Melinda and Hank stood next to their unadorned, small submersible. James thought Melinda looked sensual in her black neoprene wet suit but she did not look happy.

"Why do I have to ride with him?" she said. "I'm just as qualified as James to detonate the EMP; in fact, I designed it." She hated the thought of riding this out with Hank. Her time spent with him during the initial Mola sub experiment had been torture. He'd tormented her with cruel comments about Dan and James' safety and rambled egotistically about his leadership on the project.

Dan held firm that she would ride with Hank. He knew Hank would not put himself in any danger. If things looked like they might go bad, Hank would get his ass out of there and Dan wanted Melinda safe and secure, thus with Hank.

"Look, James and I are a team," Dan said. "He and I have done this before. We're simpatico when it comes to smoke-screening Titan." She didn't look mollified. He moved between the two small submarines and fiddled with a clasp on the outside of the Mola sub.

"I can't worry about you when I'm doing this. James can't either. You mean too much to us; to me." He kept his head down as he spoke, fiddling with the clasp. It fell off and clanged on the floor of the sub. Melinda's feet were visible in his periphery; they never budged. He finally looked at her and saw tears falling silently down her cheeks. She turned and got into the other sub, taking the driver's seat.

The three men remained on deck. A sailor awaited their signal to launch them into the water. James' wet suit stopped inches short of his boney wrists and ankles, emphasizing his large hands and feet. The ill-fitting suit made him feel awkward. He cradled the Faraday Box in his left arm. "We should synchronize our watches," he said as he lifted his scrawny right arm. "I do hope *you* remembered one, Dan," James voiced guiltily as he dangled his wrist – sans watch. Dan nodded; he and Hank adjusted their timepieces.

"Brasco said we will have forty-five minutes to one hour of Internet disruption once I discharge the HERF gun," Hank said. He knew he looked fit in his neoprene suit. He wished the weapon he held in his right hand looked less like a NERF gun and closer to a bazooka – a more suitable accessory today.

Dan reviewed the plan on his tablet; once the internet was down, he would rely on memory. The mission was sparse; first to launch would be Hank and Melinda's sub. Outfitted with several external cameras, it would capture images of Titan and the Mola sub simultaneously.

Hank would deploy the HERF to disrupt the internet and approach Titan from the port side. Dan and James would approach in the Mola sub head-on and fire their EMP squarely between Titan's eyes. Then the researchers would board Titan and secure the control room, keeping the nanos off-line, then wait for the refrigerated cargo ship in a holding pattern nearby to come and secure the carcass.

Dan checked on Melinda inside her sub. She also reviewed her tablet. There was little legroom so she rested the PC on the sub's dashboard. He sent her a silent goodbye and entered his sub. By now, James had folded his gangly frame into his seat in the Mola.

"See you on the other side of this," Dan said to Hank as they boarded their respective submersibles. Hank nodded his acknowledgment and closed his hatch.

Dan turned to the seaman who was waiting for the signal to deploy the subs.
"We're ready; sixty seconds and counting," he said retreated into his sub.

Sailors rolled the subs to an expulsion tube. The plain sub queued up first and
was ejected. Melinda activated her video receiver; its images came from the camera
anchored to the front of her sub. Hank crowded in to see what was unfolding, but
Melinda did not attempt to make room for him to see comfortably. A panoramic
view of the ocean filled the screen. In the distance, through a school of blue fin tuna
that swam into view, she saw Titan's outline suspended in the water. She quickly
put in the earplugs. Hank followed suit.

Chapter 54

L ike a giant pendulum, the one hundred and twenty foot mutant whale hung upside down in the water. Fluke up, its torpedo shaped body gently swayed with the current.

Lately the surface waters had cooled and the chatter he picked up from his pod included talk of exodus. Titan listened as they planned their migration northwest between the Hawaiian Ridge and the Mid-Pacific Mountain Range. The trough between these two massive mountains were guaranteed to be rich with giant squid. The deep clefts and crevices, in the towers of stacked basalt bordering the ridge, provided plenty of crannies for their prey to skulk.

Titan's longing to join his pod for their journey to the Sea of Okhotsk jumbled with his fear of what lurked beyond the static. This caused a spike of emotions that threatened to overwhelm the mainframe; as a result, the nanos wired and rewired circuits in the anterior cingulate cortex.

Titan detected the return of the Mola mola. The nanos battled through the static to retrieve data on the fish. While creating the information system, the nanos had developed a wireless network router for access to the internet and file sharing. They did not construct a fixed spot for data storage since information was readily available through radio waves.

All information sites were inaccessible.

The mutant whale turned his attention to his pod. Access to long-distance acoustical monitoring systems was denied – he could not locate his family.

The whale calf panicked. The harmonious relationship maintaining the nanos' primary objective (maintenance of the vessel) and the whale calf's instinctive need to protect his pod, ruptured. The nanos' inability to connect to the internet caused chaos.

Chapter 55

Concurrently, Dan powered the Mola sub closer to Titan. The EMP's impact would be more powerful the closer they were to their target. With teeth clenched and a death grip on the steering wheel, he navigated the sub to within two hundred yards of Titan's bow. They just had one chance to get in position. He needed to be close.

James interrupted the silence. "You planning to take his temperature?" he asked. "'Cause we're getting pretty close, and its googly eye is looking directly at us." Despite the fact that he'd sucked down a shot of his inhaler before he'd boarded the Mola sub, he'd broken a sweat as soon as the hatch banged shut. Now he checked his forehead for rising temperature – no heat, just cold and clammy. *Good*, James thought, *I'm just scared.*

The leviathan's telescoping eye snaked out toward them. Dan checked his watch and counted down as the remaining seconds ticked away to when Brasco would jam the internet. Reaching into his vest pocket, he retrieved the earplugs. "Better put your plugs in and pull the trigger," he said. "It's now or never, Buddy. The internet should be down.

Chapter 56

In the *Edison*, Captain Rogers stood in the conning tower, peering through the periscope, and monitored the researchers' sub. The image of the beast's eye snaking out of its socket and slithering toward the researchers shocked him.

They've been detected, he thought. "We're need to create a diversion," he said. "Fire number one torpedo!"

As if Titan heard the captain's command, he fired his sonic cannon at the *Edison* a split second after the submarine's torpedo left its tube. The deflector shield Dan installed on the ship held firm as the sonic blast silently echoed through the submarine. The earplugs and headsets the crew wore protected them from brain trauma, but the bio-effect on the central nervous system caused vertigo and vomiting.

"The second attack won't be as severe! Fire number two torpedo!" Gil took great gulps of air in an attempt to avoid puking; he swayed and held white-knuckled onto the com center. The room swirled around him. Titan met the second torpedo with a sonic blast as quickly as he had the first. Gil was right; it was inferior. But still the sub shuddered and an eerie rumble traveled stem to stern as the blast blew through. Bells and whistles sounded. The putrid smell of vomit mingled with sweat, and the sound of retching competed with the alarms clanging throughout the sub. Disoriented, Gil willed himself to focus. "Damage?" he barked at his first officer.

Still dry-heaving, Robinson wiped vomit from his communication center. He fought to remain upright and watched as the panels flashed red warnings. Sailors reported extensive damage but not critical. "We'll remain afloat," Robinson replied.

Titan's sonic blast swept through the Mola sub. The camouflaged vessel reacted to the assault and spontaneously released mucus. Pressure inside the sub rose dramatically and Dan waited for his eyeballs to explode. Nausea threatened to overwhelm him. Vertigo slammed into his brain and his ears rang loudly. He fought to stay focused on keeping the mini-sub pointed toward Titan.

Turbulence tossed the Mola sub about like a popcorn kernel in a hot air popper. Dan steered like he was driving a bumper car. He rotated the steering wheel violently to the left to keep from pitching to the right. As the Mola sub wobbled to the right, he needed to steer just as violently to the left.

James wrenched himself into position and grabbed the control stick that manually kept the sub level. Using Titan as the horizon, he jerked ferociously on the joystick to keep them horizontal.

Dan didn't wonder how the blast affected James; the evidence dribbled down his shoulder. As soon as the first explosion had rumbled through the Mola sub, James had puked. Thankfully, James hadn't eaten very much, and produced little more than a sticky bile.

James longed to reach up and hold his head tightly to stop the sound reverberating through his skull. His body convulsed. He wrestled to control the joystick.

"You've got to hold on!" screamed Dan as he pressed the Mola sub into position. "I'm pretty sure there will be another blast!" James never took his eyes off the horizon. The next blast echoed through at a reduced effect. Dan grabbed the control from James.

"Deploy the EMP!" Dan shouted. Still heaving, James opened the Faraday box and flipped the switch.

Immediately, James felt every hair on his body stand on end and the Mola sub's small compartment crackled with electrical current.

The turbulent pitch and sway from the backwash of the torpedo attack subsided, and they listened fixedly to the purr of the Mola's engine, mercifully protected by the sonic shield. Sea creatures tumbled past, stunned or killed by the energy bursts emitted by Titan. Dan thanked his maker they'd survived the battle between Titan and the *Edison* as they idled a mere two football fields away from their target.

Chapter 57

The whale calf went wild. Agony occupied every corner of his mind. The EMP blast fried the nanos controlling all of Titan's systems, catapulting the calf into emotional and physical torment. The working relationship developed between the nanos and the limbic system relieved the emotional distress by creating alternative neuro-pathways – redirecting waves of excess emotional energy to different systems. Without nano intervention, his memories felt like shards of glass ripping into his consciousness. Nano eyes no longer presented him with images, but that didn't stop him from visualizing the deaths of his mother and the matriarch. Paralyzed, the huge nano infused carcass of a ship, leveled in the water and floated to the surface.

With 97% of the nanos destroyed, the 3% remaining assembled and worked to stabilize the mainframe.

Titan floated to the surface and the water around the Mola sub calmed. James slumped back in his seat, still heaving; the raging noise in his ears eased. Next to him, Dan closed his eyes and took deep gulps of breath. In an effort to calm, he willed himself to breathe through his nose. Years of tactical training paid off and Dan regained composure. "Are you okay?" he asked.

"I think so," James replied. "The convulsing has stopped. I'm shaking but I think it's just from fear. The God-awful noise in my head is down to a dull roar, and I've stopped barfing. Yep, I'm okay." James tried to look out the windows, but the panting and puking that had taken place produced so much condensation that the windows were fogged over. He scrubbed at the window closest to him and spied the wake of Melinda's sub as it passed them by.

"Can we get to Titan?" James asked.

"It won't be pretty," Dan replied, "but I think we can limp over." Dan steered the Mola sub forward.

Chapter 58

Melinda watched as Titan floated up to the surface; once there, it bobbed twice, stopped, then listed to one side. "It looks dead," she said. During the skirmish between Titan and the *Edison*, she and Hank had fared better than Dan and James in the Mola sub. It may have been their position in the water, or the over-sized parabolic reflector Dan installed on her sub, but Melinda and Hank experienced mostly gut-churning whoopsies – the kind you get on a roller coaster – as the acceleration force created by Titan's sonic weapon slammed through their sub.

"We need to approach it as if it is temporarily immobilized," Hank said. Time seemed to stand still as the behemoth leveled onto the surface, but in fact, several precious minutes had passed. Brasco had guaranteed no more than one hour of blocked internet access.

Melinda scowled at him. "Why temporarily?" she said. "I have no data to support that the nanos will reanimate."

"We have done very specific research in the past few days," Hank countered. "We have not done long-term studies. Therefore, we cannot calculate what will happen next."

Melinda snorted in response.

They glided past the Mola sub and Melinda twisted her body and smashed her face to the winshield in hopes of getting a peek inside, but the foggy glass veiling the Mola windows, denied her a glimpse of her friends – however, a foggy windshield meant heavy breathing – she felt thankful for any proof of life.

The closer they got to Titan, the less organic it looked. An eerie sheen highlighted its hull and the exterior lacked the soft, supple look of flesh. Melinda stopped the sub several feet in front of Titan's mouth, which was agape, half out of the water.

"I think we should surface. We can enter through the mouth," Hank said.

"I thought we were going to enter somewhere around a fin on the left?" Melinda said. She remembered Dan saying it looked like there was an opening there.

"Right now, the mouth seems like the logical place," Hank said. "The fin entry Dan and I discussed is below the surface. It would take more time." *If she questions one more thing, I'll strangle her, right here, in this min-sub*, Hank thought as their sub sat stationary at the maw of the beast.

Damn it, Hank is right, Melinda thought. Clearly, Dan would figure it out as soon as he arrived. It would be stupid not to agree. She knew she was stubborn but she wasn't stupid. She maneuvered the sub to the surface. Even without comparison to their mini-sub, the creature was colossal. The enormous construction tilted and rested on the cobalt ocean, as if it was taking a nap. The immense mouth gently dipped in and out of the now calm sea; water sloshed in between its cone-shaped teeth.

"We need to get in there ASAP," Hank said. He fumbled for something under his seat. "If it fills with water, it will go down and be of no use to anyone."

"What are you groping for?" she asked. They wouldn't need any of the underwater gear they'd stowed in the back. It would be a dry entry into Titan. Melinda watched Hank pull up a backpack and slide his arm into the sling. "Open the hatch," he commanded.

"Hey, wait a minute, what's in there?" She said, fuming mad – again. Just like Hank to bring along something that hadn't been agreed upon.

Hank reached above them and manually opened the hatch. He needed to get inside Titan before it sank – if it sank. *Better to get on board and take control*, he

thought. He snaked himself half out of the hatch. "Is there something we can attach
to one of these teeth here – to tie the sub to?" he said, ignoring her question. He
would not allow himself to be left here without an alternate means of transportation
if the cold cargo ship failed to show up.

"Yeah, we can use your backpack," Melinda said sarcastically. She looked
around the sub; *they could buckle the weight belts together*, she thought.

Ignoring her snide comment and coming to the same conclusion, "Grab the
weight belts," Hank said, "We can buckle them together."

He shaded his eyes, looked into the distance and saw the Mola sub wobble
toward them. "Here comes lover boy," he taunted. Melinda jumped up and
smacked her head, hard, her eyes filled with tears. She blinked them away. Hank's
body blocked the exit. "Move you buffoon!" she cried. She tugged on his
backpack, pulling him off-balance.

"Stop that, you little bitch!" Hank bellowed as he grabbed the handles at the
sides of the hatch to catch his balance. *So much for ignoring her*, he thought. He
held himself firmly on the ladder, effectively blocking her from leaving the sub.
"Buckle the weight belts together and give them to me, then I'll let you out!" he
said through clenched teeth.

Melinda twisted around to the back of the sub, yanked the belts out of the
wetsuits, and fastened them together. She yanked her own belt out and added its
length to the others. She passed it up to him. It was easy enough for Hank to loop
over one of the many teeth snaggling out toward him.

Hank popped out of the sub and took a tentative step inside Titan's mouth. The
floor, unexpectedly firm, tilted at a gentle slope. Melinda scrambled quickly up the
hatch. The sun shone brightly, she shaded her eyes and searched the horizon for
signs of the camouflaged sub. Also finishing its trip above water, it bobbled into
sight. It too listed to one side, but steadily got bigger as it motored toward them.
Cautiously Melinda stepped inside the beast.

"It's not springy or mushy," she said, slowly moving around on the tongue. She
lead with her toe, tapping it in front of her as if she were looking for a loose board.
Moving closer to a later wall of the mouth, she examined the structure closely. The

teeth, skin, buccal mucosa, -- everything appeared synthetic. The entire structure was infused with nanos!

"Look," Melinda said, her hand brushing the wall of the cavity.

"What?" said Hank.

"Look closer. This thing is clearly as much nano technology as it is biology."

The drone of the Mola sub's engine stopped, interrupting her examination. "I think we should wait for them." She planted herself next to her sub, shaded her eyes and willed the hatch to open.

The hatch opened and Dan stepped out into Titan's mouth. He felt his heart rate increase and his breathing quicken as a burst of adrenalin shot through his system. He relied on his navy seal training and prepared for action.

In contrast, James flopped up and out of the opening. The continuous retching he experienced earlier had taken its toll on him. Every muscle in his body ached.

Dan gave James a hand and hoisted him upright. "Good move to enter through the mouth," James said, his voice gravely and throat raw. "An underwater entry would have wasted time," James blabbed. He didn't want anyone to comment on his weakened condition – anyone meaning Melinda. She took the hint.

"It looks like there is an entry this way," Melinda said. She nodded to a tunnel descending into the gullet. Hank stood at the access at the base of the tongue. Melinda and Dan trotted cautiously down toward him; James staggered after them.

"I told you to wait for us!" Melinda carped, tired of keeping track of Hank.

"Fuck off," Hank snapped. "We don't know how much time we have before the internet reboots." He was just as tired of her

All four stood before the complicated barrier between the outside and the inside of Titan.

"I think we can pry this open without much trouble." Hank ran his hand along the edge of a frond that formed a whorl separating the outside from the inside.

James stumbled up to the entryway and stared at the dilating aperture that formed a shield between the inside of Titan and the elements. "Jesus Christ, Hank. Are you seeing this?" he said as he watched Hank carefully fiddle with a leaf-shaped segment of the opening.

"I've read about these!" Dan stared at the access point in disbelief. "When I was a kid I had a subscription to Boys Life. I loved *Have Space Suit –Will Travel* and *Farmer in the Sky* by Robert Heinlein," he said. "I read Heinlein novels -- *Beyond this Horizon*, and *Star Ship Troopers*! This door was described in one of those books!" Dan reached past Hank and stroked the extraordinary entryway.

Melinda looked closely at the entrance. "I've actually seen these on several occasions. This type of closure is an extremely effective barrier – when they work right." Leaning close with her eyes closed she carefully palpated each petal's edge to find the one minutely raised.

"They often get stuck," she said. "Too many gears to keep aligned if opened and shut often. Aha! Here it is!" Her fingers rested on the slight raise.

"We should be able to rotate this open," she explained. "This can be tricky; grab ahold and visualize us dialing the door open – we need to get it right or we'll just jam it."

James stood back and watched as the others dragged the frond downward and an opening appeared in its wake.

Chapter 59

Hank pushed to be first inside. Dan nodded to James, indicating he should be next. Melinda hung back; she felt her heart beat deep in her gut, and stars smudged the edges of her vision as she fought off dizziness. For a moment, she thought she might turn and run back to the sub.

Already on the inside, Dan held out his hand toward her. She took it and stepped through the rabbit hole.

LED headlamps, worn by the researchers, illuminated the interior a florescent blue. The design was definitely a submarine. Arranged throughout the organic cavity, recognizable submarine structures jutted up from the floor. Each appeared as if it had begun as a biological seed, grew into crude equipment and then was encased in nano-infused skin. Dan touched the wall; it felt several degrees warmer than the ocean water. The nanos regulated the interior temperature.

At the fore position of the cavity stood a weapons station. Dan recognized a torpedo data computer (TDC) and a gyro angle setter. The setter looked like the old fuse box his grandparents had in their cellar. He identified the TDC by the large screen and the arrangement of hand cranks, dials, and switches to track a target. The base of the station was rooted in the nano-skin.

James closely examined the TDC; his nose nearly touched the hand crank. "Visual inspection identifies very fine – almost undetectable – repair patterns," James said. "I can confirm that my nanos used found material – probably from the exploded sub that carried them – to rebuild this computer screen." He looked at Melinda for confirmation.

Melinda wasn't listening. Upon entering the alcove, an outcropping in the center of the bay had drawn her attention. Cradled in a crib of whale skin, lay the charred remains of a whale calf; brain exposed with wires leading to the motherboard. Cables coiled out of the circuit board, progressed down the crib, and embedded themselves into the floor of the cavern. Melinda knelt beside the casket and held her hands inches from the charred and scarred calf; she felt the warmth and humidity radiating from the organic framework. She detected respiration from the calf.

"Jesus, he *is* alive," she said,

"Do you think he is in pain?" she said, staring at the wires winding out of the brain.

"Is it dangerous?" Hank asked simultaneously.

"I don't know," answered Dan. *That should satisfy both of them*, he thought.

Less concerned about the biology than he was interested in technology, James walked over to the sidewall and kicked it.

"What are you doing?" Melinda stroked the outcropping in front of her.

"I was checking to see if any of the nanos are active. If they were, I suppose we would've been attacked," James said as he carefully maneuvered his way through the tilting cavern to the command center.

"Don't do that again!" Hank barked. "Unlike you, I do not have a death wish."

"Stop it James; he's still alive," Melinda said quietly.

"What's alive, Melinda?" James challenged. "The ship? The whale? What the hell!" James surveyed his surroundings. In addition to the obvious weapons station, he could identify a fiber optic sonar array (defined by the three flat panels mounted on either side of the interior), and a VLF (very low frequency) communication device located in the same space as the communication center on the *Edison*.

"The ship's alive and the whale's alive," she said. "The nanos – your nanos – have done their job! They have used the materials on hand to rebuild their vessel. Once we get this – him – secured, we can discover how and why they decided to use this design." She swept her hand around the cavity.

"There's been a change in plans," Hank stated; a sleek, .32 automatic Colt handgun pointed at her. "You all will listen to me. James, if you kick the wall again, I will shoot Melinda. Dan, if you try anything, I will shoot Melinda. Do you all understand?" The three looked at Hank, stunned into silence.

Melinda was speechless. Hank's behavior during the project had generated nothing but contempt. He'd strutted and swaggered throughout this assignment; in response, she'd insulted him repeatedly. She'd purposely left him out of the loop and ignored his very presence and *now* he was threatening her with a gun? She should have been terrified, but she was, again, furious.

"What the hell Hank!" Melinda finally blurted out. "You're a bad guy as well as an ass; and why will you shoot me? Is it because I think you're an ass? Well, Dan and James think you're an ass, too, right?" she said.

Dan realized Melinda was mad, not frightened – he knew this was a mistake on her part. He tried to take control of the situation.

"I guess we underestimated you, Hank," Dan said.

"Yeah, he's a big ass," James said.

Dan continued, "Why do you think you need a gun?" He noted Hank's position with his back to the wall while they, scattered around the interior, were more vulnerable.

"I need a gun to get things done my way," Hank replied. At first, Dan didn't recognize the Faraday box sitting in front of Hank. Melinda saw it and paled. It was different from the one the team developed and James deployed on the Mola mola. She just knew that there was some kind of weapon inside it. She felt for her earplugs, which hung uselessly around her neck. If she was correct and he had a weaponized something inside that Faraday box, she needed to get them on.

Dan noticed the box and had the same thought: it was an unknown Faraday box, probably containing an unknown weapon and they needed to get their earplugs in without Hank seeing them. He hoped James and Melinda had figured that out, too.

He continued to draw Hank's attention to him. "What's the gun for, Hank?" he said. "Is it to get us to agree with whatever you're going to do with the Faraday box? Titan is already subdued. What do you need that Faraday box for?" Dan saw Melinda put in her earplugs and James hurried to do the same.

Melinda turned Hank's attention to her. "I still don't get why you're only going to shoot me, Hank. I'm puny. If anyone tries to stop you, it certainly won't be me." She hoped she'd given Dan enough time to insert his earplugs.

"I just want to shoot you, Melinda." Hank sneered. "You are a bitch and a know-it-all. You can't ignore me now, can you?" He cocked the hammer back.

"Whoa, whoa Hank, don't be stupid!" cried James; he knew without a doubt Hank would easily kill Melinda.

Hank let the hammer fall back into place. "Keep talking James, convince me." He rummaged through his backpack with his free hand.

"I'm in this real deep, so convince me that I don't need the money," he said and extracted a small black device from his bag. It fit snugly in his hand, and he placed his thumb on the plunger pad at the top of it. He continued to talk to James. "Convince me I won't be happy with my new identity, or that this plan can't possibly work. Convince me James, that I'm better than this." Hank didn't wait for anyone to answer. "From where I stand, you three are in the way of me getting what I deserve."

Hank pulled something else from the pack, a blue braided lanyard that held a yellow case the size of a deck of cards. "Brasco provided me with this." He dangled the lanyard at James. "Very top secret – from the Pentagon – it's a personal ground fault circuit interrupter. It will protect me from this." He waggled the ominous black appliance at him. "This gadget produces very high voltages of electricity and will drop you like a stone. I understand from Brasco this is going to hurt like hell," he said and pressed down the plunger.

James, Dan and Melinda felt electricity invade them; body hair stood on end each was thrown backward several feet; they were consumed by the "pins and needles" feeling as paresthesia set in;. Blood trickled from their eyes and they tumbled into unconsciousness.

Hank walked over to Melinda and kicked her. "This is what happens when you ignore me. Oh, and I'll be back to finish this." He kicked her again and walked out through the mouth of Titan. Time was of the essence. Inside the Faraday box was a small Morse code transmitter. A contact on the cold cargo ship had a similar Faraday box with its sister Morse code translator.

Dan fought to regain control of his motor functioning. Having been only temporarily blacked-out, he had awoken to witness Hank's parting attack on Melinda. There was not a doubt in his mind Hank would kill them. Dan knew he had to find a way to subdue Hank. Irony wasn't lost on him – they'd spent the past several days developing a method to subdue one monster, and now they had another monster to contend with. As he pulled himself upright, the command center started to reboot with a whirring groan.

Outside, Hank felt the change as the nanos worked to get back on line. He saw Dan's silhouette standing near the exit to Titan's mouth. Without a second thought he aimed his gun and shot Dan in the head. He went back to work contacting the cargo ship.

The blast sent Dan flying backward, smashing him against the com center. A small hole just to the left of his nose oozed blood. His body slid lifelessly to the floor. The small caliber bullet entered a tiny channel of fluid running through his brain. This small defect turned slightly several times, carefully skirting any vital areas, and finally shriveled to an end at the base of the skull. The bullet tumbled through the channel like a marble through a tube, rolling harmlessly to a stop at the base of the skull. A sliver to the left or right and the brain would have been destroyed and evil would have triumphed.

James labored to keep from retching. It took the effort of Hercules to keep his body motionless. When he had fallen to the ground unconscious, he'd landed with his back to the others. He could only imagine the worst, after hearing the gunshot.

Melinda had watched in horror as Dan's body flew back into the com center. Her grief was paralyzing. She lay motionless on the floor and let sorrow wash over her.

Chapter 60

The nanos labored to get their ship back on line. The remaining fraction of functioning nanos worked together to render essential programs operational.

As they came on line, the nanos interpreted the gunshot in the com center. Upon investigation of the gunfire, the nanos discovered an energy signal, erratic but strong, originated nearby. They considered this new power source to replace the unpredictable whale brain.

A small metallic string of nanos snaked out of the com center, searching for the new energy source. This nano-coil reached Dan and began work.

Repair damage and bring the vessel back on line: The original mission of the nanos. The new energy source was stronger and less fitful than the previous power supply. The bullet caused minimal damage to this new resource; the nanos noted marginal external damage.

It was essential for the nanos to link this new power supply to their ship's power source. This biological collaboration would fire up the vessel.

Several more nano cables snaked out of the com center and linked with Dan. Similar to the original repair to the whale calf, the nanos stabilized Dan's biology by repairing critical organic damage while rewiring the electrical currents in his brain to accomplish their single-minded goal – keep the vessel in working order. Dan took long gasping breaths as the nanos wired him into the com center.

Dan's ragged breathing caused James to chance turning to see what was happening. Incredulously, he witnessed nano cables wind around Dan's injured head and snake into the com center. Shocked into action, he pulled himself to standing and staggered toward the mouth of Titan.

Melinda heard James struggle to his feet. *Where was he going?* She willed herself to look away from Dan and caught James' eye; he signaled her to be quiet. She understood. He needed to draw Hank's attention away from the interior of the whale.

"Who are you contacting, Hank?" James said as he walked out onto Titan's mouth, his voice still raspy from heaving.

"I don't really know. Someone Brasco hooked up with." He looked at James. "You look awful again," he said.

I've got to keep his attention focused on me. "Are you going to kill us, or will you leave that to whoever shows up?" James asked.

"You know, I think I already killed Dan," Hank said. "It was surprisingly easy. I thought this would be where I'd choke." He said calmly. "I could kill Melinda six times over." He continued, "She's treated me like shit from the beginning. But you, killing you should be hard. We had a relationship. You even liked me once, right James?"

Boy, he's more of a whack job than I ever imagined, James thought. "Sure Hank, I liked you once. But you poisoned me, and as this has all unraveled, I've begun to think it was on purpose; not so much of an accident, right buddy?"

Hank looked to the horizon. "Yep" he said. "That very deliberately placed Kup-o-Koffee was there for the taking. Just the way you like it, tepid, two creams and a sugar. Don't you remember James? I like my coffee steaming hot and black as coal."

"You son of a bitch," said James.

"Human trials were years in the future," Hank said. "We even talked about it. By the time human trials were finally indicated, we'd be the old guys, pushed off the project by aggressive young researchers. Hey, I got to continue our research and even discovered a cure," Hank finished, as if he was defending a research abstract.

"I repeat, you son of a bitch," James said as Titan lurched in the water.

Chapter 61

Melinda crawled over to Dan, each movement cautiously coordinated, her concern for Dan winning over her fear of Hank. She watched as nanos meandered purposely between the com center and Dan's injured head. Fearful she would disturb their progress, but wanting to comfort him, she cradled his foot in her lap.

The nanos stabilized the biology and focused on connecting the whale source with the Dan source. This connection would be critical. The nanos still viewed gathering useful information from the whale calf difficult because the whale relied on imagery and sensation to problem solve. Dan's mainframe and the complex language contained within his communication center promised to provide ample functional information. However, reprogramming the new source would take days
  – *unacceptable timeframe—*
a gunshot indicated that there was imminent danger within the vessel.

The outcome of linking the whale calf's cognition and Dan's consciousness was unpredictable. Nanos sorted the information from both sources and networked essential functions. Survival motivated the original power source. The new power source utilized more logic. By weaving information contained in the two mainframes the nanos hypothesized: 1)they never succeeded in repairing any vessel as they had been programmed to do; 2) They created something altogether different, and 3) this creation had been the danger in the pacific these past few weeks.

The melding of instinct and logic provided the nanos with insight. These nanos achieved a level of awareness. This new acumen decided to channel system control to the new power source, Dan.

For the time being, Captain Rodgers and his crew monitored Titan's movement from the deck of the *Edison*. Rodgers' submarine sustained significant damage during Titan's attack, but remained operational. His crew regained their sea legs and operated at high alert. Glued to his periscope, Rodgers watched as two of the men stood in the maw of the beast.

Hank scanned the horizon for the cargo ship, but saw nothing. He considered asking someone from that ship to get rid of James and Melinda, then he'd only have Clair and Dan's death on his conscience. He stopped fiddling with his pistol. The once shiny nickel finish was now smeary, and the handle was damp from his clammy palms. He aimed the pistol and shot James in the leg.

The bullet passed through James' thigh, knocking him to the ground. "What the fuck-" James, sputtered, white hot pain sliced through his quadriceps into his hamstring. Why the hell did you do that?" James said. Adrenalin dulled the pain, but did nothing to lessen his frustration. *Now he had no chance of overpowering Hank.*

"I've got a lot of reasons," said Hank. "First, I'm not a son of a bitch, and I'm tired of being called names. Second, I don't want you to try anything stupid and I'm tired of keeping an eye on you. And third, it's for drinking the fucking coffee. If you hadn't done that, I wouldn't be standing in the mouth of a goddamn monster, waiting for some goddamn stranger to come and take this monstrosity off my hands!"

Inside Titan, Melinda did nothing to acknowledge the second gunshot she heard. She sat with Dan's foot in her lap and rocked back and forth. All of her swagger gone. She'd labored her entire career – no life – to radiate confidence and in seconds, it was gone. She closed her eyes; unable to bear another minute of watching pieces of nano-infused whale flesh being delivered to Dan's head and melding into his damaged tissue. Tears streamed down her cheeks as she listened to the gibberish his damaged brain made him speak. Every now and then she felt Dan flinch. If she'd seen the whale calf, she would have noticed its movements synchronized to Dan's.

The nanos finished the essential repair on Dan's mainframe, and the connection of both biological energy sources was complete. However, the initial power source – the whale calf – remained in a chaotic pattern.

Dan sensed pain, but did not experience it. His thoughts were in disarray. Hank had shot him. Melinda cried in the distance, and he heard ragged breathing. One thing he did know: something had hijacked his thoughts.

Images of an explosion overwhelmed Dan. He saw his mother burst into flames, and pieces of her float away. Crushing sadness enveloped him. Images appeared again – his mother in her favorite blue sundress running to him, smiling, waving, and happy to see him. BAM! Explosion. Fire and pieces of her drifted away.

This image looped repeatedly and it threatened to drive him insane. His special ops training reminded him that when fear threatened to overtake judgment, he needed to disconnect his amygdala by concentrating on a difficult task to engage his neocortex. Starting at one hundred, he counted backwards by threes – in Farsi. This worked. He felt his heart rate start to slow. He counted backward in Tuyuca, a language of the eastern Amazon combining an excess of vowels that, to be understood correctly, required the speaker to produce sound from deep in the throat. His symptoms of panic subsided; his breathing deepened, and the waves of nausea crashing through him like a tsunami receded.

Dan heard a sad whale song in the distance. The song was so meaningful to him now that he could see, feel and taste the sadness of it, each of his senses understanding the loss. The nanos had tried and failed for months to create a neural network to erase this destructive engram – Titan's memory of his mother's death.

Operating under the conclusion of behaviorist Karl Lashley that memories are distributed throughout our brain, not saved in a single area, Dan carefully picked through the riot of images invading his hippocampus. His goal was to search out good memories and replace the destructive images flooding his limbic system. He located a memory of a whale and her calf as they played – racing through the cool, clear ocean, the mother whale encouraging the calf upward through a frothy wave. Dan felt the fizzy crest of the wave tickle his skin as he propelled up through the water. The warm dry air was a welcome contrast to his cold wet skin.

Dan found his own memory of his mother and him at the park. That summer – so hot – they'd soaked themselves in the sprinkler before running to the swing set. His mom lifted him and swung him around and around, then plopped him into the brown plastic baby swing. His sopping wet shorts cooled the scorching seat. The metal felt hot as he snagged his thumbs through the links of the chain that hung the swing. He listened to her sing her favorite song as she pushed him.

Your love, lifting me higher

Than I've ever been lifted before

So keep it up

Right here in the song, she would stop the swing high in the air and he'd feel his innards swoosh forward. Dan's prefrontal cortex filled with joy.

The song continued, and a moment so treasured and fondly remembered over the years was now a vibrant sensory experience.

Dan relished the moment his mother repeated the chorus "higher and higher." He felt his cool, wet skin; dry in the hot breeze.

The end of the song snuck up on him, as it always did when he was a child.

. . .and he soon departed

And you know he never

Showed his face again

When she sang this, she always cried.

Dan blended his and Titan's memories of mother; the games played, the songs sung and painful lessons learned. *These are the memories we need to hold on to*, he told Titan.

Titan recognized Dan's sadness as his mother wept at the thought of her lost love. Mirror neurons fired; now linked to a complex language system Titan empathized with Dan's sadness, and echoed a fundamental principle of the pod.

There is sacredness in tears, Titan responded. *They are not a sign of weakness.* In turn, Dan urged Titan to lessen his grip on sorrow and recalled a passage from Emerson his grandmother would recite, *'We do not live an equal life, but one of contrasts; now a little joy, then a sorrow.' You need to embrace the joy.*

The nanos searched through the images that had guided them for so long for an image to join with the descriptive words from Dan's complex language center that explained the change for both biologies. Each knew the beauty of the butterfly. Several times the pod noticed a butterfly resting on a piece of floating sea junk. Ever so carefully, members would swim up and gaze at the delicate, but energetic creature. Titan wondered at its choppy movement – no grace, a random voyage.

Metamorphosis

Titan had encountered many sea creatures in differing stages of transformation. He particularly liked to watch the flat fish develop from the round fish; at first, free swimming, then flattening out and eventually sinking to the bottom. That metamorphosis was complete when the eyes migrated to the topside of the fish and jutted upward.

As the caterpillar lives in the butterfly, you and I are one. Dan felt a shift in his consciousness; Titan's memories were his, the alteration was complete.

The nanos receded back into Titan and Dan eased back into awareness. He felt his body lying on the floor; Melinda cried softly near him, and Titan was definitely in his head.

Maybe I died, Dan contemplated. *Great, I finally find out there is an afterlife and my soul ends up trapped with Titan's. No heralding angels, no pearly gates for me. I'm going to be part of the scourge of the sea.*

Information flowed in.

Not dead

Nano technology responsible

WE NEED TO SAVE JAMES

He knew what he needed to do. Melinda grabbed tighter to his leg as he struggled to get up.

"You have to let go," he said, gently.

Melinda opened her eyes. Dan was alive. She let go of his leg. "I don't understand what's happening," she whispered.

"We don't have time for me to explain. Do you trust me?" he asked, and pulled her to her feet.

Melinda had no answer. She reached out and stroked the glistening nano flesh at his temple. "What's in your head?" she asked.

"Ahh, now that's a tricky question." He pulled her close and kissed the top of her head. "You better come with me. I'm not sure what's going to happen next but you'll be safe." They walked through the unfurled portal onto the mouth of the ship.

James watched them come through the tunnel. Hand pressed tightly to his thigh, "We thought you were dead," he said.

"The reports of my death were greatly exaggerated," Dan replied, recalling a Mark Twain expression. "Melinda, stay with James."

Hank looked away from the horizon. "I killed you once. I'll do it again," he said.

Dan sensed desperation. Hank looked at Melinda and James.

Dan he needed Hank's attention back on him. "You know why I'm still alive," he taunted, "but you don't believe it. You want me to say it. OK, I've been mutated by nanos."

Dan tapped the glimmering new nano flesh on his cheek. "You can shoot me again, but it won't matter. The nanos will repair me. But guess what? The nanos are really mad at you, Hank." Dan continued, "We've already contacted Captain Rodgers on the *Edison*. They're on the lookout for unauthorized ships in the area. You're done now. No one's coming for you."

Hank grabbed his Colt; he was going to kill someone. Dan dove forward and knocked Hank to the ground. The gun discharged into the fleshy part of Hank's side.

Hank clutched his side, and drew his legs up; he moaned and rocked himself as he lay in the fetal position.

"It's a through and through," Dan said as he looked at the wound. "You deserve more." Hank turned on his back, his hand pushed against the wound; blood oozed between his fingers

With a pop, a tiny metallic string sprang from within the dermis of the vessel, and snaked its way to the wound. Hank watched in fascination as the filament entered the injury.

"Ha! You're wrong! The nanos did come to save me." Hank watched as his wound changed before his eyes. His fascination turned to terror as the wound began to fester. "What's going on?" His face distorted with pain and horror. The putrid wound expanded and extended up his side and began to consume his arm. Like a flesh-eating virus, skin bubbled open, stench and puss oozed from the growing lesion. "Make it stop!" he cried, as a stain of puss and blood soaked through his shirt. He screamed once more and fell over as his body turned into a putrid mush.

"Dan! We need to save James," Melinda shrieked.

Dan turned and saw Melinda slapping at the nano connection coiling toward James. "It's okay. They won't hurt him," Dan said.

"No, it's not okay," Melinda countered. "Look what they did to Hank!" She took off her shoe and beat down emerging nanos like she was playing the whack-a-mole game.

Dan assessed the scene unfolding in front of him. Several nano filaments were sprouting around James, who frantically ripped at any connection he could find.

A gelatinous mass puddled where Hank used to be.

The Titan vessel lurched in the water. The merging of nanos, Titan and Dan was complete. The trinity in control worked together to steady the helm; engineer nanos successfully rebooted parts of the remodeled mainframe and several systems were on line.

Dan knew this was no longer a U.S. recovery project; Hank had gone rogue and an unknown vessel was approaching. While employing the unique spectrum of sound used by sperm whales in echolocation, the fellowship in control identified the distinct signature of an acoustic invisibility cloak shielding a very large cargo ship.

Titan knew the cargo ship intended him harm.

Dan's emotional knowledge and ability to express and regulate sensorial responses modulated Titan's rage. Instead of directing the excess energy to the whale calf's enlarged cingulate gyrus – the area of the brain that coordinates sensory input and emotional responses – he directed the nanos to guide it to the frontal lobe – the area of the brain dedicated to decision making and behavioral control.

We need to stand down

Rage had been conquered.

Chapter 62

The *Edison* sent a message to Dan, "Have you secured Titan?"

What in hell was going on over there, Gil worried; he could see two men down and the girl was stomping at something on the deck around James.

Dan ignored the question. He replied with the nautical metaphor for last hope. "We're going anchors to windward Gil, balls to the wall." He walked toward James and Melinda. Both finally stopped attacking the nanos, realizing the nanos purpose had clearly been to repair James.

"Have you lost your mind?" James said. "Look at us!" He lifted his hand off the wound in his upper thigh and blood oozed through the nano patch. "We're not going balls to the wall anywhere!"

Dan stared at James, but continued his communication with the *Edison*. "James and Melinda will off-load on the Mola sub. You will pick them up. We have located a cloaked refrigerated cargo ship and we will intercept. I repeat, you will pick up James and Melinda on the Mola sub and withdrawal. We will intercept the cargo ship."

Gil could see Dan in the mouth of the beast. There was every indication Titan was back on line. Gil's ship was in bad shape; he knew the *Edison* would not survive another conflict. "Dan, I repeat, is your team secure?"

Dan looked around. Hank was a puddle of puss and blood; James sprawled on the deck, his left hip bloody and exposed, and Melinda was, well, she looked angry.

"We are safe," was his reply.

Gil alerted his men they would retrieve the Mola sub and then retreat to a safe distance. An audible sigh of relief emanated from his battered crew.

"What is wrong with you?" Melinda demanded as her anger transcended her fear. She had given up her fight against the nanos – there had been too many of them. Without her assault, the nanos repaired James' wound.

"What makes you sure we are safe? And who are you talking to?" She stamped her foot that still had a shoe on it.

"Melinda, you need to get James back on the Mola sub," Dan told her as he mentally prepared for battle. He walked to James and helped him to his feet, and turned to her. "You need to get off the ship," he urged.

"What ship?" Melinda shrieked, something she'd never done before. "We're in the mouth of a freaking mutant whale! What ship?" The hollering left her breathless. "James, do you know what is going on?" she gasped.

James had studied Dan since he'd emerged, hale and healthy from Titan's gullet. He came to two conclusions: one, Dan appeared to be too much in his head, and two, he was not alone there. "I think Dan is connected to Titan. We need to listen to him, Melinda, for once just do what you are told!" He turned to Dan. "Are you coming with us?" he asked, gingerly entering the Mola sub. The last of his energy spent, he collapsed in the passenger seat.

"Not on the Mola sub," Dan answered. "If we need to get away, there is the other submersible." He looked at Melinda. "I love you. You have to go." Melinda lowered herself into the driver's seat, letting the shock take over; she pulled the hatch closed behind her. *I love you, too*, she thought. She started the engine, pulled away from Titan and never looked back.

Gil watched as Dan sent the Mola sub off. He and his crew were indebted to Dan because of the extra equipment installed below deck. That gear had probably saved them all. "We've got the colorful sub in our sights," he reported to Dan. "We'll pick them up quickly. Godspeed."

Chapter 63

Certain Gil would keep James and Melinda safe, the triad in control severed their connection with the *Edison*. Titan listened for his pod and heard their peaceful coda safely in the distance while the nanos considered the biologic vessel's chance of survival.

Repair and maintenance had once been their primary objective. The addition of perception to their diagnostic system rearranged their priorities.

There was no longer a need for the biological vessel.

The vessel was a liability.

The triumvirate all agreed – they would save Dan and the body that once housed Titan would be sacrificed.

As the cargo ship continued its approach, the nanos prepared to attack. Shrugging off the husk of the Titan vessel would not be difficult for the nanos. There would be no regret. Like the tale of the trapped hiker who hacked off his arm to escape a certain death, the nanos instinctively knew it had to be done. They severed non-essential connections between the Titan ship and Dan.

They imported engrams of whale/nano experiences – impressions, language and knowledge – for storage in Dan's working and long-term memory. The newly formed cooperative left a squad of nanos, running a simple search and destroy program, in the carapace to operate the ship.

Dan ran toward the small submersible tethered to Titan. *How will I get into this thing and shove off in time?* He thought. The surface under his feet shuddered, and the small sub inched toward the open sea.

Dan laughed. He wasn't alone. Jerking free the lines that secured this sub to Titan, he jumped into the driver's seat, closed the hatch and thought, *Go! Go! Go!* If anyone was watching, it would have looked as if Titan spit the small sub into the water.

Chapter 64

The ten-thousand-ton, eleven-hundred-foot cargo ship filled the horizon. It lumbered toward them at a steady twenty-nine knots. The captain of the ship saw the giant whale carcass bobbing in the water and rubbed his hands together in satisfaction. His contact in control of the aberration confirmed the whale-boat was ready for transfer.

His orders: to deliver it whole, if possible. The skeleton crew he'd assembled included a team of Japanese whalers. He directed them to ready their equipment. He had paid dearly for the tortuous looking grappling hooks and the heavy-duty pulley system he'd installed.

The team of scientists aboard readied themselves to enter the carcass and photograph anything unusual. Entering a dead whale seemed damn unusual to the captain, but his silence had not been cheap, and he questioned nothing. As the cargo ship approached the body, the unthinkable happened – it trembled and righted itself. He watched in horror as the creature now turned toward them.

Dan did not look back, but his shared consciousness imagined the terrifying image of the Titan vessel as it-thundered toward his target.

On the cargo ship the crew stared as fifteen feet of massive head loomed high and mighty into their seascape. His hide, carved with telltale pockmarks and deep gashes earned from marathon battles with giant squid, shimmered as the nano-infused skin reflected the sunlight. The familiar hollows and gashes left by orcas, caulked with a glittering glaze, winked eerily at the terrified crew. The Japanese whalers recognized these battle scars of a great warrior.

In their final moments, the crew witnessed Titan's eyes telescope out from the sides of his head, like snakes erupting from the gorgon Medusa's head, as the whale-ship fatally rammed the cargo ship.

The collective could not have anticipated the physical pain caused by the death of the Titan vessel. If they could have screamed, they would have.

Dan clutched his head in agony, his nanos pulsating as Titan exploded. On the *Edison*, James arched and fell to the ground, as his nano-repaired gluteal muscles contracted in reaction to the explosion.

Captain Rogers and his crew watched the Titan ship and the cargo ship burst into flames. "We need to sweep the area," he said. "If Dan got out alive we need to find him."

Seeing the Titan ship ram the cargo ship, and the explosion that followed, devastated Melinda. Her knees buckled and she fell next to James. The noise around her sounded muffled and far away. Something slammed into her side, knocking her out of her stupor. She realized James had kicked her; a rude but effective way of getting her attention. Weakly, she kicked him back.

"You cannot fall apart on me Melinda Jean Davenport," he yelled as he flopped closer to her. "I need you to help me up."

Melinda pulled her knees up and slumped her head between them. She concentrated on a beginner yoga mantra: *regulate; breath and the body and mind will follow*. Slowly and deeply, as she continued her breathing, the buzzing in her head softened. James banged into her again.

"Stop it," she said, looking up from her knees, "I'm fine." She brushed her hair back as if to demonstrate, but the gesture was hollow. She was anything but fine.

Chapter 65

Inherent to the whale pod was the unique sensation created when a member died. The death of their beloved leader reverberated through the close-knit group. The water churned as loved ones nudged and bumped against each other. They torpedoed through the water and breached the top of the ocean. The sound of whales crashing against the surface replaced the clattering clicks and clacks typical of the pod. Bursts of staccato tail slaps accompanied the uproar as they grieved noisily.

Chapter 66

The *Edison* found Dan quickly. Melinda and James stood by as they pulled him, unconscious, from the sub. The ship's medic checked his pupils for reaction; the pupils contracted, and the nano-infused sclera sparkled; he wiped the strange scar to the left of Dan's nose with a sterile pad.

Dan moaned, nano-repair throbbing in his head. "It feels like my head exploded," he groaned, batting at the medic trying to assess his condition.

Melinda gently took Dan's hand and moved close to him. "Your head didn't explode," she said, holding his hand to her cheek, "Titan did."

James paced as he watched the medic evaluate Dan's condition. He tried everything to ease the pain in his ass. He backed into a door and massaged his aching gluteal muscle against the metal frame. He contorted his body backwards - reducing the strain on the muscles around his burning butt. Nothing worked for long.

"Is he going to be ok?" he asked the medic with a voice stronger than he felt. "When this pain started," James slapped his hip, "nanos started trickling from my wound – and my repair was minor compared to Dan's repair. I don't think he can survive the loss of many nanos."

Nanos labored to maintain the power source.

Dan's blood vessels would not maintain tension on their own. Nanos were essential in maintaining enough pressure to allow blood to pump up in Dan's body.

Melinda took the discarded dressing to examine; dirt, blood and the telltale glint of nanos twinkled on the pad. She gave it to James for inspection and chewed on her fingernails as she watched the EMT examine Dan.

"Nanos are leaking out of his repair," she said, and spit out a scrap of fingernail she'd chewed off. "Yours oozed out your butt, but his are coming out of his head!" She tried not to panic as she stared at Dan as if he were a multivariable in vector calculus.

"They oozed out of my hip," James corrected her. "When Titan exploded, something happened to the nanos."

"Treat me for shock," Dan said. "The nanos need to reboot. They're using all their power to keep me from going into shock. If they don't reboot, there is a good chance we will die."

James heard a helicopter approaching, its telltale thwops growing louder as it came closer. "Do it," James told the medic, "treat him for shock."

The medic didn't break his concentration as he spoke, "Pulse strong, blood pressure and breathing normal – His body shows no signs of shock."

As if on cue, the nanos initiated a hard reboot of their system and Dan's blood pressure plummeted. The medevac helicopter descended onto the *Edison's* helipad.

Two seaman hoisted the stretcher and took Dan to the helicopter. "I'm going with him," Melinda said.

"Me too." James hobbled along after her.

The nano reboot would take time. They needed to Block most of the operating system to update and install the modifications made during the integration of the Titan system into Dan's mainframe. They would rely on medical intervention to keep the biological scaffolding linking Dan, the nanos and Titan's memories alive.

Their patient was in shock. The medevac team worked to regulate blood flow and pressure. His pulse weak and his breathing shallow. Melinda and James huddled closely on a bench seat away from the medical team, allowing space for them to do their work. Traveling over one hundred miles per hour, the MD 550

Medevac helicopter zoomed to shore. As the helicopter approached the hospital, the medical team called for equipment to treat Dan's failing organs. They added a biohazard alert when they spotted the trickle of silver oozing from his head injury.

Melinda and James followed Dan off the helicopter, through a corrugated hazmat tunnel that led them to a small, sterile room. An Emergency medical team wearing Gray tyvek biohazard suits met them. Pressurized air pumped into the suits from a pack on the back of each medic, which produced an arrangement of eerie whooshes. Three decontamination responders, in matching green suits, sat sentry at the doorway of the room.

"What exactly am I looking at?" the middle-aged woman examining Dan asked. She peered through her Plexiglas visor at the shiny discharge.

"We have a very secure situation," James said. "I'm not sure what I can tell you."

Dr. Helen Latamir, chief medic, snorted in disapproval. "We all have clearance here," she said. "If you want me to treat him, you need to tell me what the hell is going on." She looked pointedly at the scar tissue glittering under the medical light.

"He's been shot in the head," Melinda said. "A bio-electronic process took place that healed his injury." Pointedly ignoring James' sputtering reference to top-secret procedure.

"Initially Dan – that's his name – was fine after his nano-repair," she continued. "You know, up and about talking, even taking charge. He put me – I mean us – on a sub and saved us. Then he followed in a different sub. When we got to him he was like this." She pointed to his recumbent body.

"What's been done?" Dr. Latamir asked. "The chart doesn't list a gunshot wound."

"They've treated him for shock," Melinda replied.

"Makes sense, with a gunshot wound to the head. I'll need to do a CAT scan," Latamir replied.

Melinda put herself protectively in front of Dan's body. "We used silicon and platinum only, James, right?" she asked. "I don't want his head to explode."

"He could be full of steel beams and a CAT scan wouldn't hurt him," Dr. Latamir said. "However, if I ordered an MRI, he might shoot out of the tube like a cannon ball. Look, I don't know how much time we have, but I'll take time to say this; you need to answer every question," she said to James, who was currently shushing Melinda. "That's the only way I'll be able to treat this guy.

"I treated Forty-Three for polyps and no gossip-rag-magazine could tempt me – even with millions of dollars – for a picture of his anus," Dr. Latimer proclaimed proudly of her treatment of the ex-president. "There is a reason I was the doctor called in for this."

She walked to a wall phone and ordered a CAT scan.

"Will we need to take any special precautions?" Latimer asked.

"Yes!" Melinda and James said in unison.

"No one in the vicinity should have an open wound," James said. "If anyone is in the process of healing, even a scratch, keep them away from this."

Continued monitoring of Dan's vitals showed signs of recovery. He remained attached to a respirator and other equipment that eased the functioning of his internal organs. The CAT scan showed significant nano scaffolding within several areas of his brain. The gunshot damage near the hypothymas was significant, and intricate nano repair had happened there. The medical team determined they would continue to provide life support as needed and monitor neurological functioning.

James and Melinda stayed by Dan's bedside and closely monitored the nanos.

Dan remained unconscious while the nanos repaired the system. His brain rehabilitated to accommodate the data collected from communication center that was once Titan. The calves' particular sperm whale culture, language and history was filed in the right hemisphere dorso-lateral prefrontal cortex, Using their new found perspective, nanos developed new programs. Although he was unconscious, Dan was an active participant of the repair team. It was as if he was watching the development of his new neuro-grid from a remote location.

Chapter 67

Brasco sped into his garage. Chatter about the fiasco around and on the *Edison* swept through the intelligence community like a wildfire. Clearly, Brasco thought, Hank had fucked it up royally and now there was only a small window of time to run before the CIA uncovered Brasco's complicity. Sweat beaded on his upper lip and began to pool at his armpits. He didn't know which was worse: getting caught by the good guys or the bad guys. He'd worked with some of the agents he thought would be breaking down this case and he did not want any one of them to find him.

His very carefully planned life in a rustic villa outside of Rome was ruined. Hank's fatal error created the possibility that Brasco would be traced, and he was unwilling to take that chance.

He focused on Plan B: set up an identity in some rat-shit country – like Sierra Leone or Chad. He returned to his house for the couple million dollars' worth of diamonds stuffed into a chicken Kiev in his freezer. He would fence a couple and swallow the rest. These diamonds had provided Brasco peace of mind over the years. If the plan had progressed without a hitch, the chicken would have expired and been tossed out by whoever cleaned up after he went missing. Going into his house was dangerous, Brasco thought, but he needed those goddamn diamonds.

He punched in the intricate security code and entered his home. As soon as he

shut his door, Brasco knew he was dead; the sound of his door closing was different
– muffled, and there was that faint familiar odor – plastic. He surveyed his living
room. His brain knew the room was draped in the transparent plastic visqueen
before his eyes recognized it. He saw the earth-tone walls and mission-style
furniture as smudgy, as if someone had taken an eraser to his living room. *Shit*, he
thought, as he felt the bite of a KA-BAR knife slip carefully between his T1 and T2
vertebra severing his spine. Paralyzed, his knees buckled and he slumped backwards
into the cradling arms of his preferred transport operative David.

He couldn't feel the knife as it was drawn out of his spine but he knew David,
well trained in Eskirma martial arts, would now slit his throat. Years of Special
Forces training told him so. He felt a gentle tugging as the knife's blade sliced
though his throat. David let go of his shoulders and Brasco slumped awkwardly
onto his side. He knew it would only be minutes; he watched the crimson pool
expand out in front of him. He slipped into darkness, coldness, and then death.

David exited Brasco's apartment in beautiful Falls Church Virginia and walked
calmly down the elm-lined street. He hit redial on his burn phone; it rang several
times.

"USA Plumbing and Cleaning," someone answered cheerily.

"The leak has been taken care of; ready for clean-up," David replied. He
approached a white frame house and a small dog ran and yapped protectively along
the fenced yard. David pulled a baggy out of his pocket with a frozen brick of
chicken Kiev defrosting inside it. He tore open the ingot of chicken, retrieved a
small packet of diamonds from the congealed butter and herbs and tossed the
chicken meat to the dog.

Chapter 68

An unprecedented mustering of Cetus came together in the Pacific Ocean off the coast of Washington state. Scores of sperm whales gathered off Puget Sound in the Salish Sea. Family pods of Monterey grays, gnarly and encrusted in barnacles, cruised up the coast. These grays met up with bands of acrobatic California Humpback whales tumbling along the Coastline, and they traveled together. Several groups of enormous blue whales trekked nosily up the western seaboard. The solitary right whales appeared in record numbers, silently weaving into the historic congregation.

This was a loud gathering. The cacophony drew curiosity seekers; the beautiful white sided dolphin, the always smiling bottlenose dolphins and the shy harbor porpoise ventured out to join the chorus. Regional pilot, pigmy, dwarf and minke whales merged into the multitude.

The mournful moans and howls of baleen whales eventually melded with the sorrowful songs of blue and humpback whales. Repetitive pulse chains of clicks, boings and thumps replaced the anxious tail lobbing and breaching by the sperm whales. This symphony played on for days. Regional Orcas scouted the parameter and kept predators at bay.

Researchers photographed and recorded dorsal knuckles, flukes and callosity patterns. Every scratch, scar and unique mottling pattern was carefully cataloged, identifying hundreds of individual whales. The information gathered would prove useful for years.

Teams of scientists and filmmakers videoed and monitored diverse species as the whales spyhopped, breached and slapped their pectoral fins against the water. Also noted, were smaller cetations porpoising throughout the group. Biologists and behaviorists theorized the cause for the gathering. Heated discussions swirled around the impact of global warming on the world Cetus population. Or an impending shift in the Cascadia fault, moving the North American Plate southwest, setting up a suduction zone earthquake. Geologists closely monitored the entire Pacific Coast, including the San Andras fault as engineers and commonwealths from Vancouver Island to San Diego prepared for a megathrust earthquake.

The Salish Tribes of Puget Sound had folklore that more closely matched the event. They believed the gathering was the acknowledgment of the passing of a great leader. Tradition dictated that the tribes suspend their own activities and join the ceremony. There was the fabled story of "ùapqin çu t sìsi" (many people celebrating long ago) as scores of "âçpümetä sätisôewç" (big fish of the ocean) gathered off the coast. At that time, the tribes did not hunt, instead the ancestral tribes of the Songhees Nation, including the Skagit, Nisqually, Muckleshoot and Swinomish tribes congregated together for "esyapqini" – a celebration.

Local, national and world news reported on the unprecedented collection of whales and the spontaneous celebration of the Salish Tribes, which included athletic contests and games similar to lacrosse, rugby and native forms of martial arts. And there was no report of the battle between a U.S. submarine and an unidentified craft.